LAST CHANCE COWBOYS: THE LAWMAN

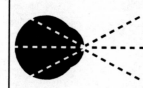

This Large Print Book carries the
Seal of Approval of N.A.V.H.

WHERE THE TRAIL ENDS

LAST CHANCE COWBOYS: THE LAWMAN

ANNA SCHMIDT

THORNDIKE PRESS
A part of Gale, a Cengage Company

Farmington Hills, Mich • San Francisco • New York • Waterville, Maine
Meriden, Conn • Mason, Ohio • Chicago

LIBRARY OF CONGRESS CIP DATA ON FILE.
CATALOGUING IN PUBLICATION FOR THIS BOOK
IS AVAILABLE FROM THE LIBRARY OF CONGRESS

ISBN-13: 978-1-4104-9942-4 (hardcover)
ISBN-10: 1-4104-9942-1 (hardcover)

Published in 2017 by arrangement with Sourcebooks, Inc.

Printed in the United States of America
1 2 3 4 5 6 7 21 20 19 18 17

For Earle Horne. Thanks for raising me to love a good Western!

ONE

Arizona Territory, October 1882

After six months on the streets of Kansas City, Jess Porterfield had come home. But he might as well have kept on riding for all the place where he'd grown up *felt* like home to him. In the relatively short time that he'd been away, everything about the Clear Springs Ranch and the town of Whitman Falls — indeed, the entire Arizona Territory — had become nearly unrecognizable.

As he slowly rode up the trail that led to his family's home, he saw the adobe house with its flat roof meant to ward off the desert heat. His father had built that house and added to it through the years as the family had grown. Jess expected to find his mother, two sisters, and younger brother inside, gathered 'round the table in the kitchen. He expected to hear laughter coming from the bunkhouse. He expected to see a light in the small outbuilding next to the house where their foreman lived. He planned to corral his horse and walk past the chicken coop and the plantings of cholla and barrel cactus and on into the kitchen as if he'd just come back from checking on the herd.

Instead, the annual party his family always hosted after the livestock had been taken to market was in full swing. The courtyard was packed with people — some he recognized, and some were strangers. Everyone seemed to be in the mood to celebrate . . . which made no sense, given that the ranch had been about to fail the day he left.

Back then the situation had been dire on all fronts. His father had just died in a freak accident. A drought that had gone on for over a year threatened to send the family and the ranch into bankruptcy. His mother had been so consumed by her grief that she refused to believe her husband was truly gone. And he was ashamed to admit he had left his sister, Maria, on her own to fend off the land-grabbing Tipton brothers, who already owned most of the land in the territory.

And yet there were lanterns lighting the courtyard and bonfires where guests gathered between dances to warm themselves

8

on this autumn night. He had heard the music from some distance away, and now that he was closer, he could also hear the laughter and excited chatter of people enjoying themselves. So who was throwing this fandango? He half expected to see Jasper Tipton and his much younger wife, Pearl, playing the role of hosts. Surely Maria had had to surrender and sell out. Truth was, his father had barely been hanging on before he died. But there were some things that didn't seem right about the atmosphere of the party — like that their hired hand, Bunker, would never have agreed to provide the music for a Tipton party. Yet there he was along with a couple of other cowboys, stomping their feet in time to the music they produced from a worn fiddle and guitar and banjo. Just like old times.

"Is that you, Jessie Porterfield?"

Their nearest neighbor and Jess's father's dearest friend, George Johnson, waited for Jess to dismount and tie up his horse at the hitching post before grabbing him in a bear hug. "Good to have you home."

"Looks like there might have been some changes since I left," Jess ventured.

George laughed. "Things are pretty much the same, only better. That sister of yours is quite the little businesswoman."

"You don't say." Jess was baffled. Was Mr. Johnson saying that Maria had managed to somehow save the ranch? "So we still own this place?"

"In a manner of speaking. Maria can fill you in, but the short version is that several of the smaller ranchers decided the only way to fight the Tiptons was to beat them at their own game. So we've banded together in a cooperative arrangement. We share the profits — and the debts. We help each other out. 'Course, having just come back from taking the stock to market, we've got a little time to get settled into this new arrangement, but you mark my words, by spring every small ranch in this territory will be holding its own."

So Maria — his sister — had held the Tipton brothers at bay. Their father would be really proud — of her.

"You've got a new foreman," George continued. "A Florida boy — came drifting in here not long after you left. Went to work with the others, and everyone's pretty sure that him and Maria will be heading down the aisle before too long."

Jess was aware that several others had spotted him, and a crowd was beginning to form as they pushed forward.

"What about Roger?"

10

"He took off. Some think he might have been involved in that business with your pa. 'Course, there's no proof, and he was a good foreman and all. Didn't get along with the drifter, though — not one bit."

"What business with Pa?" Jess was reeling with these bits of information that made no sense. But George didn't get a chance to answer.

"Jessie!" his younger sister, Amanda, squealed as the crowd parted to let her through. Jess scooped her up and swung her around.

"Look at you," he said, glad for the diversion. "I go away for five minutes, and you go and grow up into a real beauty." He set her down, and his expression sobered when his other sister stepped out of the crowd. "Hello, Maria."

He saw Maria hesitate as she ran through a range of emotions that went from anger to confusion and wariness. After what seemed like an eternity, she opened her arms to him. "Welcome home, Jess."

As he hugged her, feeling hesitation even in her embrace, they all heard a shrill cry. Jess looked up to see his mother — Constance Porterfield — running across the yard, her skirts clutched in one hand as she reached out for her eldest son with the

11

other. Jess steeled himself to accept the fact that she was probably thinking he was his father. When he'd left, she'd lapsed into a fantasy world of unreality, refusing to believe her husband was gone.

But when she reached him, she pushed his hat off and ran her fingers through his hair, brushing it away from his forehead. "Jessie, at last."

She recognized him — surely that was progress. He smiled and bent to kiss her cheek. "Kill the fatted calf, Ma," he said with a laugh. "I've come home."

"To stay?"

"Yes, ma'am."

"Let the dancing begin," his mother shouted, and the band struck up a lively tune as she pulled him into the center of the lanterns that outlined the dance floor.

"You look older, Son," she said, frowning as she studied his face closely.

"And you look . . . better," he replied, searching for any sign of the glassy-eyed, distracted woman he'd left behind.

She frowned. "Stop looking at me as if you expect me to start speaking in tongues. I had a rough time of it, but one cannot hide from reality forever." She quirked an eyebrow, and he understood that her words were her subtle way of saying that she had

12

not been the only one hiding from reality.

"Well, you're still the prettiest woman around," he countered, reluctant to get into the details of the last several months.

"Prettier than Addie Wilcox?"

Addie — the reason he had gone, and one of the reasons he had finally come to his senses and returned. She was the only person he had not yet allowed himself to think about. His intent had been first to settle things with his family, and then . . .

"She waited for you to come to your senses, you know," his mother continued. "Why didn't you at least write to her?"

"I don't want to talk about Addie, Ma. It's you I've come to see." He was glad to see her well again . . . and sorry that he'd had no part in her recovery. It was, after all, a key reason for his return — the realization that while he was not and never would be his father, the family needed him, and he had a responsibility to be there and care for them. But it appeared they had managed quite well on their own. "How are you feeling?"

She laughed. "Well, if you're thinking that I'm the batty old woman you left six months ago, stop worrying. I needed some time. I'm still missing your father every minute of every day, but now that the culprit who murdered him is in . . ."

Jess stumbled to a stop. "What are you saying, Ma? He died in an accident and . . ." Maybe she wasn't better after all. His heart sank.

She heaved a sigh of resignation. "You have a lot to catch up on, Jessie. We've all had to face some hard truths lately."

Jess thought of what George Johnson had been saying when Amanda interrupted — something about there being no proof that their foreman, Roger Turnbull, had been involved in "that business with your pa."

"Murdered?" he said, unable to take it all in. The news shook him to his boots. Could it be true that his father's death had been no accident at all — but cold-blooded murder? He was speechless, first with disbelief, and then rage, as he tried to think of what signs of foul play he could have missed that day they'd found his father's body on the trail.

"Now you pull yourself together, Jess," his mother ordered as the band hit the final notes of the tune. "The culprit — Marshal Tucker — is in custody at Fort Lowell. This is a matter for Colonel Ashwood and his men to handle, and you need to stay out of it. Is that clear?"

"Tucker? But what kind of beef could he

14

have had with Pa?"

His mother looked away and then back at him. She linked her arm through his, but it was less a gesture of consolation than one that felt as if she was trying to make sure he stayed put. "You'll hear it soon enough, so it may as well be from me. At least then you know you're getting the truth of it. Tucker was working with the Tipton brothers. It appears that he decided to take matters into his own hands when your father refused to sell. I suspect he hoped he would endear himself to the Tiptons with his actions."

He slapped at a biting bug that attacked his neck. Some things, he realized — like the bugs and the dust and the underhanded Tipton boys doing whatever they found necessary to control the territory — did not change. "You're saying they had nothing to do with this?"

"I'm saying there is no evidence that points to that. I am saying that Tucker is in custody, and Colonel Ashwood assures me he will be tried and punished to the full extent of the law."

"But what about . . ."

"Now you listen to me, Jessup Porterfield — I have lost my husband, but I will not lose my oldest son in the bargain. So you just contain that temper of yours, and let

15

the colonel handle this. If the Tiptons are involved, then they will be arrested."

"If? Ma, we both know . . ."

"No, Son, we don't know anything. We suspect, but we do not know, so stay out of it, and let the federal authorities do their job. If you're so all-fired interested in taking up the law, talk to Doc. With the arrest of Tucker, Whitman Falls is in need of a new marshal. Now, about Addie," she added, so smoothly changing the subject that Jess felt his head spinning like the dancers whirling around the courtyard. That seemed to be happening a lot tonight. "The boys just struck up a ranchera, and it looks to me like a certain young lady is standing over there itching to get out on that dance floor."

She gave him a nudge and then went off to dance the reel with his younger brother, Trey, who waved and grinned as if Jess had just come back from a day on the range, not six months gone with no word.

His mother couldn't have engineered a better distraction. Jess looked about, dazed, and saw Addie Wilcox tapping her toe in time to the music. She wanted to dance all right. Question was, would she dance with *him*? After all, he hadn't just left Whitman Falls and his family's ranch — he had left Addie as well.

16

Well, the one thing he had always been able to count on with Addie was that she would tell him the truth. She would know what had really happened with his father. Of course, first he had to get her to speak to him. Addie had a temper that matched his own. And the fact was that he hadn't written her, but *dabnabit,* he'd sure thought about her and, more to the point, he'd come back because he'd realized that without her, his life was pretty bleak.

He nodded to friends and neighbors as he threaded his way through those watching the dancing. "Welcome home, Jess," he heard more than one of the women say. "Learned your lesson, did you?" He expected he was going to hear that sentiment a lot in the coming weeks. He'd even heard one man mutter, "Well, all hail the prodigal son." It was what he'd expected — and probably deserved — people assuming he'd come running home because he was out of luck and money. He wasn't of a mind to set them straight. He had far more important matters to attend to.

Addie had to be hearing these comments, and she had to be aware that he was making his way toward her, although she refused to acknowledge him. Clearly, she hadn't changed a bit in the months since he'd left.

17

She was every bit as stubborn and mule-headed as she'd always been. He ought to just turn right around and ignore her. He ought to ask Sybil Sinclair to dance and see how Addie liked that. He ought to do half a dozen things, but he didn't.

"Evenin'," he muttered, sidling up next to her. He kept his eyes on the dancers. "Good to see Ma looking better," he added.

"No thanks to you," she replied as she clapped her hands in time with the beat of the music.

He bristled. Addie had this way of saying exactly what was needed to get under his skin. "Meaning what?"

Of course, he knew what she was saying. *The prodigal son.* He'd seen more than one person's lips murmuring those words as they had watched his mother come running to welcome him back — as she had enfolded him in her embrace.

"I asked you a question, Addie."

"Rhetorical, I'm sure." She kept right on clapping and tapping her toe, smiling at the dancers as they passed.

"Don't you go throwing around those fancy words with me, Dr. Wilcox."

"And don't you go playing like you're some uneducated country bumpkin, Jess Porterfield. You owe that much respect to

18

your parents, who made sure all their children got a solid education." Her smile tightened. "Besides, I'm not a doctor for real — not yet."

He had to clench his fist to keep from touching her bare forearm below the lace trim of her sleeve, comforting her as he had in the past whenever she got discouraged. "You wanna dance or not?" he grumbled instead, holding out his hand to her.

Just then, the music finished on a crescendo, and everybody applauded. "Looks like your timing is perfect, as usual," she said. She turned to go, but was prevented from moving by the throng of dancers leaving the floor in search of cider to quench their thirst.

Jess decided to try a different tactic and moved a step closer. "Ma hinted that I ought to apply for the marshal's job," he said. "Your pa being head of the town council and all, do you think he might . . . ?"

She wheeled around and looked directly at him for the first time since he'd come riding up to the ranch. She was staring at him, her dark brown eyes large with surprise behind the lenses of her wire-rimmed glasses. "Are you serious? Why would Papa trust you? Why would any of us living in town trust you not to up and leave again?"

Her eyes filled with tears.

"Addie, I had to . . . I never meant . . ."

Her mouth worked as if finding and then rejecting words before she could spit them out at him. She held up her hands to stop him from saying anything more before she brushed past him, losing herself in the crowd. He glanced around to see others looking at him. Obviously, they had witnessed the scene and were now passing judgment, as they always had. Well, he would show them. He would show all of them — even Addie. Especially Addie.

The question was how. He could hardly take over here at the ranch. From the talk he'd had with George Johnson, it sure seemed like Maria had done a better job than he would have thought managing things — or than he could have done. In spite of the attempts of the Tipton Land and Cattle Company to buy out all the smaller ranchers in the area, including — no, especially — theirs, Maria had found a way to hang on.

So maybe he should think more seriously about applying for the lawman's job. After all, even though a local marshal had no jurisdiction over crimes that took place outside the town's borders — like the murder of his father — it would be a way he could look into the matter without raising suspicions. As head of the town council, Addie's father would be the one to hire a new marshal.

That gave Jess pause. No doubt Doc would be as down on him as Addie was, so why bother? On the other hand, he needed work — work that would give him the time and the cover he needed to solve his father's murder by tracking down the real killers.

The town was in need of a new marshal. And why wouldn't Addie's father hire him? He'd make a fine marshal. After all, how hard could it be?

"Hello, Jess."

Jess looked around to find Sybil Sinclair gazing up at him. "I was on my way to get some punch," she said, "but . . ."

"How about we enjoy this waltz first?" Jess offered her his arm, the way his mother had taught both her boys a gentleman would escort a lady, and led her onto the dance floor.

Addie could not for the life of her figure out why she continued to allow that man to get to her. Why couldn't she be more like Jess's younger sister and her good friend, Amanda — calm and sophisticated? She searched the gathering for Amanda, but

hesitated when she saw her friend surrounded by the usual trio of admirers.
Amanda had been planning this party for
weeks now. She certainly deserved to enjoy
herself and not have to sympathize with
Addie. Besides, Jess was Amanda's brother,
newly returned to the fold from his travels
following his father's death — a death
everyone now knew had not been the accident they'd first thought.

She stopped dead in her tracks. Her hand
flew to her mouth. What was she thinking?
Maybe Jess had overheard some of the talk.
Maybe that was why he was talking about
applying for the marshal's position. After
all, Jasper Tipton had built that big house in
town to please his bride, Pearl, and his
brother Buck lived there as well. While the
local marshal had no jurisdiction outside
the town limits, Jess might just think the
fact that the Tiptons resided in town opened
the door for him to go after them — and
more than likely, he would get himself killed
in the bargain. Her mind raced as she tried
to think the issue through from every side.

"This is not one of your medical cases,"
she muttered to herself. "This is Jess." And
when it came to figuring out what Jess Porterfield might be thinking, she fully appreci-
ated that logic was not part of the process.

22

She was still mad at him for leaving all those months ago, but that didn't mean she didn't care about him, and, knowing his temper, he was bound to get into trouble.

With a sigh, she headed off to find her father. Maybe he could talk some sense into Jess — the man she had fallen in love with and once upon a time planned a future with. But as she moved through the throng of party guests, pausing now and then to exchange a greeting, it wasn't her father she saw.

It was Jess.

He wasn't spoiling for a fight at all. No, he was laughing and flirting with Sybil Sinclair. Sybil with her blond curls and her bright blue eyes and a cupid's bow of a mouth that made her look like a porcelain doll. Sybil with her tiny waist and her flawless skin and giddy laugh that actually came out as "tee-hee-hee."

"My brother is trying to make you jealous," Amanda murmured, coming to stand next to Addie. "Do not let him know that it's working."

"It's not," she insisted, pushing her glasses firmly onto the bridge of her nose. She straightened to her full height, still a good three inches shorter than Sybil's willowy five foot four. She brushed back a strand of hair that had drifted from the practical bun she preferred and tried not to think about how her stick-straight locks would look worn down like Sybil's long curls. "I really couldn't care less if your brother wants to make an utter fool of himself with that —"

"Good to know you aren't affected," Amanda said wryly. "But two can play this game. Come on. Dance with Harlan Stokes."

Just like Jess, Harlan Stokes had a reputation with the ladies. He had never paid the slightest attention to Addie, but he had definitely set his sights on Amanda. She could get him to do anything — even dance with plain Addie Wilcox. Of course, even as he led Addie to the dance floor, Harlan's eyes remained on Amanda, who had accepted another cowboy's invitation to dance. Addie couldn't fault Harlan because her own gaze kept drifting to where Jess was dancing with Sybil. The song was "Sweet Betsy from Pike" — a favorite of Addie's — but she barely heard the tune as Harlan guided her around the floor.

"You think I've got any chance at all with Amanda?" Harlan asked.

Addie glanced up at him. He was only a few inches taller than she was, and she knew the other cowhands teased him a lot about his short stature. They even called him Pee-wee. He looked miserable as he turned her for the sole purpose of keeping his eye on Amanda. Addie knew that her answer called for diplomacy of the highest order.

"Well, you know Amanda is still unsettled in her ways. She's not yet decided on the path she wants to take."

"Not like you, huh? I mean, everybody knows you've been planning on taking over your pa's practice just as soon as you finish your schooling and all."

"Well, not taking over. More like working with him."

Harlan looked surprised. "You've been doing that since you were a kid."

The fact that Harlan's full attention was now focused on her made Addie uncomfortable — so much so that she stumbled, and he tightened his hold on her, pulling her closer. "Easy there," he said. "You got your bearings?"

"I'm fine," she said, and knew it came out as a rebuff when he loosened his grip. "Thank you," she added. "I'm not very good at dancing."

He frowned. "You're fine, Addie Wilcox. Just fine."

She was surprised to feel a lump in her throat at his kindness. Blessedly, the waltz

25

ended just then. "Thank you, Harlan. I know that Amanda asked you to take pity on me and . . ."

"You shouldn't do that, Addie. Put yourself down that way. You're worth two of most of the women at this party."

This had to stop. Addie could feel the heat rise along her neck up into her cheeks. "There's not a whole lot of competition," she said, looking around at the gathering, where men outnumbered the girls and women by a factor of at least three to one.

"You know what I'm saying."

"Why, thank you, Harlan. Does that include Amanda Porterfield?" She was teasing him now.

It was his turn to blush. "Well now, Miss Addie, it would take a lot to measure up to Amanda Porterfield — at least for me."

"You're a good man, Harlan. Thank you for the dance." She punctuated her appreciation with a slight curtsy and laughed when Harlan bowed in return.

"Pleasure was mine, ma'am."

They were both laughing when Addie spotted Jess scowling at her as he carried two cups of punch back to where he had left Sybil waiting.

"Hey, Jess," Harlan called out, " 'bout time you got home. The other boys and me

26

have been missing you and your money at the poker games."

Jess kept walking, acknowledging Harlan's greeting only by raising one of the punch cups in a toast. Addie wondered if the cowhands had spiked the drink. She wouldn't put it past them. It was not all that uncommon for the men to add a little whiskey, hoping the spirits might make the girls a little more amenable to their advances. But Jess had never pulled such a trick. Truth was, Jess didn't need to do anything but be his charming self to make a girl like Sybil sit up and take notice.

Stop it, she ordered herself.

Seymour Bunker, the oldest hand on the Porterfield spread who was as good with a fiddle as he was with a lariat, struck up a reel. Harlan took Addie's hand and joined the other dancers. At the same time she saw Jess set down the cups of punch and lead Sybil into the circle. Addie's pulse raced as she realized there was no way she could avoid taking her turn with him in the change of partners required by the dance.

Sure enough, a few minutes later they came together and then circled away and then came together again, sashaying their way down the line of other dancers. She refused to look at him, her mouth drawn

27

into a tight line and her brow furrowed in concentration, as if the steps of the dance were every bit as complex as her study of the thick anatomy text she'd left on the kitchen table back home. Jess tightened his hold on her waist as they made their way down the center of the other dancers. When they reached the end of the line, he let her go without a word.

When the dance finally ended, Harlan's cheeks were flushed. "I'm sorry, Addie. I wasn't thinking. I mean, Jess is a durn fool, if you'll pardon me saying so. Leaving a woman like you the way he did . . ."

"Please don't concern yourself, Harlan. Thank you for the dances. Oh, there's Amanda, and she's looking this way. Maybe she's free for the next waltz."

Harlan gave Addie a little bow and hurried off. Addie sighed. He wasn't the only one who thought that Jess had left her. Jess's stupid pride had never allowed him to admit the truth — that he had begged her to go with him, and she had refused. Well, now he'd come back. She had no idea why, but she'd be willing to bet that it was because the life he'd been so sure was waiting for him in the city had never materialized. It surprised her to realize she got no satisfaction from that thought.

She watched him drink down his punch in one long gulp while Sybil sipped hers. The one thing that no amount of irritation at the man could change was that he was undeniably good-looking. He was tall, and his muscular frame gave evidence of his ability to work hard. Tonight he was wearing black trousers, a blue shirt, and a leather vest, as if he'd known he was dressing for a party. And boots, of course — new, from the look of them. When he'd first arrived he'd been wearing a black Stetson, but his mother had removed that as soon as she ran to embrace him. She had thrown the hat aside and combed his straw-colored hair away from his forehead with her fingers, all the while repeating his name over and over as tears of joy rolled down her weathered cheeks.

A hank of his hair had now fallen over his forehead, and Addie saw Sybil reach up to push it back, but Jess stepped away from her touch. He said something to her, smiled, and then walked away. Addie's breath quickened, and she closed her eyes, preparing herself for what she might say when Jess came her way. But when she opened her eyes again, she saw that he had not only walked away from Sybil — he had also walked away from her.

■ ■ ■ ■

Jess sought out the shadow of the cotton-wood trees that stood between the house and the creek and watched his neighbors and friends dance. He saw their family's housekeeper, Juanita, bring his mother a shawl — defense against the coolness of the autumn night. He watched as Maria danced with a man he'd been told was the new fore-man. He still didn't have the whole story of what had happened to Roger Turnbull, the foreman his father had hired a few years earlier — the man who he'd been pretty sure would have married Maria by now. He was also surprised to see how his younger brother Trey — always sickly, with his nose buried in a book — seemed to be a favorite among the ranch hands. He'd certainly filled out some and was looking more like a man than a puny kid.

Eventually, there were bound to be ques-tions about where Jess had gone, what he'd done and, most of all, why he'd come back. He dreaded those questions because there was no way around the fact that he'd walked away when his family needed him most. His father had built this ranch from nothing, always with an eye on the future and his dream that the ranch would be his legacy for his children. And now, Isaac Porterfield was dead — not from the tragic accident Jess had thought, but by the deliberate hand and malice of others.

He watched Trey cross the yard, a border collie at his heels. "Ma wants you to come sit with her," his brother said.

"You've grown, Squirt," Jess replied, ruffling Trey's shaggy mop of hair.

Trey ducked away from him. "I'm not a kid anymore."

"Hey, I wasn't gone that long."

Trey's expression sobered. "Why'd you leave, Jess?"

Jess thought about his answer for a long moment. "I guess I thought it was the right thing to do."

"But this is home."

Never felt like that for me, Jess thought, but what he said was, "I'm glad you think that way, Squirt."

"Got me a new nickname," Trey announced. "The men call me Snap."

"Not sure I get that one."

Trey grinned. "It's 'cause I'm what they call a whippersnapper. Bunker shortened it to Snap."

Jess saw their mother watching them from her chair under the trees. When he'd left, she'd been so struck down by grief over her husband's death that it made her loopy. She'd wander through the house at all hours neither bathed nor properly dressed and insist that her husband would be home at any moment. Jess vividly remembered the afternoon he'd gone to her room to tell her he was leaving.

"What does your father have to say about this idea?" she'd demanded.

"Not much," Jess had stammered, understanding for the first time what his sister Maria had been trying to tell him.

"You haven't told him, have you?"

"Not exactly, ma'am." He'd been at a loss as to how to handle her delusions. If he told her straight out that his father was dead, what might she do? "Look, Ma, we always knew the ranch wasn't for me."

She had sighed and gazed out the window. "I know, but the least you could do is wait until your father returns. This feels like you're sneaking off behind his back. He's going to be deeply hurt, Jess."

"How about I write him a letter and leave it with Maria?"

"You're that anxious to be on your way?"

"There's a train out of Tucson tonight. I'd sure like to be on that train, Ma."

"Have you got money for the ticket?"

"Yes, ma'am." He had bent and kissed her forehead. "Don't worry, Ma, okay?"

He remembered that she had smiled then — a little wistfully, the way she was smiling as she watched him with Trey now. "Mothers are meant to worry," she had told him as she brushed his hair away from his brow. "Take care, and I want a letter from you at least once a week, understood?"

"Yes, ma'am. And I'll write that letter for Pa before I . . ."

"You let me handle your father. Just be careful." She had cupped his cheeks between her hands, then given him a little push, sending him on his way.

He closed his eyes against the memory of that moment. "How's Ma doing?" he asked his brother.

Trey glanced back toward where Constance Porterfield sat, and he gave her a little wave. "She's all better. Maria says she just needed time enough to find her way. Chet helped."

"Who's Chet?"

"Chet Hunter. The guy Maria's gonna marry. That's him over there." He pointed to the man dancing with Maria. "This is his dog, Cracker. These days Cracker follows me or Maria around when Chet's off doing something else."

"Sounds like the guy has made himself at home." Jess tried to keep his tone even.

"Chet's the best," Trey exclaimed. "He came riding in here sometime after you left. I'm telling you for sure that Roger Turnbull didn't like him one bit, but he had a way about him. There were two times when Ma thought he was Pa." He chuckled. "That really set Roger off. Then Chet and Maria started spending time together. Oh yeah, and then this woman shows up claiming to be Chet's wife, and she brought this kid with her, no more than a baby, and you shoulda seen how Ma took to that young'un like he was her own, and —"

"Hold on, Squirt. Maria can't marry a man who already has a wife. It's not only illegal — it goes against —"

"He ain't married," Trey explained. "Never was. She pulled a trick, trying to cover up having the baby and all."

"That toddler there? That's his kid?"

Trey sighed. "Not *his* — that was part of her trick. But the woman ran off with Turnbull, and now Ma has decided to take little Maxwell in. Juanita pretends to be upset at the extra work and all, but it's pretty clear that she's not the least bit mad about it, and . . ."

Jess's head hurt from the lack of sleep and

the surprise of everything he'd learned in the last hour or so. How could so much have changed in just a few short months? It was one thing that his life had been turned upside down. After all, he'd gone off looking to make changes — not that he'd been happy with how those changes had turned out. But the Clear Springs Ranch had been the same from the time he could remember, and even with his father gone, he had expected to come back and find not much different. Instead, his father had been murdered, one sister was planning to marry a complete stranger, their foreman had run off, his younger sister was surrounded by a trio of men looking at her like she was fresh meat, and Trey was babbling on about this boy who wasn't really the foreman's son but who now had been taken into the family.

"I better go see what Ma wants," Jess said, interrupting Trey's bright chatter. He crossed to where his mother had taken the toddler onto her lap and was playing a game of patty-cake. "Who's this big fella?" he asked, forcing a grin.

"This is Maxwell. Max, meet Jess."

The boy looked up at him with wide, dark eyes and promptly burst into tears.

"Oh, there, there," Constance crooned,

the way she used to when Jess was the kid's age.

He felt an unreasonable bolt of jealousy as Juanita hurried to take the child away. "Past his bedtime," his mother said, giving Jess her full attention. "Come sit with me."

"Trey tells me the kid belongs to some drifter Maria hired a few months back?"

His mother waved her hand as if shooing away a bee. "It's a long story, but the short version is that Chet is not the child's father, and yet he is determined to care for the boy as if he were."

"Seems to me you and Juanita are the ones caring for him."

"Jealousy does not become you, Jess. You have been away, and I would remind you that in spite of your promise to write, we have not had a word about you for months now. Your sisters wrote to you, but their letters were returned unopened. So it would be prudent for you to reserve judgment on others until you have all the facts." She watched the dancers spin by. "Did you dance with Addie as I suggested?"

"I asked. She refused. Looks like she prefers Harlan Stokes." He spotted Addie laughing as she and Harlan and Amanda stood together drinking punch and watching the dancing.

"Now, Jess, that's not like you. Addie has every reason to be . . . disappointed. After all, you didn't write or . . ."

"I was a little busy," Jess replied, shifting from one foot to the other, trying to figure out the best way to escape what he knew was coming next.

"I'd like to hear all about that," his mother said, patting the arm of the empty chair next to her. "Why don't we begin with where you've been all this time?"

To his surprise, Jess realized that spilling out the tale of his months away would be a relief. Ma would not blame him or reprimand him. She would find a way to forgive and get the rest of the family to do the same. But he had other, more pressing things on his mind. "We've got time for all that. Right now, I need you to tell me everything you know about Pa's murder."

"No." There was no arguing with that single word, and Jess knew it. "Now, where did you go on this grand adventure of yours?"

He sat on the edge of the chair, his hands dangling between his knees, his eyes on the ground. "I went to Kansas City."

"On the train. That much I know."

"I . . ." Jess searched for the right words. Suddenly the music seemed too loud, and the voices of the partygoers too rowdy. "How 'bout we do this tomorrow, Ma? Right now, I'd like to dance with my best girl." He held out his hand to her with a crooked smile and, in a voice filled with the struggle to keep his emotions in check, added, "It's so good to see you feeling all better, Ma."

His mother touched her hair and smoothed her dress as she stood and accepted his hand. "You should be dancing with Addie."

"I'd rather be dancing with you," he said as he escorted her to the center of the courtyard and nodded to Bunker. The fiddler raised his instrument to his chin and drew the bow across the strings as all the other guests stepped away and watched Jess dance with his mother.

Addie felt Amanda's elbow jab into her side as the jig ended and the musicians started playing a slower waltz. She looked up and saw Jess dancing with his mother. He held her as if she were one of the fragile figurines that Addie's mother kept behind glass in their parlor. Addie knew the feeling of Jess's arm around her waist, his large hand flat against the fabric of her dress, while he held her other hand as if it were a butterfly that had landed on his palm. She closed her eyes to dismiss the memory, but found herself lost in the vision of his blue eyes sparkling as he looked at her and the way his deep voice seemed in perfect harmony with the music as he spoke to her about his dreams for the future — always assuming that his future naturally meant *their* future.

She forced her eyes open and deliberately concentrated on running her finger around the rim of her punch cup. It had never really been about their future for Jess. It had always been what he wanted now and how she might fit into his plans. "You can doctor anywhere," he once had the audacity to tell her. She was certain he hadn't meant it as dismissively as it sounded. He had been pleading with her to come away with him to the city, laying out the promise of an actual hospital and lots of patients, not to mention an opera house and restaurants and shops where she could find anything she wanted. She had not been able to make him understand that what she wanted was right here in Whitman Falls, Arizona — the town where she had grown up and where her family and friends lived, and where one day she hoped to continue the role her father had played for generations as the town's doctor.

"We can find all of that and more out there — new friends, new opportunities. I have to go, Addie," he'd said. "I want you to go with me. I'm asking you to go with me."

"Can you find a new family?" she had asked, unable to believe that with his father barely in the ground and his mother overcome with grief, he would choose this as the time to go.

"You'll be my family," he'd told her. "You and the kids we'll have."

He had never once said a word about marriage, although there weren't three people in the whole region who didn't believe that one day the two of them would wed. Now suddenly, he was talking about children, just assuming what everybody else did, that they would be together.

"You go do what you have to do, Jess."

His features had collapsed into an expression of utter disbelief. "You don't want to marry me?"

"You haven't asked," she reminded him, then laid her finger on his lips before adding, "and now would not be the best time to remedy that. Good-bye, Jess."

She'd slipped into the house and gently closed the front door. She had leaned against the cool surface of the hard wood until she heard him mount up and ride away, the clip of his horse's hooves growing faint as the sun set.

Every day for weeks she had scanned the horizon, jumped at the sound of anyone stepping onto the front porch, and kept a vigil for his return. She had been so sure that he would realize his mistake, that he had been driven by the sudden change in his family's circumstances that came with his father's death. She had been so sure that his love for her would bring him to his senses and he would come back, begging her forgiveness and pleading with her to become his wife. At night she lay awake listening to the lonely call of the distant train as she wept the tears she had kept hidden behind a smile all day. And finally, as the days and then weeks and months passed, she stopped hoping and buried herself in her studies, determined to become the best doctor in the territory.

When she heard the other guests titter, she risked a peek and saw that Jess had led his mother in a pirouette and then pulled her close to steady her. As the waltz ended, he bowed to her curtsy, and everyone burst into applause. Jess grinned. Oh, how she had missed that smile. But when his gaze met hers, the grin faded. The scowl that replaced it could not be entirely hidden by the tight smile he gave others as he led his mother back to her chair.

"I have to go," Addie murmured, brushing past Amanda and Harlan — only to run straight into Buck Tipton.

If there was one person that Addie dreaded seeing more than Jess, that person was Buck Tipton. He was a large man — at least a foot taller than she was, and he was barrel-chested and broad-shouldered to boot. He dominated a room not with his personality — as Jess did — but with his sheer girth. He had a mustache that drooped around the corners of his mouth, giving him the expression of someone perpetually upset with whatever might be happening around him. He wore one of the newfangled tall-crowned and wide-brimmed Stetsons so popular with cowboys. For reasons Addie could not fathom, she suddenly recalled that the most popular style — according to her brother — was something called "Boss of the Plains." No doubt Buck would have chosen that for the name alone. The hat's brim placed his eyes in shadow, making it next to impossible to gauge what he might be thinking. His hair, as well as the mustache, was flame red-orange, and there was almost always the stub of a foul-smelling cigar clinched between his teeth.

And yet, with all of that going against him, he and his brother were the wealthiest and most influential men in Arizona. For that reason alone, there were several people in the area who thought Addie ought to count her blessings once the younger Tipton brother had taken a shine to her.

"Evenin', Miss Addie." Buck moved in close. Addie took a step back and found herself pushed up against a tree. Buck smiled and placed one hand on the trunk above her shoulder, blocking escape. "You're lookin' especially fine this evening."

"Thank you. I was just about . . ."

"How about you and me dance this next waltz?"

Stall! her mind screamed as she looked around for help. The last thing she wanted to do was make Buck Tipton mad. He had a temper, and there was no telling what he might do.

"I promised the next dance to Harlan," she lied.

"Harlan who?" Buck glanced over the gathering, then laughed. "You mean Peewee? Now why would you want to waste a dance on that bow-legged cowboy when I'm right here?"

"I promised," Addie managed weakly, just as Harlan led Amanda into the thick of the dancers.

"Looks to me like Peewee there don't honor a promise the way you do." He pushed himself away from the tree and held out his hand. "So let's dance."

It was not a request.

TWO

"Go talk to Addie," Jess's mother counseled as he led her back to her chair. "Get this settled tonight, Son."

"She doesn't want anything to do with me, Ma."

His mother's eyes went wide with fury, and for a minute Jess thought he was in for a lecture. But she was looking at something over his shoulder. "What is that man doing here?"

Jess followed the direction of his mother's pointed finger and saw Buck Tipton standing a lot closer to Addie than was right. "I'll handle this," he muttered, and strode across the yard.

"Are you lost, Tipton?" he called out. Several guests stopped in mid-sentence and turned to watch the confrontation unfold. "Because I'm pretty sure you weren't invited."

Buck tipped his fingers to the brim of his

hat. "Heard you were back, Jess. I'm guessing things didn't work out?"

The fact that Buck was saying aloud what others were probably thinking was infuriating enough, but the way he had backed Addie up so she was trapped between him and a tree made Jess see red. He clenched and unclenched his fingers and heard somebody murmur, "Fight!"

Still Jess was not the impulsive young man he had been when he left. He had learned more about choosing his battles than he cared to think about as he found his way through situations he couldn't control. Right now, he wanted more than anything to keep hitting Buck Tipton until the man's teeth were scattered on the ground and his face looked more like a slab of raw meat than human flesh. Right now, he wanted to make the man admit he and his older brother had orchestrated Isaac Porterfield's murder and that their only motive for that murder had been greed. Right now, he wanted most of all to get Buck the hell away from Addie.

He forced himself to steady his breath and keep his fists in check. Instead, he held out his hand to Addie. To his relief, she took hold of it and allowed him to move her away from Buck. "You didn't answer my question, Buck."

"I was just passing by and heard the music. Thought I'd see what was happening."

"So now you've seen, and you can move on." Next to him, Addie was actually shaking. If Buck Tipton had so much as laid a finger on her . . .

"Is there a problem?" Doc Wilcox stepped to the other side of Addie, and Jess saw the drifter from Florida and three hands from the smaller ranches take their positions just behind Buck. He noticed the dog, Cracker, was also on guard, his tail down and his eyes on the big man.

Buck held up his hands. "No trouble, Doc. Just paying my respects. Good to see you back, Jess. I guess my brother and me will be dealing with you now."

"I guess your brother and you won't," Jess replied.

"Oh, that's right. You gave up your birthright to your sister there."

"Maria has done a fine job managing this ranch, Buck. That's no thanks to you and Jasper. The fact remains that we've got no business with you or your brother — and more to the point, you've got no business with us. So I'm asking you nicely to get off our land."

"Or?" Buck sneered.

Jess felt Addie tighten her grip on his hand and only then realized that from the time he'd pulled her away from Buck, she had not let go. He felt ten feet tall and certainly able to take Buck Tipton out with one solid punch to the jaw. He took a step closer, and as he did, he was aware that Chet Hunter and their hired hands had also moved in. "Or I might just have to ask these men to escort you."

Buck glanced around, aware for the first time that he was surrounded and outnumbered. He pushed himself away from the tree he'd been leaning against and sauntered in the general direction of his horse, taking a route that brought him close to Addie and Jess. "Nice talking to you, Miss Addie. Guess we'll have to save that dance for another time." He winked at her and then smiled at Jess. "If your sister ain't hiring, Jess, there's always a place for you over at our company."

The dog growled as Chet and Harlan moved in. Buck stepped past them. "I'm going, gents. No need to upset the ladies."

It was only after they saw Buck mount his horse and ride off that Addie released Jess's hand. "Thank you," she said softly.

To Jess's surprise, Doc Wilcox offered him

a handshake. "Yes, Jess. Thank you. Your mother mentioned that you might have an interest in the marshal's position. Next time you come to town, stop by, and we can talk about that." He wrapped his arm around Addie's shoulders and led her away. "I think your mother is ready to head for home, Adeline, if that would be all right with you."

"Yes, please." Addie's voice shook, and seeing the way she clung to her father, Jess couldn't decide what he wanted more — to track Buck Tipton down and give him the lickin' he deserved or escort the Wilcox family back to town just to be sure Addie was safe.

Addie had managed to avoid Buck Tipton for several weeks before the party. Partly that was because he and his brother were busy with the cattle drive that took place every autumn, when ranchers took their stock to market in Yuma. Partly that was because Buck did not stay at his family's mansion in town as much as he had right after Jess left. Either way, she had been relieved and had allowed herself to lapse into complacency when it came to worrying about Buck. But at the party, he had made it quite clear that his interest in her had not waned in the least.

As the Tiptons' power over the town and region surrounding it grew, so did Buck's confidence. He strode around town as if he owned the place — which he and Jasper pretty much did. And although Addie had made it clear numerous times that she had no interest in Buck, he continued to act as if the two of them were destined to be together. His advances had escalated in the weeks just after Jess left, to the point where Addie was more than a little afraid of him. Of course, she had said nothing about that to her parents. Why worry them? She had worked hard to show her family and others that she was a grown woman and that she could handle her own problems, especially once Jess left. For way too long people in town had assumed that Jess would handle Buck Tipton — and tonight he had. But was that really what she wanted? To be in Jess's debt?

She sat bolt upright in bed, wide awake as she recalled how she had clung to his hand. She had learned the hard way with Buck that men had a terrible habit of taking the slightest gesture the wrong way. Men made assumptions that were simply not realistic. It was a wonder to her that the males of the species could excel in the sciences — a profession that demanded decisions be made strictly on the basis of fact.

"Well, not all men," she muttered as she got out of bed and paced the perimeter of her room. Her father did not fall into that category, nor had Amanda's father, nor did Chet Hunter, from the little she knew of him. Perhaps it was a matter of maturity. In time, Jess — and Buck — would understand that just because they wanted something to be true, that did not make it so.

A light knock at her bedroom door sent her scurrying back to bed.

"Adeline?" Her father's voice was soft enough that if she had been sleeping, she would not have heard him, nor would he have disturbed her.

"Come in, Papa."

She scooted to one side of the bed, leaving room for him to sit. He set a cup of steaming milk on the bedside table. "Your mother's remedy for achieving a good night's sleep," he explained, and they both smiled. Alice Wilcox had her own methods when it came to healing — methods that had nothing to do with books or research, potions or pills. "It was quite an evening," her father continued. "First Jess returns, and then that business with Buck Tipton."

"Why did you invite Jess to come speak with you about the marshal's position?"

51

"I wasn't going to — in spite of Constance. I know she's looking for some way to keep her son close, but if he's determined to go . . ."

"He'll go, or worse, he'll try to use the position to make a case against the Tiptons for his father's murder," Addie said. "So why even consider him?"

"I was impressed with the way he held his temper tonight. Everything about him said he wanted more than anything to light into Buck, but he didn't. Maybe he learned something while he was away — grew up some." He watched her sip the milk. "It occurs to me that having him here in town where I can keep an eye on him might just help keep him out of trouble. Of course, if you'd rather I not speak with him, I won't."

"It's hardly my decision. The town needs a marshal, and right now, Jess seems a likely candidate."

"He would not be staying at the ranch," her father reminded her, his gray eyes probing her expression. "He'd be right down the street there."

She shrugged. "I know."

"So that won't be a problem for you?"

"Not at all."

But it would. Having Jess Porterfield not a hundred yards away, seeing him every day

52

— maybe even several times a day — just knowing he was nearby? Big problem.

Two days later Jess lingered across the street from the Wilcox house. Mentally, he ran through what he wanted to say to Addie's father. He tried to anticipate the questions the man would ask. Why did he think he was qualified to serve as the town's marshal? That would be the first thing Doc Wilcox would ask him, and then he would peer at him over the tops of his wire-rimmed spectacles so similar to those Addie wore. He would wait patiently for Jess to answer him, not like some who would keep talking, keep prompting. No, Doc would wait to see what he would say.

The doctor's buggy was outside the house, so Jess knew he wasn't out on a call. No doubt Addie and her mother were inside as well. That was a problem, because he really didn't need to see Addie. His jumble of feelings, along with thinking about what he could do to get at the truth about his father's murder, had kept him from getting much sleep since the party.

"You gonna hold up that wall all day, Porterfield?"

He looked up to see Doc Wilcox standing outside the side door that led to the room he used as his office and examining room.

"No, sir. I reckon we've got some business to discuss, if this is a good time."

"Good as any," Doc replied, and waited for Jess to cross the rutted and dirt-packed street and follow him inside.

The office was smaller than he remembered. The couple of times he'd been there as a boy — once for a broken arm, and again, after getting into a fight with both Tiptons — the room had seemed much larger. He noticed the screen that separated the examining table from Doc's desk, the one wall with bookcases that ran from floor to ceiling and were still not enough to hold all the books, the model skeleton that dangled on its perch in one corner, and the tray of shiny metal instruments ready for use that sat atop a metal cabinet next to the privacy screen.

"Sit," Doc invited, indicating one of two wooden armchairs on the visitor's side of his desk. He took the swivel chair across from Jess, set his pipe on a large ashtray, and rested his elbows on the cluttered desk. "So, you gonna be our marshal?"

That took Jess by surprise. It sounded like Doc had already decided to offer him the job.

"I'd like to talk about it, sir." He could

hear someone moving around in the kitchen. Addie? Her mother?

"All right. What do you want to know?" Doc leaned back and folded his hands over his stomach. He was wearing a white shirt and a brocade vest that covered his suspenders. His suit coat hung on a coatrack behind him, along with his hat. His black bag sat on the floor next to the rack, as if at any moment, he might be called into action.

"Ma thinks . . ." Jess began.

"I know what your ma thinks, Jess. What I need to know is what you think."

"Not sure I get your meaning."

"Well, for example, are you hoping that taking the position will give you free rein to go after the Tiptons?"

Maybe. "Why would I do that?"

Doc arched an eyebrow. "Don't play me, son. We both know why."

"You mean because of them trying to get their hands on the ranch?"

Doc reared back in his chair and studied Jess for a long moment. "Well, there's that, and the fact that you think they killed your pa."

Jess felt bile rise in his throat. "So do you and just about everybody else in these parts. But nobody seems to be interested in proving they were calling the shots."

Doc leaned forward and removed his glasses. "Here's the situation, Jess. The town needs a lawman to keep things under control — in town. Duties will include breaking up fights over at the Dandy Doodle Saloon; locking up men like Lucas Jennings, Gus Abersole and others so they can sleep it off; and maybe even organizing a posse to hunt down some gang that decides to rob the bank. What it does not include is anything that might happen — or have happened in the past — outside the town limits."

"But . . ."

"No buts, son. If you take this job, you do it the way it is — the things I laid out, plus a lot of paperwork and collecting taxes and back payments and such. It does not now, nor will it ever, involve going after the Tipton brothers for your pa's death. You try and take on Jasper Tipton and his brother, you're gonna end up dead. If you want this job, those are the terms."

He hesitated.

"I mean what I say, Jess. Make one move outside your jurisdiction as town marshal, and I'll fire you on the spot."

Jess wrestled with the choice . . . that really wasn't a choice at all. "I understand. I want the job." He sure hated lying to Addie's father.

56

"Good. The pay is a hundred a month, and you can set your stuff up in the back room over at the jail. My wife will bring you breakfast every morning, and you can pick up a hot meal at the hotel every evening. The job is pretty much 'round the clock and every day and night of the year. You can sleep, of course, but if somebody needs your help, you go — like I always have. And it's good for folks to see you out and about — gives them the idea that all is well. Think you can handle that?"

It sounded like the world's most boring job, but Jess needed work, and he also needed time to get to the bottom of his father's murder. "Yes, sir."

"Like I said before, the bulk of your day will be spent doing paperwork. I'll stop by later and go over all that once you get settled in." Doc stood and offered Jess a handshake to seal the deal. Then he opened a drawer, pulled out a tin badge and a ring of keys, and tossed both on the desk. "That badge tells folks you got the job. The keys open your room and the two cells over at the jailhouse. I assume you've got your own gun?"

"Yes, sir."

Doc eyed him closely. "That all you got to say?"

"Yes, sir . . . I mean, no, sir . . . I mean, thank you, sir." He picked up the badge and keys then turned back to face the town's doctor and mayor. "What about the deputy? Didn't he want the job?"

"He's a good man, but not up to the work. He's decided to move on to Yuma, so in time you're going to need a deputy. I'll leave that to you."

"I appreciate that — and this." Jess fumbled with the badge, trying to pin it to his vest.

"Give me that," Doc said, nodding toward the badge as he came around the desk and faced Jess. He pinned the badge to Jess's vest and then patted his shoulder. "Don't let us down, son. There are folks here in town who think I'm making a big mistake giving you this job. Don't prove them right."

Jess bristled. "Who?"

"Now, you see, son, that's one reason folks have some concerns. You've got a temper. Who thinks you should be marshal and who doesn't shouldn't be a concern for you. Just do your job, and in time everybody will come around."

"Addie?" Jess asked, unwilling to let it go.

"I expect she's not especially pleased to know you'll be here in town, where she's likely to run into you on a regular basis, but she hasn't said anything to try and convince me not to hire you. The important thing for you is to keep your mind on your job. You hurt my daughter again, and I promise that you won't have to speculate about who doesn't like you. Do we understand each other, Porterfield?"

"Yes, sir."

"Good. Now get to work." He turned to the coatrack to get his coat and hat. "Adeline," he shouted, "you coming?" He picked up the black bag and headed for the door, but stopped when he saw Jess still standing by the desk. "You still here? Job started five minutes ago."

Jess hesitated, glancing back to the entrance to the living quarters.

"You hard of hearing, son?"

"No, sir." Jess slammed his hat on and picked up the ring of keys. "Thank you, sir. I won't let you down."

Doc looked like he doubted that, but he nodded. "Remains to be seen."

Blessedly, Addie did not see Jess for the next few days. The truth was she did everything she could to avoid that happenstance and was pleased with how successful she was. She left early each morning to make house calls around the region with her father or stayed with him in his office as he saw patients in town. She helped her mother prepare meals and do other household chores. She avoided going to Eliza McNew's general store as she usually did at least a couple of times a week, telling her mother she needed to study. And in three days she did not see Jess Porterfield even once.

But on the fourth morning, Jess arrived at her father's office just as she was coming down the hall that connected the office to the family's living quarters. She had intended to get her medical bag and accompany her father on calls to a very pregnant ranch wife and a cowhand who had badly injured his leg after a fall from his horse.

" 'Mornin', Doc." She heard the familiar bass of Jess's voice and through the partially open door saw him standing respectfully just inside her father's office.

"Is there a problem, Marshal Porterfield?" Her father was always formal in business situations.

"Miz McNew over at the mercantile told me she gave Marshal Tucker some back bills that needed collecting some time ago. I thought I might ride out today and see what I could do."

"All right."

"I just wanted to be sure I wasn't overstepping. I mean, I won't be here in town."

"But the business you're investigating is town business, is it not?"

"Yes, sir. That was my thinking."

"Then get on with it. One of the Johnson hands took a bad fall yesterday, and I need to get out there. Adeline!"

Addie saw Jess glance toward the door and pressed herself against the wall. She scooted quickly behind the door and did not answer her father's call.

"Was there something else, Marshal?" she heard her father ask, his tone impatient.

"No, sir."

"I suggest you be on your way then and let me get back to my business. Adeline," he barked again, "if we don't get going, Millie Jennings is going to have that baby without our help — not that she couldn't manage on her own with four children already."

Jess glanced toward the kitchen once more as her father walked to the outer door and held it open. "I don't know where that girl has gotten to," he muttered as the two men walked outside.

Addie waited until she heard the office door close before she tied on her bonnet and stepped into the office to pick up the medical bag identical to her father's. She lifted a corner of the lace curtain that covered the glass on the door and saw Jess headed down the street. It was safe to go out.

Her father was hitching their horse to the buggy. He did not look up when he said, "Millie Jennings is near her time, and those kids of hers need checking on as well. I'll drop you off there while I go on to George Johnson's place."

"All right." She chanced a look toward the street and saw Jess opening the door to the jail. The reality that she would not be able to avoid him forever hit her hard. After all, he was living and working within plain sight of her family's home — of her bedroom window. He would be around every time she went to the store or to the bank or . . .

"We need somebody to wear that badge, honey. I'm no more certain than anybody else that Jess Porterfield is the right man for the job, but for now, he's what we've got." Her father had come to stand next to her and place a comforting hand on her shoulder.

She knew he was right. The cattle from the ranches in the region had just been taken to market. Following that, there was always the chance that some cowhands with money in their pockets and no work for the time being might drift into town, get drunk over at the Dandy Doodle, and then decide to go on a tear, shooting up the town just for the sport of it. This was no time to be without a marshal.

"And what if Jess hadn't happened to show up?" she asked as they climbed aboard the buggy, and her father snapped the reins.

Doc shrugged. "Guess then we would have had to make do with Tucker's deputy, but the truth is I'm not sure he wasn't somehow involved in that business with Porterfield's murder, and I know for a fact that he would do whatever the Tiptons asked. Given that, I guess Jess Porterfield is the lesser of two evils."

They rode along in silence, leaving the town behind. In the distance, Addie spotted the adobe walls of Fort Lowell, the regimental headquarters for the 5th U.S. Cavalry. The soldiers billeted there were responsible for keeping the peace between the local ranchers and those native tribes that had not been moved to the reservation. As she and her father continued on their way, they passed what seemed like miles of barbed wire fencing that separated the acres of land belonging to the Tipton brothers from that of the other ranchers.

"He's going to want to know what really happened to his father," Doc mused, as if they had been holding a steady conversation ever since leaving the house. "He's already thinking the Tiptons were the real culprits, but he's smart enough to know he's got no proof."

"He's bound to find a way."

"Yep. That's why we're going to be sure he stays busy enough with this job that he's got no time for that."

We? "You mean you and the town council."

"I mean anybody who cares about that young man not getting himself killed." He glanced sideways at her and then clicked his tongue, sending the horse into a faster pace as they turned off the main trail and followed a narrower path to the Jennings place.

Millie Jennings was not yet twenty-five, but she looked and moved like a woman at least ten years older. Her face was mapped with deep lines — her skin weathered and dry, her hair thin and lank. She had four daughters — the oldest one was twelve years old — and Millie was large with her fifth baby as she pushed herself off a rickety stool to her bare feet and watched Addie climb down from the buggy. The two older girls came running, while the younger two —

64

twins — clung to Millie's patched skirt. Millie's husband, Lucas, was nowhere in sight, and Addie was glad of that. Lucas Jennings was a bitter, angry man who appeared to blame his wife for the fact that he had no sons to help manage their small plot of land.

Addie remembered the night she and her father had come to deliver the twins. After the birth, she'd gone out to the lean-to where Lucas was brushing his horse to give him the news. "You have twin daughters," she said quietly.

He continued to stroke the horse with the curry brush. "So now she's giving me girls two at a time," he had muttered before throwing the brush against the wall and stalking out, pulling the unsaddled horse with him and nearly knocking Addie over in the process. She'd run after him, afraid he intended to go inside and berate his wife for her failure, but he mounted up and took off, riding bareback in the opposite direction — the direction that took him away from his wife, children, and responsibilities. The direction that took him to town and the Dandy Doodle.

He'd come back a week later reeking of sweat and liquor. Addie had been there when he arrived. She'd taken to checking in

65

on the family, trying her best to make sure Millie and her children had what they needed to survive. "Get out," he'd growled at Addie.

Addie's instinct had been to stay for the sake of Millie and the children, but the expression on Millie's face begged her to follow his orders. "I'll be back tomorrow," she assured the children. And she had come back — day after day for weeks — but Millie refused to answer the door that Addie could easily have breached, since it hung half off its hinges. And it finally occurred to Addie that she might be causing Millie more stress by calling on her than if she just left her alone.

Now, four years and two stillbirths later, Millie would soon deliver her fifth child. Addie prayed it would be a boy, and at the same time, shuddered at the responsibility that male child would be expected to carry.

"How are you feeling, Millie?" Addie called out as her father drove on after shouting out a promise to Millie to return soon. Addie walked toward the hovel that passed for the family's home.

"She's been right poorly," Sarah, the eldest girl, reported.

"Shush up," her mother said, her voice barely a whisper. She was clutching her stomach, and as Addie came nearer, she realized the woman's face was contorted in pain.

"Papa!" she shouted, but her father was too far down the road to hear. "The doctor will be back soon," she told Sarah and the other children. "He has to go check on a man over at the Johnson place, and then he'll be back. In the meantime, help me get your mother inside."

"Is the baby coming?"

"Looks that way," Addie grunted as the full weight of Millie's bloated body pressed against her. She was half carrying the woman now. Should she send Sarah to get Lucas? Not that he would be any help. No, better to leave him out of it. She would manage until her father returned.

She got Millie to a rumpled bed pushed into one corner of the small house, then turned to the children who stared at her, wide-eyed and terrified. "Your mother is going to be fine. I just need all of you to go outside while I get her settled. Watch for the doctor, and as soon as you see him, Sarah, you must run as fast as you can to let him know he is needed inside."

Sarah nodded. "But what do we do until then?"

Addie searched her brain for ideas to stem

the children's natural curiosity about their mother and keep them occupied so they would not get into any trouble. She focused on the dying fire, a broom in the corner of the room, and a bucket filled with rags that she realized might well be clothes.

"While Mama is not feeling well, she's going to need you girls to take over doing her chores."

"Like what?" The second eldest child eyed her suspiciously.

"Sweeping the front porch, getting water from the creek, and washing out those . . . things there, hanging them on the line to dry, and . . ."

"We ain't got no clothesline," the girl, who looked a good deal like her father, persisted.

"Then drape them on the porch chair and railing. They'll dry in no time at all." She turned her attention to the twins. "As for you, we are going to need fuel for that fire there." From the smell, she knew they normally used dried cow chips as fuel, but she could hardly send them out into the pasture alone. "Maybe on the floor of the chicken coop or lean-to there's some dried straw you could gather in this basket?"

One of the twins grabbed the basket and toddled off, her identical sister in pursuit. "Wait for me, Sissy," she cried.

Addie heard Millie muffle a moan.

"Shouldn't one of us go get Pa?" Sarah asked.

"Not yet. Just watch for the doctor."

"I'll go down to the end of the lane," Sarah said, "and wait there."

"And get out of doing any real work, as usual," her sister muttered as she took the broom and headed outside.

"Before you go, Sarah, I'm going to need this pan filled with fresh water and any clean towels or bedding or rags you might have."

"We got nothing more than what you see here, miss."

Addie's heart sank. "Go fill the pan then," she said.

With all the girls gone, Addie turned her attention to Millie. Sweat poured off the woman's face as she clutched at the thin blanket and grimaced in pain. Casting around for anything she might use to ease the woman's suffering, Addie pulled a spindly wooden chair close to the bed and sat down. As she did, her skirt caught, and she saw the edge of her petticoat. It was clean — maybe not at the hem, but the skirt of it. Quickly, she lifted her dress skirt and unfastened the petticoat, letting it puddle at her feet. She snatched it up from the dirt floor and began tearing at it with her teeth until she was able to convert it to strips of fabric that would do for bandaging and padding, should either become necessary.

Sarah returned with the water, hurrying so that a good deal of it sloshed over the sides. "Good, now go to the road and watch for the doctor," Addie instructed as she dipped one of the petticoat cloths into the water and began wiping the sweat and dirt from Millie's ravaged face. When she'd done what she could, she plunged the cloth back into the cool water, folded it, and laid it on Millie's forehead, and then prepared to examine the mother-to-be as she had seen her father do dozens of times.

Oh, why had she not insisted that he observe her instead of the other way 'round? She positioned Millie on the bed with her knees bent and legs spread open. The woman wore only a dirty shift and skirt with no underclothes beneath it. Addie took one of the larger pieces of her petticoat and spread it under Millie's hips. It was so dark in the smoky cabin that it was hard for her to see what she was doing, but her father had taught her how to use touch to determine what she needed to know. Thankfully, the baby was positioned perfectly to move through the birth canal and out into the world. The head had not yet crowned, and

Addie knew it could be hours before this child came, or given Millie's history at birthing, it could come much sooner.

Meanwhile, she realized that the labor pains had stopped, and Millie's breathing was even and natural. "Millie?"

The woman's eyes fluttered open, and her face now held a heartbreaking expression of hope. "Is it a boy?"

"Too soon to know. It could be some time before the baby comes. Get some rest while you can."

As Addie got up to soak the cloth and replace it on Millie's forehead, Millie grasped her hand. "Promise me," she whispered, "if it's another girl, let her go to Jesus. Promise me," she demanded as she tightened her hold on Addie's wrist.

"I can't make that promise, Millie. You know that. Get some rest, and we'll hope for the best."

Millie's hand dropped like a stone cast into the river, and she closed her eyes and turned her face away from Addie.

"Oh, please let Papa get here soon," Addie whispered as she took advantage of the reprieve to stand at the open door and breathe in some fresh air.

As an hour passed and then another, she alternately took turns checking on Millie

71

and watching the girls go about the tasks she had set for them. She noticed that once she finished sweeping the front stoop, the girl who looked like her father went to help the twins gather straw. What was that child's name?

"Emmie," one of the twins shouted. "Can I take this for the fire?" The girl held up a piece of dried cactus.

Of course, Emma — named for Millie's mother. She remembered now. Lucas had even been happy at the time of the birth. "It'll be a boy next time," Millie had told him as he held their second daughter.

"She's beautiful, Millie, just like you," Lucas had said as he bent to kiss his wife's forehead and hand her the child.

Everything had been different then. The house had still been small, but spotless, and had included little homey touches that Millie loved to add, like a jam jar filled with wildflowers on the table. Now the table was cluttered with unwashed and chipped crockery and a crust of bread that was starting to mold.

"Help!" Millie's cry was so weak that Addie thought at first what she'd heard was a cat mewing. But there was no cat. She turned and found Millie struggling to sit up. "It's comin'," she muttered. Then she

72

looked around, wild-eyed. "Baby's comin' now."

"Emma!" Addie hurried to Millie's side even as she heard the child run inside. "Take that pan and get more water, and then make sure the little ones stay outside."

"Yes, ma'am." She took the pan and then froze and pointed. "Mama's bleeding."

Addie stepped in front of Millie, blocking Emma's view. "Not to worry," she called. "Just get me the water."

But there was plenty to worry about. Millie's face was ashen, and her eyes had rolled back as she collapsed onto the bed. "Stay with me, Millie," Addie begged as she worked furiously to get the woman settled so she could see what had happened.

Emma brought the water. "Set it here on the floor," Addie instructed, "and then keep your sisters occupied outside."

"Would a lamp help?" The girl did not wait for an answer, but unhooked a lantern from a nail by the door, and set it next to the pan of water. Then Addie heard the scratch of a match and the screech of the lantern's casing opening, and suddenly, there was light.

"Thank you, Emma. That's so much better."

"I could hold it for you."

Addie knew she could use the girl's help, but at the same time she saw from the corner of her eye that the twins were crowded together in the doorway. She glanced around and saw the window ledge next to the bed. "Let's just set it here for now. When my father gets here . . ."

"Somebody's comin'," Emma said.

Addie listened, praying for the familiar creak of her father's buggy and the clop of their horse's hooves on the hard-packed ground. But this was no buggy. This was the sound of a lone rider on horseback. "Emma, whoever that is, go get them, and bring them here as fast as you can, okay?"

Addie's first thought was that she would send whoever the rider turned out to be right back down the road to fetch her father. But when she heard Millie groan, she realized that waiting any longer was not going to be an option. She could see the baby's head, and Millie's breathing was growing weaker by the second.

"Come on, Mister," she heard Emma shout. "There ain't no time. The doc needs you right now." There was a beat, and then she heard a man step onto the porch. "You deaf or what? Doc needs you now," Emma shouted.

Addie looked over her shoulder at the

74

figure standing in the doorway, his six-foot frame and broad shoulders blocking a good deal of the light as, behind him, Emma herded her younger siblings into the yard.

"It's Mrs. Jennings," Addie started to say. "I'm afraid there's no time to waste. The baby's coming and . . ."

He stepped forward, and she swallowed the last of her words.

Jess Porterfield looked from her to the woman on the bed and back again. Then he tossed his hat in the general direction of a chair, rolled back his shirtsleeves, and plunged his hands into the pan of water. "Tell me what to do," he said.

"Well, for starters we're going to need more water now that you've contaminated that supply."

He stepped back and held up his hands. "Sorry, I just . . ."

"Emma! Find a pot you can fill with clean water, and put on the fire to boil. The marshal will go with you so he can refill this pan and help you carry the pot. And then keep your sisters outside until I say it's all right to come in. Understood?"

"Yes, ma'am."

With two hands, Emma grabbed a large hanging iron pot from the hearth and hurried away. Addie was all too aware that Jess was still just standing there.

"Maybe I should go get your pa?"

"This baby is coming within the next thirty minutes, so I doubt you could get him here before things start happening. In the meantime, I'm gonna need that water."

"Yes, ma'am," he said softly, and she wondered if he was mocking her. She had no idea what it was about Jess Porterfield that seemed to bring out the worst in her. Around him she could practically feel herself closing up in a tight ball, and when she spoke to him — *if* she spoke to him — it always seemed to come out angry or impatient. She sounded shrewish even to her own ears.

"Addie?" Millie's voice was weak, and she plucked at Addie's sleeve. "You got to . . ."

"Shhh," Addie whispered before the woman could finish asking her again to kill her child if it was a girl. Millie was crazy with the pain of birthing, and afterward she would not want to recall what she'd asked of Addie. "Let's get this baby born."

She heard Emma and Jess return. While Emma set the tin pan of water next to Addie, Jess hung the heavy iron pot over the fire and had the good sense to stir the embers and add more fuel.

"Emma, outside," Addie instructed. "Jess,

76

look in my bag there, and bring me my stethoscope and the bottle of rubbing alcohol. We're also in need of scissors or a good sharp knife and some string or twine."

Wordlessly, he followed her orders.

"Help me lift her toward the bottom of the bed," she asked, and noticed that he didn't so much as flinch when Millie cried out with the pain of a fresh contraction.

"I'll hold the lantern," he said, and Addie nodded as she positioned herself on a short three-legged stool at the foot of the bed.

"Millie, I see the head," she said. "It won't be long now."

Millie's answer was a low, guttural groan that trumpeted into a high, keening shriek. "That's it, Millie, push hard." She cradled the head of the child as it emerged and frowned when she saw the umbilical cord wrapped around the baby's neck. Her hands were shaking so bad, and the child was so durn slippery that she was afraid she might drop it or . . . "Jess, set the lantern down a minute and very carefully lift that cord free of the baby's head."

Jess hesitated only a second and then knelt to do what she asked. She couldn't help but notice that his hands were also shaking, and a trickle of sweat ran down his cheek. "Like that?"

"Good. Okay, Millie, here comes the first shoulder." Shoulder, and then an arm, and a tiny hand firmly clinched in a fist. Addie lifted the child's half-exposed upper body toward Millie's stomach as she'd seen her father do, and miraculously, the other shoulder came free. Then, in an instant, the full body of the baby was lying in her hands.

"It's a boy, Millie," Jess said, his voice filled with excitement and awe. "A big boy."

Addie tilted the child's head so that fluids could drain from his nose and mouth and waited for the cry that would tell her he was breathing free and on his own. She was just about to panic when the child gave what sounded like a cross between a cough and a hiccup and started to wail.

She grinned up at Jess. "A big boy with a big voice," she said as she handed the newborn to Millie, careful to watch the connected cord as Millie gathered the child to her breast.

"Addie?" Jess looked like he might be ready to pass out. He certainly couldn't seem to find any words, so he just pointed to the stream of blood oozing from Millie and onto the floor.

"It's all right," she assured him, not willing to admit that in the excitement she had forgotten all about the need to birth the pla-

78

centa. "Get me that stack of rags there." She pointed to her petticoat, now reduced to cloths of various sizes. "Use the ones with the lace." The placenta could be wrapped in the cloths that had come from the hem of her petticoat. They were going to need the cleaner ones for washing the baby and Millie.

"Okay, Millie, one more big push."

Millie grunted and strained, and the slippery mass fell into the wad of cloth that Addie held in readiness. She wrapped it tightly and set it aside. "Go find Lucas, and tell him he has that boy he's been wanting," Addie told Jess.

Then Addie stared at the cord. Millie, being the experienced mother that she was, had already freed one breast and given it to the child to suckle. Mother and child both seemed content, but that cord would need to be cut. Going over in her mind all the times she'd observed her father performing this essential task, Addie went to the fire and used a dipper to soak pieces of string in the hot water. Then she soaked a cloth with rubbing alcohol and wiped the blades of the scissors.

Gently, she turned the baby so that she could tie off the cord a few inches below his belly button. Then she made a second tie a few inches below that. "Cut between the two," she whispered, as if this were her father giving her the process as he performed the task. But her father wasn't there, and if she made a mistake . . .

"You can do it, Addie." Jess had returned and was standing with Millie's husband just inside the cabin door.

"Don't you hurt my son," Lucas Jennings snarled.

"Shut up, Luc, and let the doc do her job," Jess said. "In fact, let's you and me wait outside. You'll be wantin' to tell those girls of yours how they've got a little baby brother."

When Lucas seemed inclined to resist, Addie saw Jess practically pick the scrawny man up and carry him back outside.

She turned back to the work before her. "It'll be like cutting through rubber," her father had told her, "but just keep at it until you work it all the way through. It won't hurt the mother or child, so just pretend you're cutting out a dress pattern or some such."

Addie set to work. Once she had severed the cord, she used the remaining clean cloths to wash Millie and the baby, adding hot water from the pot on the fire to the cooler water in the pan. Finally, she helped

Millie sit up against the bed's headboard while she pulled free the covers that had gotten stained in the birthing process.

"Just set those over there," Millie directed. "I'll see to them tomorrow."

"The girls and I will see to them," Addie corrected. "You need to rest and regain your strength." She glanced around the cabin, hoping to see something clean she might help Millie change into, but it seemed the shift she'd been wearing was all she had. Addie had been out on enough calls with her father to be fully aware of the poverty that had stricken so many families in the area, especially as the drought went on and on, but she had never really seen anything as bad as the conditions here in the Jennings household.

"Addie, what I said before . . . about if it came out a girl . . ."

"Shhh," Addie said. "I think I hear my father's buggy." Her heart throbbed with pure relief as she ran to the door and saw the buggy coming up the lane with her father driving and the eldest Jennings daughter at his side.

"We got a brudder," one of the twins shouted.

"I did it," Addie said as she ran to her father and hugged him. "Oh, Papa, it was so thrilling, and I was so nervous and . . ."

"Doc, you'd best take a look at my boy." Both Addie and her father turned, but Lucas locked his gaze on the elder Wilcox. "I want to make sure he's all right."

It galled Addie that the man thought only of the child and not his wife. It infuriated her that he would dare to question her work. But the worst thing of all was what she saw as she stood in the yard and looked around — at the hovel that passed for a home, at the girls in patched shifts that barely covered them properly, at the neglected land and outbuildings, all in need of repair. To Addie's way of thinking, she had done Millie Jennings no favors today.

"Addie," Jess said, coming alongside her while Lucas Jennings and her father went inside, "I can't believe you did that — that you knew how, that you could be so . . . brave. Weren't you scared?"

"A little," she admitted. "I mean, I've watched Papa deliver a dozen or more babies, but that was just watching. This was different."

"I'll say."

His praise made her uncomfortable, and she cast around for any way she might take his attention away from her. "What brought you out here anyway?"

He grinned as he used his shirt cuff to polish his badge. "Official business. Seems Lucas Jennings has run up quite a tab in town at the mercantile and the Dandy Doodle. I came to see how he might be able to start paying off that debt so I won't have to arrest him."

"He needs a proper job," Addie said.

"He's got this place to run."

She raised an eyebrow and was pretty sure Jess had observed what she had. "This ranch is not going to pay any bills, and now, with a new baby and the girls to feed and . . ."

"Got to be something we can do to help them out. That girl you sent with me for water is smart like you. She and her sisters ought to be in school, not here trying to keep this place up."

Neither seemed to have more to say on the matter until Addie spoke her mind. "It's Luc that's the problem," Addie muttered.

"Now, Addie, him and Millie both were our friends growing up. He's a man who's lost," Jess replied, and he sounded like this was something he understood better than most might. "Doc did say that I could hire a part-time deputy," he added after a moment. "The pay isn't much, but . . ."

"What about this place?" Addie asked.

"I could probably help out some, and the hands at the Clear Springs could as well. My brother Trey would jump at the chance to take on more responsibility. I'll speak to Ma."

Addie felt a lump form in her throat. This was the Jess she had known when they were kids — always trying to look out for others. This was the Jess she had admired . . . and thought could do no wrong.

This was the Jess she had loved.

THREE

On his ride back to town, Jess could think of nothing but Addie delivering that baby, which led him to some disturbing thoughts about the two of them *making* a baby. That led to an obvious problem. Addie would have to agree to marry him, and that was about as likely to happen as his horse sprouting wings. Besides, she was good at doctoring, clearly loved it, and her father wasn't getting any younger. With the way the town and surrounding areas were growing, it was going to be important that there be a doctor living there.

But then she could be the doctor, and he could be the marshal, and why wouldn't that work out just fine?

Because she can barely stand to look at you, Porterfield.

Maybe with time. After all, speaking of doctoring, didn't the saying go that time heals all wounds? Of course, that might be true for some, but in the case of Addie and him, he was pretty sure there would be scars — at least on her part. But not going off with him had been her choice. He hadn't had a thing to do with it. If a guy looked at it from that angle, he was the wounded party here, so why was Addie acting like he'd been the villain?

"I came back, didn't I?"

His horse snorted.

"Okay, so I didn't exactly come back for Addie. I mean, I hoped she would be here waiting, but I came back because of Ma."

Another snort.

"And I had no place else to go," Jess admitted grudgingly. "You satisfied?"

His horse plodded along, sending up little puffs of sandy dirt as he followed the rutted and well-worn trail that led to town. Jess relaxed in the saddle, letting the reins go loose while he looked around. There wasn't a house or sign of a neighbor in sight — hadn't been since he'd left the Jennings place. All around him was open land pocked by the occasional Saguaro cactus set in among clusters of saltbush and desert willows. The only things moving were a couple of wild boar in the distance and a hawk circling overhead. How did anybody survive out here with nobody to talk to, nothing to really see except the same open range for miles around? At least the Clear Springs Ranch had some life and community with the cowhands and their housekeeper Juanita and her big extended family. Lucas and Millie Jennings had their kids and each other, and that was it.

And Lucas had changed. When the two of them had been in school together, Lucas had been the jokester — the kid always getting into trouble with the teacher. He'd been popular — somebody the others all looked up to and wanted to be like. And he'd been so in love with Millie. But each passing year, Jess had grown more restless, while Lucas became more silent and sullen. He began to drink — a lot — and he always had some excuse why he and Millie and the girls could not come to social gatherings. Come to think of it, Lucas had been the one to encourage Jess to leave. He'd been at Isaac Porterfield's funeral, and it had been the first time Jess had seen him in some time.

"Been busy," his friend had muttered as an explanation.

When Jess had hinted that he was thinking about moving on to a big city, Lucas's eyes had brightened for the first time. "Do it," he'd urged, grabbing Jess's shoulder and squeezing it hard. "Do it, and don't look back."

Jess thought Lucas's enthusiasm for the idea was born of one man supporting the dream of another. But now — seeing how Lucas and his family were barely getting by — Jess realized that his friend hadn't been thinking about him at all. He'd been wishing for a better future for himself, and he'd known there wasn't likely to be one.

Well, maybe Jess could help Lucas and his family out. After all, Doc had said he could choose his own deputy, and if he put it just the right way, maybe Lucas would agree to take the position. Back in the old days when they'd been in school and rode the range together, they'd made a pretty good team. If he put it that way, maybe Lucas wouldn't think Jess was offering the job out of pity.

He heard voices and horses and looked up to see a group of soldiers from Fort Lowell riding his way. He'd been intending to ride out to the fort to talk to Colonel Ashwood, the commanding officer, about his father's death — his murder. Doc had told him the man responsible had been arrested and would have his day in court, and had warned him to stay out of it. But when Jess had gone home to the ranch for Sunday dinner that week, he'd cornered his sister,

88

Maria, demanding details.

She, too, had begged him to stay out of it. "They've got the man who did the deed in custody at the fort, Jess, so let it go. Nothing you do will bring Papa back, and you're likely to get yourself killed in the process."

Later Trey had confirmed that both Maria and Chet were sure the real culprits were the Tipton brothers. Jess tended to agree with that. There had always been hard feelings between the Tiptons and Isaac Porterfield. While other ranchers had bowed to the pressure to sell out and move on, the Clear Springs Ranch — prime real estate for the Tiptons — had never been for sale. But when he'd tried to talk to Maria about going after the Tiptons, she had snapped at him. "Ma's been through enough, Jess. Pa's death, and then you leaving. Now you want to come back and stir everything up again? Just leave it to me — and Chet."

Jess had taken Sunday dinner as an opportunity to look over Maria's new beau. After all, whether Maria liked it or not, technically, Jess was the male head of the family now that his father was gone. He felt some responsibility to make sure his sister wasn't stepping from the frying pan that had been her association with their former foreman, Roger Turnbull, into the fire with this drifter. Before heading back to town, Jess had stopped by the bunkhouse where their cowhand, Bunker, had had nothing but good to say about the guy. Fact was that if Bunker liked someone, you could bet that fella was all right.

Besides, apparently Maria intended to marry the cowboy from Florida and stay on the ranch at least until Trey was old enough to take over. There was no doubt that Trey thought Chet Hunter practically walked on water, and their mother clearly respected the man, so as far as Jess could see, he had no worries there.

On the other hand, there was the business of Buck Tipton and Addie. Way before Jess took off, Buck had made it clear that he was sweet on her — not that she had the slightest interest in him. But the Tiptons did not like not getting what they wanted. Jess would have to watch out for Addie now that he was back. Of course, he'd have to do that without her knowing it because she wouldn't like it, much less thank him for it. That woman was just about the most pig-headed female he had ever met.

And that brought him full-circle in his thinking and within talking range of the soldiers. "Howdy," he called out. The lead soldier acknowledged his greeting with a raised hand and reined in his horse as his men followed suit. "Marshal Porterfield," Jess added by way of introducing himself.

He had to admit he liked having that title in front of his name. Addie would say it was nothing but pure pride, but what was wrong with taking a little pride in rising up in the world? Wasn't she one day going to be calling herself a doctor? Same thing, as far as he could see.

The sergeant was saying something about the weather.

"I understand the guy who had this job before me is in jail," Jess said, interrupting the mundane exchange.

The soldier looked down, and his men glanced nervously at each other. "You said your name is Porterfield?"

"That's right. The victim was my father."

"Then you'll understand, sir, that we really can't discuss the matter." He tipped two fingers to his hat in a kind of salute and signaled his men to move on.

"Just tell me this: Are you looking past Tucker?"

The soldier hesitated. "I don't get your meaning, sir."

"Yeah, I think you do. The Tipton brothers were pretty tight with the former marshal. Seems to me I recall him doing them a lot of favors over the years, looking the other way and such."

The sergeant turned his horse and signaled his men. "Nice talking to you, Marshal Porterfield. Good luck with your new position in town." He put the emphasis on the last two words, making it clear that he was reminding Jess where his jurisdiction began and ended.

Jess smiled as he watched them ride on. Clearly, they didn't know him well. A warning for him to stay out of something was like an invitation. And given the fact that it was his father who had been murdered, the idea that he might not go snooping around for answers was pure folly.

On the ride back to town with her father, Addie waited for him to say something about how she had handled herself in the face of the emergency delivery, but his mouth was drawn into a tight, thin line, and his hands gripped the reins as if at any minute the horse might decide to bolt. "Mark my words, Adeline," he said in that way he had of conversing with her after a long silence. "That woman is not long for this world."

"Millie?" Addie's mind raced as she tried to figure out what she might have missed.

"Was there more bleeding? I mean, did she . . ."

"Her body's not the problem. It's her mind that's going to go first. All those children, and Lucas not a lick of help. She's cooped up out here with no female companionship, no one she can talk to or seek help from. Did you see her eyes?"

"Her eyes?"

"The way she looked at her husband. It was like she was pleading with the man. 'Here at last is your son. Now leave me be.' "

"Luc would never hurt Millie," Addie said.

"I know that. He's a good man who's lost his way. I'm not talking about him taking a hand to her. But I'll wager you the fee we'll never see from Lucas Jennings that he'll be on her again before the week's out. Got one boy, so why not try for two?" His tone was filled with mockery and bitterness that made Addie uncomfortable.

"Papa!" Sometimes she had to remind him that she was his daughter, and some things he said out loud to her he would never say in the presence of his wife or other females.

He glanced over at her and shrugged. "Sorry."

Still she knew he was right. Millie had not

been herself the last few times that Addie had stopped by to check on her. Aside from the condition of the cabin and the girls, there was the matter of there being little to no food, and the way Millie avoided eye contact was not good. "Jess mentioned something about hiring Luc as his deputy."

To her surprise, her father laughed. "How's that gonna work when more often than not it's Jennings who needs to be locked up so he can sleep off a binge?"

Addie stifled the tendency to take offense. Her father was not fond of Jess — never had been. "You don't think Jess will stay, do you?"

"He left before."

"And came back."

"Yep, but have you asked yourself why he came back, Adeline? Things didn't go his way up there in Kansas City." He reached over and squeezed her hand. "Just don't go getting your hopes up again."

That made her mad. In the first place, she was a grown woman and certainly smart enough not to be taken in by the likes of Jess Porterfield twice. She hardly needed this fatherly advice, and besides . . .

"If you're so sure he'll take off again, why hire him at all?"

"As I told you earlier, he'll do until the

other council members and I can find somebody else."

Her father expected Jess to fail and disappoint everyone again. Probably half the town thought the same.

"I don't want you getting mixed up with that boy, Adeline. He broke your heart once. Don't let him do it twice."

"He's not a boy, and I'm not that girl. Oh, why is it that everyone — including my own family — assumes he left me? The truth is that I refused to go with him. He asked, and I said no."

"So you have said, and I believe that is precisely what happened. But, Daughter, sometimes doing the right thing is very different than what you truly wish to do. And it is my hypothesis that placed in the same circumstances a second time, you might well reconsider your original decision and —"

"Papa, please. I do not wish to talk about Jess Porterfield. I have just delivered my first baby, and that is what I want to think on now."

He looked straight ahead and said no more.

They were nearly back to town. Her mother would have supper waiting. She could see the roof of their house — the house where she'd spent her entire life. The house where she would more than likely spend the rest of it delivering babies, treating injuries from falls and gunshot wounds, and dealing with the usual rounds of stomach upsets and colds and such. But wasn't that what she had wanted? Wasn't that why she had pored over her father's medical books teaching herself, writing letters to medical colleges in the East, and being turned down by every one of them? Thankfully, her father had seen her passion and had taken her under his wing.

"Things are different out here," he'd told her. "You can apprentice with me, and when the time comes, we'll figure out how to get you whatever the law says you need so you can take over my practice."

At the time, it had seemed a dream come true. Addie had not been able to imagine wanting more. But even though Jess had not so much as written her one letter in all those months he'd been gone, she had been unable to put aside the feeling that medicine was never going to be enough. And on this day, after helping Millie birth her son, she found herself thinking a lot about how she would handle things if she were a mother.

"Go on inside and wash up," her father said as he pulled the buggy to a stop behind the house. "Tell your mother I'll be in directly."

The irritation she had felt for her father just minutes earlier faded as she studied his weathered face and saw how deep the shadows under his eyes were. He'd had a long day — they both had. "Let me take care of unhitching the buggy," she said, resting her hand on his forearm. "Mama will be wantin' to hear how the Johnsons' cowhand is faring with that leg of his."

If she needed further proof that her father was exhausted, it came in the form of his ready agreement. He climbed down and headed for the back door. Addie noticed he did not even pause to take his bag. She remained next to their horse, stroking its muzzle, as she watched her father slowly climb the back steps. When had he gotten so old?

She had unhitched the horse and was removing the harness when her brother came outside. Brian was five years older than Addie, married with kids of his own, and managing a successful law practice down in Tucson. To her way of thinking, he had a tendency to take his role as big brother a little too seriously.

"I understand Jess Porterfield is back," he began as he relieved her of the harness and then led the horse inside the lean-to.

"Really? I hadn't heard," she replied, making no attempt to temper her sarcasm.

"Don't be smart, Addie. Mama and Pa are worried."

"If Papa's so worried, then why did he hire the man to take over as marshal, which means he's working and living just down the street?"

"You know why. He did it for Miz Porterfield. Ma says she was finally starting to come back to herself, and then Jess shows up."

"I would think his return would be good news for the Porterfields. I know they've been awfully worried about him since he never wrote to let them know where he was."

Brian started brushing down the horse. "He never wrote you either, did he?"

"No. What's your point?" She gripped her medical bag in one hand and then walked around the buggy to retrieve her father's with the other.

"My point is that I don't want that guy to hurt you again, Sis."

"He won't. Now, can we talk about something else?"

"What?"

"Anything but Jess Porterfield."

Brian grinned. "Pa mentioned you delivered your first baby today. How did that feel?"

And, as if the sun had come out, Addie felt all her annoyance disappear. "It was incredible, Brian. I mean, I held this new life in my hands, and it was the most wonderful feeling. I was so scared and happy and excited all at the same time, and when that baby cried, I thought I would start bawling too."

Her brother set the curry brush on the shelf and pitched some fresh hay for the horse. "You're gonna make a fine doctor, Addie."

Brian's praise pleased her, and for the moment, she relived the time when she'd thought all she would ever want or need in this world was to practice medicine. And then Brian spoiled it by taking their father's bag from her, wrapping his free arm around her shoulders, and saying, "Just don't let Jess Porterfield mess that up for you."

After supper Addie sat outside on the front porch swing. She could hear her father and Brian talking inside, while her mother and sister-in-law, Ruth, washed and dried the supper dishes. She could smell her father's pipe smoke mingling with the scent of Brian's cheroot. It reminded her of the time she and Jess had decided to steal one

99

of Brian's cigars and try it. How Jess had gagged and then pretended he was just fooling around. But the greenish cast to his complexion had told her he was as close as she was to throwing up. Both their mothers had known exactly what they'd been up to and had punished them by making them each take two more puffs.

"Waste not, want not," Mrs. Porterfield had said, her voice dripping with sweetness and her eyes twinkling with mischief.

"Ma!" Jess had protested.

Those had been the good times — the times when their families had come together often, when everyone had teased Jess and her about the future it was assumed they would share. But they were no longer those two children. They were adults now, and as much as she and everyone else might have hoped they'd just go on spending their lives together, times had changed, and so had they.

They had been fifteen when her father had first started to question their relationship. He and Jess's father were friends, and he knew how Isaac Porterfield worried about his eldest son. "He has no ambition," she'd heard her father say one night.

"He has dreams," she had countered, interrupting the conversation between her parents. "Just as I do. You've always encouraged that in me, so why isn't it the same for Jess?"

"Do not be so impertinent, young lady," her father had said. "A young man like Jess has certain responsibilities. There are expectations that come with being the eldest son. It is not the same as your situation at all."

Sometimes her parents could be so old-fashioned. Times were changing. And certainly, living out on the frontier meant things were vastly different from the way her parents had grown up back east. But she realized now that this had been the start of her father's turning away from the idea that Jess would be a good match for his only daughter. Following that conversation, he had never again teased her about a union with Jess. In fact, he had more often than not turned the conversation to medical matters whenever Jess Porterfield's name came up.

She pushed the swing into motion and stared out at the empty street. Probably things were livelier at the far end of town where the saloon was, but here all was quiet. She saw Pastor Hudson exit the newly established Methodist church that sat across from the Catholic chapel that she and her family attended. The minister crossed the

101

front yard to the parsonage next door. His wife and the younger two of his five children came to greet him, and the scene made Addie wonder what things were like at the Jennings house. Had the older girls managed to put supper together? Was Lucas caring for Millie at all? More likely he was right here in town, down at the saloon, boasting about his newborn son and hoping the other patrons would celebrate by buying him shots of whiskey.

Brian and Ruth came to the door to say good night, and shortly after they left, Addie's father stepped out onto the porch. "Getting late," he said, although it couldn't yet be much past eight. "Ma and I are going up."

"Good night," Addie said as she propped her feet on the seat of the swing and hugged her knees to her chest.

Her father hesitated. "You coming?"

"In a bit. It's been a pretty special day for me, Papa. I want to just sit here awhile and take it all in." Her father walked to the edge of the porch and stared out at the town. She knew what he was thinking. "I'm not waiting for Jess," she said.

"All right. I'll say good night then."

"Good night, Papa."

At the door he paused. "Adeline? You did

some impressive work today. I'm very proud of you."

Her eyes welled with tears, and when she spoke her voice was husky. "Thank you, Papa. That means a good deal to me."

Her father continued into the house, and she heard him climbing the stairs. As soon as she was sure she was truly alone, she let the tears come — tears of relief that she had somehow kept her wits about her and brought the Jennings baby safely into the world, tears of disappointment that it seemed her life was already set and that beyond being a frontier doctor there would be nothing more. Jess would find someone else — half the single girls in town were already plotting for ways they might catch his eye. Certainly, after the party, Sybil Sinclair thought she had a chance of winning his heart.

Addie had run into Sybil at the mercantile. "Oh, Addie," she had said, her expression one of pity, "I do hope having Jess Porterfield back in town is not too upsetting for you."

"Not in the least," Addie replied. "I'm pleased for his family — especially his mother."

"Yes, of course. We all are, but then it must be difficult for you. I mean, before he left, the two of you were practically . . ."

Addie had known exactly what this was about. Sybil was fishing for information, wondering just how much of a problem Addie was going to be.

"That's all in the past, Sybil. Jess and I are different people than we were then." She had taken both of Sybil's hands in hers and patted them. "You go ahead and go after Jess, if that's what you really want."

She remembered how Eliza McNew had turned away to hide her smile.

Now, as Addie rested her forehead on her knees, she heard the clop of a lone horse's hooves in the distance, and moments later she saw Jess ride into town. The way he dismounted and led the horse around the side of the building told her that he was exhausted, and her instinct was to go to him, perhaps with a cup of hot tea. But no, that would be a mistake. Let Sybil bring the man tea.

Her father and brother were right. The only way to handle this situation was to keep her distance, and then maybe, in time, she could be in the same town with him without wishing things were different.

Jess was beat. He couldn't recall a time when he had so looked forward to kicking off his boots and hitting the hay. He stabled his horse at the livery next door and picked up the supper that Mrs. King at the hotel had kept hot for him. The route from the hotel back to his office took him by the Wilcox house, so he forced himself to keep his eyes on the street as he passed. He would not look to see if a light burned in Addie's window.

But then he heard the familiar squeak of a porch swing — a swing he had sat on with Addie many a night as they shared their dreams and planned what he had thought would be their future.

He glanced over, and sure enough, there she was, her face burrowing into her arms, which were folded around her knees — all huddled into herself the way she used to sit with him. Well, he wasn't just going to pretend he didn't know she was there, so he crossed the road and stopped at the front gate. "Nice evening," he called.

Her head shot up, and her feet hit the porch floor, stopping the motion of the swing. "I . . . yes, it is. I was just about to go inside."

"Quite a day for you," he said, wanting more than anything to keep her talking. Maybe if they could just talk like they used to, they could come back to where they used to be.

"Yes. My first delivery." She paused, and then added, "Thanks for your help. I don't know what I would have done if you hadn't shown up when you did."

"You'd have done just fine, Addie."

The silence between them stretched on. He was vaguely aware of shouts from the saloon at the far end of town — nothing unusual. The smell of the stew Mrs. King had saved for him made his stomach growl. "Well, suppertime for me," he said finally. "You have a good night, Addie." He tipped the fingers of his free hand to his hat and turned to go.

"Jess?"

He paused but did not turn back to face her.

"You're going to make a fine marshal," she said.

He chuckled. "Your pa and half the town think I'll up and quit."

"Yeah, they do. So what are you gonna do about that?"

"Prove them wrong," he replied, and headed back toward his office.

He'd barely had time to set his supper on the scarred wooden desk when the door banged open on its hinges, and Pete Townsend burst into the small cramped room. "Marshal, you better come quick. Lucas Jennings is 'bout to tear up the saloon, and Miss Lillian says you need to start earning your pay."

Jess grabbed his hat and gun belt as he followed the bartender out the door and up the street to the Dandy Doodle. The closer they came to the saloon, the more he was aware of the sound of glass breaking, followed by a series of gunshots. All of the saloon's patrons, as well as Miss Lillian and her dance hall girls, were standing in the street. Miss Lillian — all five feet and a hundred and fifty pounds of her decked out in a satin dress the color of an Arizona sunrise — came storming toward him.

" 'Bout time you showed up. Somebody needs to shoot that man before he completely destroys my business."

"Now, Miss Lillian, if I shoot the man, that'll leave five little ones without a pa," Jess said, trying to placate the woman while he assessed the situation.

"You'd be doing them and Millie a favor," the saloon owner huffed just as a chair came crashing through the swinging doors of her establishment.

"Just give me a chance to talk to the man."

"He's roaring drunk," Pete said as he followed Jess closer to the entrance.

"Is he out of ammunition?"

"Must be. We ain't heard no more gun-fire."

Jess stepped onto the boardwalk and picked up the chair, then pushed open the swinging doors. "Hey, Luc," he called.

The man staggered as he turned and studied Jess through half-closed eyes. "What do you want?" he snarled.

"Never got the chance to offer my congratulations," Jess said as he slowly set the chair down and moved to put the ornately carved Brunswick bar between him and Lucas. "A son — that's something to celebrate all right."

" 'Bout time," Lucas muttered, but then he gave Jess a loopy grin. "He's big — Doc says he's probably the biggest baby born around these parts in some time."

"Is that right?" Jess slowly poured two jiggers of rye and stepped around the bar, holding one out to Lucas. "Well, I'll drink to that." He downed his and set the glass on the bar, then watched as Lucas downed his as well. He stepped around the bar and held out his hand to the man. "Congratulations," he said again, and as soon as Lucas accepted his handshake, he grabbed his old friend around his shoulders, pinning his

108

arms so he couldn't move, and steered him outside. The crowd parted as he continued walking Lucas down the street.

"Hey, where we going?"

"Got a fresh pot of coffee on the stove over at the office and a nice clean cot for you to sleep it off on. Then tomorrow, we'll talk some more, okay?"

Miss Lillian was not satisfied with the solution Jess had worked out. "Lucas Jennings, you are going to pay for every nickel of the damage you did here tonight, and you are never to set foot in my saloon again. Is that clear?"

Lucas actually giggled. "Women," he sighed as he staggered along beside Jess.

"You married one of the best," he reminded his friend.

"Yep. I did. She's too good for the likes of me. I can't . . ." He started to blubber.

Jess hauled an inconsolable Lucas into one of the two cells, dropped him on the cot, and then locked the door.

Lucas curled away from him, facing the wall, his shoulders shaking. "Will you see she's all right, Jess? Her and the young'uns?"

"On my way," Jess replied as he headed out the door and back to the livery to saddle his horse. As he rode out of town, he saw Miss Lillian and Pete sweeping up the broken glass. Tomorrow he'd have to figure out how to deal with that. No way Lucas could pay for the damages, and putting him away didn't solve anything.

When he'd decided to apply for the law-man's position, Jess had been certain that he could also use the position to find a way to settle the score once and for all with the Tiptons. They might think they'd gotten away with murder, but he had other ideas. Problem was that Doc had kept him so busy with the duties of his new job that he'd hardly had time to think about, much less do anything about, the Tiptons. He expected that was what Doc — and his mother — had planned. On the other hand, riding off at this hour of the night to check on Millie instead of getting some much-needed sleep had been his doing. He probably should have told somebody where he was going just in case there was more trouble in town, but this was what he was — a man who acted on impulse. As far as he was concerned, the good people of Whitman Falls could take him as he was or let him go.

It was pitch black when he reached the Jennings place. He slid from the saddle and approached the house, one hand instinctively on the handle of his gun. The door hung lopsided, and from the other side he heard a woman's voice. Millie was singing softly. He pushed the door open enough so he could see her sitting by a banked fire, breastfeeding her baby and humming a lullaby.

"That you, Luc?" she said softly, without turning. Her voice held no fear.

"It's me, Millie," Jess said, stepping fully into the room and keeping his voice low so as not to wake the girls he saw sleeping on the floor. "Just came to check on you."

She glanced over her shoulder at him. "It's late." Then she stood, her free hand going to her mouth. "Is it Luc? Has something happened?"

"He's all right, Millie. I had to take him over to the jail to sleep it off. He got a little carried away celebrating that boy there."

"He'll be home by morning then?"

Jess didn't want to lie to her. "Well now, you know how Luc can get when he's had a few too many."

Her sigh as she sat back down was somewhere between relieved and defeated. "How long?" she asked.

"Couple of days. I could send over one of the men from Clear Springs Ranch to help you out 'til then." She stared at the embers of the fire for so long that he thought perhaps she hadn't heard him. "Millie?"

"Thank you for coming all the way out here to tell me, Jess. We'll manage 'til Luc gets back. Good night."

"Have you got food enough and . . ."

"Good night, Jess."

He'd been dismissed. Not knowing what else to do, he stepped outside, but before he mounted up to leave he made sure the lone milk cow had fresh hay and feed, and that there was a stack of kindling next to the door. He was pretty sure one of the older girls could handle the milking.

On the way back to town he tried to think what else he could do for Millie. Like Lucas, she was a friend — somebody he'd known his whole life. Addie and Millie had been two of the prettiest girls in the region.

Addie.

She'd know how to help Millie, and it would make perfect sense that she'd come calling to check on her and the baby. That was the ticket. Addie would know what to do. He spurred his horse to a gallop and rode full out across the barren range until he saw the buildings of town outlined against a sky filled with stars.

FOUR

Addie woke to the sound of something splattering against her window. She opened one eye — the one she could see best out of without her glasses — and waited, listening for rain. The sounds came again — not rain, but something lightweight hitting the glass.

"Addie?"

The past filled the room as Addie recalled all the nights Jess Porterfield had stood below her window, throwing stones to wake her and calling out to her in that same hoarse whisper. Thankfully her parents' room was on the other side of the house.

She sat up, thrust her arms into the sleeves of her robe — a cast-off from her brother — and hurried to the partially raised window. "Shush," she ordered, then whispered, "What do you want?"

She expected to see the grin Jess always wore the minute he saw her at the window, but tonight he was not smiling. "I need to talk to you." His voice was dangerously close to normal — a fact noted by the neighbor's dog, who set up a ruckus. "Come down," he said, and headed for the back porch, obviously certain that she would follow his instructions.

Had it not been for the fact that Jess looked worried, she might have told him to go away. But everything about him told her he had not come for courting as he had in the past.

Barefoot, she tiptoed past her parents' closed door and down the stairs to the kitchen. The late October night chill made her pull the robe tightly around her body as she eased open the back door and stepped outside. "What?" she said, squinting up at Jess.

"Are you planning to call on Millie tomorrow — I mean, later today?"

"Why?"

Somewhere, a rooster crowed.

"I had to lock Luc up."

"It's not the first time," Addie said, stifling a yawn. But then she looked directly at Jess. "What about Millie and the girls? I mean, they're out there all alone and . . ."

"They're all fine. He went on a toot down at the Dandy Doodle, shooting up the place and breaking stuff and all."

114

"But Millie . . ."

"I rode out there. She's fine."

Addie squinted, trying to see him clearly without her glasses. "Yet you came here in the middle of the night to be sure I was planning to check on her. Why?"

Jess heaved a sigh of pure weariness. "Because, like you, she's stubborn. I offered to send some help over to take care of chores and such until Luc gets home, but she refused."

Resisting the urge to place her hand on his cheek to comfort and reassure him, Addie chose instead to soften her tone. "How long will you keep Luc locked up?"

"I don't rightly know. If it was just that he was drunker than a skunk that would be one thing. But Miss Lillian is demanding he pay for the damage he did to her place, and how is he going to manage that when he can barely put food on the table for his family?" He stepped away from her and stared off in the direction of the jail. "He's my friend, Addie, and he's lost his way. He loves Millie — and his kids — but the deck is so stacked against him right now . . ."

He was right. Lucas and Millie were caught between a rock and a hard place with nowhere to go. "Millie won't listen to me either," Addie said. "I mean, I can go check

115

on her, but if I try to convince her she needs help, she won't accept it."

"Well, we've got to do something. We can't just stand by and watch them lose everything — and each other — in the bargain." Jess sat down on the top step of the small back porch and rested his chin in one hand.

It seemed perfectly natural that Addie would sit next to him while they thought through the possibilities of how they might help their friends. "Lucas has almost no cattle left," she said. "So no real reason to farm that land. The house is practically falling down. Those girls should be in school, and . . ." She ticked off the obvious problems one by one, and with each item she added to the list, she could practically feel Jess grow more jumpy.

"Tell me stuff I don't already know," he grumbled.

"All right. If Luc had a paying job and Millie could take in some sewing or something, and the older two girls could go to school on a regular basis, then maybe they'd have a chance."

"And how's all that gonna happen?"

"Well, you did mention the idea of taking Luc on as your deputy."

Jess snorted in derision. "That was before he shot up the Dandy Doodle. Miss Lillian would have a cow if I hired him now. And who do you think is going to ride all the way out to their place to drop off sewing?"

Addie stood, prepared to go back to bed. "Do you want my help or not?"

He looked up at her. "I came to you first, didn't I?"

It was a challenge, another memory of their past. It was a memory she'd just as soon forget — all the times they had thought they were walking the same trail only to end up snapping at each other like two stray dogs.

"I'm going back to bed," she muttered, and headed for the back door.

He caught her wrist as she passed him. "Hey," he said softly. "I'm sorry. I'm just so frustrated and worried and . . ." He tugged on her hand and patted the place beside him. "Sit back down, and tell me why you thought about the sewing part."

Reluctantly, she sat again, making sure to leave at least half a foot of space between them. "Millie is an excellent seamstress. Maybe Eliza could use somebody to do alterations now that she's gotten into selling more ready-made clothes. Of course, Millie would have to come to the store to work because she doesn't have a sewing machine, and of course, who would care for the baby and the little ones while she did that, and of course . . ." She was beginning to realize that Jess had a point. With Millie and Lucas it seemed like solving one problem always meant creating two or three more.

The two of them sat in silence as the night sky turned gray, and then the horizon was streaked with the orange haze of the rising sun. Finally, Jess pushed himself to his feet. "We've got a day or so to figure on this. I'll talk to Pete Townsend. Maybe he can get Miss Lillian to listen to reason, and you go check on Millie and the kids."

"And talk to Eliza," Addie said.

Jess hesitated. "Times are hard for everybody, Addie. I wouldn't want Eliza to feel obligated."

"Well, she will because that's just who she is. But the fact is that offering alterations is a way she can expand her business — it pays for itself."

Jess grinned. "I never thought of it that way." But instantly, his smile turned to a worried frown. "I don't see Luc being all right with letting Millie come into town, especially if the reason she's coming is to work."

Addie stood again, and this time she went directly to the back door. "Jess Porterfield, you've got a lot of nerve accusing Millie and me of being so stubborn when you and your good friend Lucas might want to consider just how often you've allowed your stupid pride to get in the way of what's best for you." She let herself into the kitchen and closed the door before she could hear his response.

The snores coming from the cell closest to his desk told Jess that Lucas was at least getting some sleep on this never-ending night. He set the bowl of stew — cold and covered in a layer of congealed fat — on a shelf. Then he collapsed into the rickety old chair and planted his booted feet on the desk with no regard for the stacked papers and files beneath them. He was beat. He couldn't remember a time when he had been so tired. His head hurt, his leg muscles cramped, his stomach growled. He glanced at the stew. Was he hungry enough to eat that? Nope. He took a swallow from the mug of coffee and made a face. Cold, bitter, and foul. What he wouldn't give for a cup of Juanita's coffee, accompanied by a pile of freshly scrambled eggs topped with chopped tomatoes and onions and chili.

Behind him the snoring ended abruptly and was replaced by a gagging cough that seemed to go on far too long.

"If you're planning to be sick, Luc, there's a bucket there in the corner. Use it." The animal growl that was Lucas's reply told Jess that a night's sleep had done little to improve the man's mood. "Did you sleep well?"

The cell door rattled. "Let me outta here, Jess."

Jess plopped his feet onto the floor and got up, stretching to his full height. "Not a chance, my friend. You've got some serious charges against you."

"Tucker never locked the cell," Lucas muttered.

"Tucker ain't here. I am."

Lucas glared at him. "You gonna feed me? You lock a man up, then you gotta give him food and drink."

"You something of an expert at this or what?" Jess grinned as he used a dipper to fill a tin cup with water from the bucket he kept by the back door. "Here's your drink. Food will have to wait until later when Doc's missus brings us both our breakfast."

Lucas downed the water and held out the cup for a refill. "Doc knows I'm here?"

"Half the town knows you're here. If I was you, I wouldn't be making plans to patronize the Dandy Doodle anytime soon." Jess pulled a three-legged stool closer to the bars

120

of the cell. "We need to talk, Luc."

"I know. I'll pay for the damages."

Jess waited for his friend to drink the second cup of water before asking, "How?"

Fear and anger warred in Lucas's bloodshot eyes. Anger won. "You're acting pretty high and mighty, Jess, for somebody who abandoned his family and all. Seems to me like you're the last man who ought to questioning me."

Jess shrugged. "Comes with the job." He nodded toward his badge, then studied Lucas's face. "So, what's your plan, Luc?"

"None of your business. You just unlock this cell, let me get on my way, and I'll worry about handling Miss Lillian."

"Can't do that."

"In case you've forgotten, I've got a wife and five young'uns who need me."

"Haven't forgotten any of that. I stopped out at your place last night to check on them." Lucas turned his back on Jess. "Don't you want to know how they are?"

Lucas nodded once, and Jess noticed two things — Lucas's fists were clenched so tight that it made his upper body a tense mass of hard muscle, and two almost identical drops of water had just plopped onto the stone floor. Lucas Jennings was crying. "My boy?" he managed.

"Sleeping in his mama's arms." Rather than embarrass his friend, Jess pushed the water bucket closer to the bars so Lucas could reach it. "It'll be full sunup in an hour. We can't do anything until then, so we might as well get what sleep we can."

He returned to his chair, propped his feet back on the desk, and lowered his hat over his eyes. A minute later, he heard the crush of the straw mattress on the cell's cot and knew Lucas had taken his advice.

Just as Jess was about to doze off, Lucas said, "Was Millie all right?"

"She seemed to be fine."

"And you say my boy was sleeping?"

Lucas bit his lip to keep from reminding the man that he also had five girls. "Yeah. Addie will ride out there first chance she gets and check on them."

"Addie's a good friend," Lucas said softly. "You were a fool to leave her."

Yeah, he thought. *I know that now.*

"I have to get over to see the priest, Addie. I promised to help clean the chapel windows," Alice Wilcox said the following morning as she put the finishing touches on two plates of eggs, bacon, and thick slices of sourdough bread. "You can run these over to the jail and then ride out to see how

122

Millie is doing."

Addie saw through her mother's excuses. Addie's father might not want her to rekindle her relationship with Jess, but her mother was an incurable romantic. She had started matchmaking the minute the family had left the Porterfield ranch the night of the party. "Obviously, the boy has realized his mistake and returned to make amends," she had said.

"Yes — to his mother and siblings," Addie had muttered.

"And to you. Did you see the way he stood up to Buck Tipton?"

Doc Wilcox had sighed heavily and snapped the reins. "Alice, no one is arguing with you, but we'll just have to wait and see what Jess Porterfield's true reason for coming home might be — especially now that he knows about his pa."

Addie's mother had pressed her hands — and lips — together then, and no more had been said about Jess or Buck or the party for the remainder of the trip home. But Addie knew that her mother was a long way from giving up, and making this lame excuse about needing to wash the chapel windows so Addie would have to deliver breakfast to Jess and Lucas was as transparent as the lace curtain covering the glass on the kitchen door.

"The jail is the opposite direction of Millie's, and besides, what's so urgent about washing windows at this hour?"

"Do not question me, young lady." Alice Wilcox thrust the two plates, now covered in tea towels, at her daughter. "It's not as if you've never been asked to do this before. No, the only thing stopping you is the idea that you will have to see Jess. Now this food is getting cold, so shoo."

Addie trudged down the street, planning her strategy. She would go in the back door — the door closest to the cells. She would knock, call out that breakfast was served, set the meals on the back stoop and leave. If Jess opened the door on her, she would wave and shout that she had to be on her way. After all, he was the one who had asked her to check in on Millie and the children.

But Millie will want to know about Lucas.

Addie frowned. She had to at least have a look at Lucas, maybe ask how he had fared overnight. She couldn't think how she might do that without also having to look at Jess. She straightened her back and quickly covered the rest of the distance.

"Breakfast," she called out as she entered the back door of the jail.

" 'Bout time," Lucas grumbled. He looked

terrible. His bloodshot eyes were ringed with dark circles. He reeked of sweat, liquor, and vomit. He scowled at her, and she tried hard to remember the time when she and Lucas Jennings had been friends.

"How are you, Luc?" She uncovered one plate and passed it through the opening in the cell door.

"Hungry."

"Mind your manners," Jess instructed. He was standing in the doorway that separated the cells from the office. "That smells mighty good, Addie."

"You can thank my mother." She unwrapped the second plate and handed it to Jess. "You've got water, I see, and I assume you can make coffee," she said as she busied herself with folding the tea towels into precise squares. "I'm going out to your place to look in on Millie and the children, Luc. Is there anything you want me to tell them?"

"I don't need you or anybody else speaking for me, Addie Wilcox. Just be sure my son is doing all right."

"And your girls?" Addie forced her voice to stay calm.

Lucas stared at her for a long moment and then returned to shoveling food into his mouth, ignoring her question.

"She's just trying to help you, Luc," Jess said. "We both are."

"Didn't ask for your help and don't need it."

"Right," Jess muttered sarcastically.

Addie's heart went out to him. It was clear that Jess hadn't had more than a couple hours sleep. He cared about Lucas, and she could see their friend's refusal to accept help ate at Jess. "I should go," she said, heading for the back door.

"Did she name the boy?" Lucas spoke so softly that for a minute Addie thought she might have imagined the question.

Addie paused, her hand on the doorknob. "I don't know. Is there a name the two of you have been thinking of? I mean, for when you had a boy?"

Lucas shrugged. "Just tell her not to call the kid after me. Give him a better start in life than taking my name."

Addie felt her throat tighten. She walked to the cell and wrapped her fingers around the bars. "I'll see what she says and stop by later to let you know what she's thinking."

Lucas glanced at her, his expression one of pure distaste. "Did I ask you to do that? No. Just do your doctoring, and make sure my boy is all right."

Addie stepped away from the cell, her fury

126

at this man barely contained. "Well, you enjoy that breakfast, Lucas Jennings, because my guess is your wife and children are not seeing anything close to food like that this morning."

She pushed open the back door and let it slam behind her.

"Satisfied?" Jess grumbled as he watched Addie go. "That woman is going out to your place to care for your wife and kids. I am going up the street here to the Dandy Doodle and see how bad the damage is and whether or not I can talk Miss Lillian into cutting you a deal. Seems like everybody's trying to clean up the mess you've made of your life. Everybody but you, Luc."

"I've done my best," Lucas argued. "Your folks had ways of riding out the drought and all, but a small rancher like me —"

"Stop feeling sorry for yourself. Everybody around these parts has seen rough times. The difference is that others have figured out ways to get around those hardships. They didn't take to drink. They didn't —"

"Turn tail and run?"

Jess knew the truth when he heard it. He had a lot of nerve chastising Lucas when he'd abandoned his own family at their hour of greatest need. "Okay, so we're both a couple of failures. Maybe if the two of us join forces, we might just be able to make it through the mess we've made of our lives."

Lucas squinted at him as he sopped up the last of the egg yolk with a crust of bread. "Meaning?"

"I'm probably gonna regret saying this next sentence, but here goes. I need a deputy, Luc, and the job is yours, if you want it."

Lucas laughed so hard that tears welled in his eyes and for so long that Jess started laughing as well. The idea of the two of them being the law in Whitman Falls was pretty ridiculous when a man stopped to think about it. Jess wearing a tin star was outlandish enough, but both Lucas and him wearing the badge was downright outrageous.

Still, no point stopping now.

" 'Course I'll have to hold back half your pay until you settle your debt with Miss Lillian and . . ."

Lucas stopped laughing and moved closer so that he was face-to-face with Jess. "You're serious?"

"Yep. Doc said I could hire you." Well, Addie's father hadn't exactly agreed to Lucas as the candidate, but he had said Jess could hire someone.

"Doc said that? Addie's pa?"

"Do you want the job or not?" Jess watched as Lucas considered the idea.

"How would I take care of my place?" he asked.

It galled Jess to realize that his first thought wasn't of Millie and the kids, but of property. He fought back against his irritation and inclination to snap at Lucas. "The job's not full-time, and it'll be mostly nights, so I can get some sleep now and again."

"So I could work the land during the day and . . ." Lucas scratched his head and frowned. "But that would mean leaving Millie and the young'uns alone at night."

Jess saw the opportunity to present Lucas with Addie's idea of Millie doing some sewing for Eliza McNew. "Well, I heard talk that the mercantile might be looking for somebody to do alterations now that the store stocks a good deal of ready-made clothes. Seems to me I recall Millie is handy with a needle and thread."

"How's that gonna work? She's got her hands full with those children."

Your children, Jess almost said, and wished Addie were there to help him find his way through all of Lucas's doubts. "We're kind of putting the horse ahead of the buckboard here, so how about I go talk to Miss Lillian and see if she would accept repayment in installments? If she agrees then we can figure out the rest."

"I'll give it some consideration, but that business about Millie working — you can forget that. I take care of my own."

Jess unlocked the cell door. "I'm trusting you not to take off, Luc. While I'm gone, why don't you get yourself cleaned up a bit?" Jess nodded toward the back stoop of the jailhouse, where he kept a wash pan, towel, razor, and bar of soap. "Wash up, and wash out that shirt you're wearing, so you don't stink to high heaven."

Lucas took a sniff of his shirtsleeve and made a face. "Shoulda told Addie to have Millie send me a fresh shirt."

"You also should've thanked Addie for going out of her way to make sure your wife and children are all right." Jess picked up his hat and headed out the front door. "Might want to remedy that next time you see her."

Addie found that without the threat of Lucas's temper hanging over the squalid house, Millie and the girls were far more relaxed. By the time she arrived, the older girls had done the morning chores — milking the lone dairy cow, collecting two eggs, feeding the three chickens and rooster, and gathering fuel for a cooking fire. Now, as Emma scrubbed one of her father's shirts on a washboard, the younger girls played a game of tag. Millie sat on an old milking stool on the front porch, feeding the baby, while Sarah combed out her mother's long, lank hair.

"Good to see you," Addie called as she climbed down from the buggy and unloaded the basket of food and clothing she and her mother had gathered. "How are you feeling?" she asked when she reached the porch. All the while she was making her own assessment of Millie's health. Her coloring was better, and although she looked tired, she did not seem to be in pain.

"How's Luc?" Millie asked, ignoring Addie's concern.

"I saw him this morning. He was having his breakfast when I left to come out here. Speaking of which, you know Ma — she insisted I bring you this basket of stuff." Somehow Addie understood that a charity basket that came from her mother was more likely to be accepted than one that came from her.

"Is he coming home today?"

"Jess says he needs to keep him there for

131

a bit until they can clear up a misunderstanding with Miss Lillian."

Millie nodded. "Thought as much.
Emma's washing a shirt for him, if you'd be
so kind as to see he gets it." The baby made
a loud sucking noise that made Millie smile.
"And thank your mother for the basket. The
way this one eats, he'll be on solid food in
no time."

Addie sat on the edge of the stoop. "Luc
asked if you'd come up with a name."

Millie frowned. "Not yet."

"We've been calling him Little Lucas,"
Sarah volunteered.

"For now," Emma added firmly.

"Girls, go down to the well, and get some
fresh water so Miss Addie can have a cool
drink after her long ride." Millie shooed
both of her older daughters away, and once
they were out of earshot, she turned to
Addie. "He's in serious trouble this time,
isn't he?"

"It's not good, but Jess is going to talk to
Miss Lillian, and maybe he can work something out so Luc doesn't . . ."

"I don't see how." Tears welled in Millie's
eyes, and she brushed them away with the
back of her free hand then looked down at
the baby. "What are we going to do, Addie?
I just seem to keep making things harder

for him."

Addie was flabbergasted — and nearly speechless. "You . . . he . . . how . . ."

"I have loved Lucas Jennings since we were ten years old. He has had to fight his whole life to raise himself — and us — up so we might have a little something to call our own. He has given everything he can to this plot of land. He built this house with his own two hands. Nobody helped him with any of it. So don't you dare put this on Luc."

Millie had tightened her grip on her son to the point where Addie was a little concerned for the baby. She touched Millie's arm and felt the tension ease. "Let me help you now, Millie — you and Luc."

"You can't. It's too late."

"Let me try." The girls were coming back with the water, giggling as they carried the full bucket between them. "Please, Millie, for them, if not for you."

She saw the merest flicker of hope in her friend's eyes.

"Well," Millie said softly, "I expect if anybody can help us, it'll be you."

And Jess, Addie thought. *The two of us together.*

FIVE

On her way back to town, Addie was so pre-occupied with trying to come up with a way to convince Eliza McNew to hire Millie that Buck Tipton had come alongside the buggy before she knew it.

"Just the little lady I was hoping to see," he said as he reined in his horse to keep pace with hers. "Although . . . you being out here by yourself worries me. No telling what might happen to a purty thing like you, Miss Addie."

All of Addie's defenses were instantly on alert. Whenever Buck was anywhere in her vicinity, she felt cornered. She also felt the need to explain herself, even though she knew the man was beyond listening to reason. "I drove out to the Jennings place to check up on Miz Jennings and her children."

"Heard she popped out another one. A boy this time. I guess if a man keeps trying, odds are he's bound to hit a winner sooner or later." He must have seen the disgust in Addie's expression because he burst out laughing. "Too crude for your refined ears, Miss Addie?"

"Lucas and Millie Jennings love all their children equally." *Just stop talking,* she mentally ordered herself.

"Well now, loving your young'uns and providing them with food and such seems to be two different things for that family. My brother and me have made Lucas half a dozen fair offers for his land and that shack he calls a home, but he turns us down every time. Maybe now that I hear Jess Porterfield has him locked up, he won't be so high and mighty. Sounds like he's got quite a debt to pay Miss Lillian." He clicked his tongue in contempt. "Imagine taking food off the table so he can down a jigger of rye."

Addie knew that Buck was just baiting her, trying to get a rise out of her, and it was all she could do to hold her tongue.

"I'm trying to have a conversation with you, Addie Wilcox," he continued, barely able to temper his annoyance at her silence. "Are you thinking now that Jess Porterfield's back in town you don't need to show me common courtesy? Is that it?"

She risked a glance at Buck and saw that his face was flushed with anger. "Jess has nothing to do with it," she said primly, and saw the mistake as soon as the words were out of her mouth.

Buck's smile was downright evil as he took hold of her horse's bit, forcing the buggy to a halt in the middle of nowhere. "Oh, I'm not good enough for you, is that it? You think all your schooling and running around the countryside playing doctor makes you better than me?"

"Let go of my horse, Buck." Addie forced herself to disguise the panic she felt rising in her chest. If she let him know she was afraid of him, there was no telling what he might do. "Now," she added quietly.

Buck loosened his grip and grinned. "Yes, ma'am." He made a sweeping gesture with his hat, as if inviting her to go on her way. She snapped the reins, and the horse started walking along the uneven and potholed trail. To her surprise, Buck stayed where he was, leaning on his saddle horn, hat back in place now.

In spite of the hot sun, she shivered. She was all too aware of how far she was from any ranch or town — anyone she might turn to for help should Buck decide . . .

All of a sudden, out of nowhere, she heard blood-curdling yelps and several shots. Then Buck came riding hard toward the buggy, firing his pistol and shrieking. His actions spooked her horse, and it broke from the trail and took off, forcing her to hang on for dear life as the buggy swayed and nearly toppled. The reins had been jerked from her hands and trailed through the dust as she cried out for the horse to stop. And all the while behind her she could hear Buck Tipton laughing as he rode off in the opposite direction.

By the time the wild ride ended, she was at least a mile or more from the trail, and Buck was nowhere to be seen. Her heart was still racing as she climbed down to check her horse, making sure the animal had sustained no injuries. She was trembling as she stroked the horse's neck, and she murmured reassurances as she pulled a sugar cube from her pocket, holding it out in her palm as a peace offering. She thought of how this could have ended in disaster — the horse crippled, her badly injured if the buggy had toppled, and most of all, lying here, praying someone would come. All the while she scanned the landscape, trying to get her bearings.

Normally, she found the silence of the open landscape comforting, but now it seemed eerie — threatening. A buzzard circled lazily overhead, and a westerly wind churned up dust. The biting flies were trying to get their last hits in before winter came. In trying to hang on for dear life and praying the buggy wouldn't capsize, she had lost track of the twists and turns she'd made. Was the trail into town behind her or ahead? If she could just find some landmark . . .

Even the barbed wire fence that marked Tipton land would be a welcome sight at this point. But everywhere she turned, the scene was the same — grassland stunted by a yearlong drought and pocked by cactus and sagebrush.

But as she shielded her eyes from the dust, it occurred to her that the dry land meant the horse and buggy had left tracks . . . if she followed those backward, would they not eventually lead her to the trail? At least she would know she was headed in the right direction.

Calmed by having a plan, she took hold of the horse's harness and started to walk, her head down as she followed the buggy's trail in the soft, sandy earth. An hour later, the sun had passed its peak, and she was soaked with sweat, but she had found her way. The trail leading back to town stretched out ahead of her.

"Let's go home," she instructed the mare

as she climbed onto the buggy seat and clicked her tongue against her cheek, urging the horse forward. There was no way she was going to allow Buck Tipton to rattle her. He'd been a bully when they were kids, and he was still one today. The best way to fight a bully was to stand up to him.

Knowing Miss Lillian rarely made an appearance before midafternoon, Jess waited until then to go calling on her. On his way, he crossed paths with Eliza McNew.

"Afternoon, Jess," she called out as she set down the bucket and rag she was using to clean the store's window. "I hear there was some excitement over at the Dandy Doodle last night."

"News travels fast."

"I live above my store — speaking of which, you wouldn't know of anybody looking to rent a room, would you? I've got a couple to spare, and with these hard times . . ."

An idea began to come together in Jess's mind. "I just might know of a family," he said. "I'll get back to you on that."

"I also understand you've got Lucas Jennings locked up over at the jailhouse. Pete Townsend was in earlier and said Lucas owes Miss Lillian a pretty penny for damages."

Jess had been so caught up in what Lucas might owe Miss Lillian that he had completely forgotten the debt his friend owed Eliza. "He's dug himself into a deep hole all right. First with you, and now with Miss Lillian."

Eliza frowned. "See what you can work out down the street there, and then we can talk about the debt he owes here. The thing we can't lose sight of is Millie and those children. They have to eat, and from what Addie tells me . . ."

"Addie tells me Millie is real handy with a needle and thread," he said.

"That she is. What's your point?"

"Well, Addie was thinking you might want to start offering alterations for the ready-made clothes you're selling now. And maybe Millie could . . ."

"That poor woman has five children she needs to care for, not to mention doing what she can to keep that patch of dirt Luc calls a ranch going. How in the world do you and Addie expect her to take on sewing, even if I was of a mind to consider it?" She shook her head at the very idea and went back to washing the window.

Jess knew he should have waited for Addie to speak to Eliza, but he'd seen his opening and taken it . . . and probably ruined any chance they might have of making this work. "I've offered Luc the job as my deputy," he said. "I figure I can take part of his wages each week and start paying down his debts."

Eliza paused in her work but did not turn to look at Jess. "And when he goes off on another toot?"

Jess shrugged. "Can't cross that river until I come to it." He tipped his fingers to his hat. "I'd best go speak with Miss Lillian. You have a nice afternoon, Miz McNew."

"Good luck, Jess."

He needed more than luck when he entered the Dandy Doodle. Miss Lillian was in no mood to listen to reason. "Do you know what it's going to cost me to replace that mirror?" she raged, pointing to the barren space in the back bar where the large beveled mirror had hung. "And glasses. Do you have any idea what shot glasses and beer mugs go for these days? Not to mention the fact that just getting somebody who knows the first thing about hanging a mirror properly will take weeks."

"I told you I would hang the mirror, Lilly," Pete Townsend said. He was sitting at the bar going over figures in a ledger.

"Shut up, Pete. I'm making my case to the marshal here," Lillian snapped. She

141

planted her fists on her ample hips and stared up at Jess. "Well?"

"Here's the thing, Miss Lillian — you and I both know Luc has no money. What he has is a wife and five children who will not eat if I keep him locked up. He can't even work his land." He thought he saw a glimmer of sympathy cross her face, but in the dank, shadowy confines of the saloon, he couldn't be sure. Still, he kept trying to come up with ways to make the case for Lucas. "On the other hand, if I take him on as my deputy, he'll make some regular wages, and I can put aside a part of that every week until his debt here is paid off. What do you say?"

"That could take years, and what happens when he falls off the wagon and you have to let him go?"

Jess cast about for the only weapon he had. "Five children, Miss Lillian. Five innocent children — one of them just born."

Miss Lillian pursed her lips and made a face. "You always did know how to charm your way out of a tough situation, Jess Porterfield. Now it seems you've taken to doing it for others."

Jess noticed Pete had stopped working on the ledger. He, too, was waiting for Miss Lillian's answer. Jess decided to press his point. "You're a fair woman, Miss Lillian. Everybody knows that, and . . ."

The saloon owner shook her forefinger in his face. "The thing you never did learn, Jess, is when to stop talking. I'm thinking here, so let me do it in peace."

She certainly took her sweet time. From outside the half doors of the saloon, Jess heard the jingle of a harness and the rumble of wheels as a wagon passed. He heard men talking and women exchanging greetings. He heard a horse whinny, a dog howl, and a rooster crow. But that was outside — inside the saloon, all was silent.

Finally, Miss Lillian sat in a chair next to a small table. "Lucas Jennings is still banned from my establishment. If he sets one toe through those doors, the deal is off."

Afraid to say anything aloud, Jess nodded.

"I want one quarter of his wages every week until the damages are paid off — with interest."

Again, Jess nodded.

Miss Lillian turned to Pete. "Give the marshal that tally sheet, Pete, so he knows the sum — and add on one tenth of the total as interest due."

Pete did some quick figuring, tore a page from the ledger, and handed it to Jess. Jess couldn't help himself — he let out a low whistle of surprise. Even if Lucas never took another drink in his life, it was going to take him a long time to pay off this debt. "This is mighty generous of you, Miss Lillian."

She squinted up at him. "But?"

"Well, see, the thing is that Luc also owes a substantial sum to Miz McNew and —"

"That is not my problem, Marshal. These are my terms. If Lucas refuses, then I guess he stays locked up until we can arrange for the case to be heard by a judge. It could take months for the judge to make his way over here from Tucson, especially with winter coming on." She pushed herself out of the chair and thrust out her hand. "Do we have a bargain?"

"Yes, ma'am. Thank you, ma'am." He shook her small hand until she withdrew it and tottered on high-heeled shoes back to her office at the rear of the saloon.

"Good work, Jess," Pete Townsend said when she was out of earshot. "I never thought she'd give an inch, but when it comes to children, she's got a real soft spot."

"Yeah, my ma's like that too."

"Good woman, your ma. Give her my best next time you see her."

Jess nodded and headed back to his office. The truth was that it had been days since he'd ridden out to the ranch for a visit.

Between Lucas and all the work Doc kept piling on his desk, he'd hardly had time to eat or sleep, much less go see his family — or work on nailing the Tipton brothers for the murder of his father. That had to change, so on his way back to the jailhouse he stopped at the Wilcox house and knocked on Doc's office door.

"Come in, Jess," Doc said, then turned back to his wife, who was clearly upset. "She'll be along directly, Alice. You know Addie when she gets involved with a patient, and in this case, Millie Jennings is a friend as well as her patient. I expect the two of them are just catching up."

Alice Wilcox twisted a hankie around her fingers and pursed her lips. "You don't believe that, and neither do I, Sam Wilcox. She's been gone far longer than is normal. This is not a case of her forgetting the time. She knows you have patients today. She wouldn't miss a chance to observe how you treat that burn Gus Abersole is coming in about. I'm telling you, something is wrong."

All thoughts of why Jess had stopped to speak with Doc flew out of his mind. "Addie's missing?" His pulse pounded in his temple.

"She went to check on Millie and the children this morning. She's not back yet, and Mrs. Wilcox is concerned — unduly, I might add."

Alice Wilcox turned her attention to Jess. "Will you go look for her, Jess?"

"The marshal has Luc Jennings in custody," Doc interrupted. "He can hardly go off chasing after our daughter."

"Well now, sir, that's why I stopped by. You see, Addie and I were discussing things earlier, and I was thinking if I hired Luc to be my deputy, that might help him get straight with his life, and it would allow me time to attend to other matters."

"Like trying to go after the Tiptons?"

"No, sir. Like setting your wife's mind at ease by going to see what's happened to Addie."

Doc glanced at his wife. "You know how Addie feels about us checking up on her." Alice Wilcox set her lips in a stubborn straight line and folded her arms across her chest. Doc turned back to Jess. "Go on then. I'll go talk to Lucas and see if I agree that he's up to the job."

Jess was out the door and headed for the livery to retrieve his horse, almost before Doc finished speaking. He rode out of town at a full gallop.

Addie was cold, thirsty, and exhausted. Not

fifteen minutes after she had climbed back into the buggy and started following the path she was sure led back to town, the trail disappeared. And as the persistent wind covered her tracks, she wandered around in circles until the sun was low in the western sky. If she didn't find her way soon, it would be dark — and a lot colder than it was now.

She shuddered as she sat on the buggy seat and stared at the landscape around her. She had traveled this country her entire life. How could she be lost?

And yet she had to admit that she was. Jess knew this territory like the back of his hand — even if he had been away from it for months. She wished he were here now.

No, she did not. Jess rescuing her from Buck Tipton a second time would just complicate matters, and no doubt send Jess off to hunt Buck down and get himself killed in the bargain. No, she would not admit to Jess that Buck Tipton was behind her predicament. Besides, it wasn't as if this were the first time she had gotten herself into hot water. She just needed to take a deep breath and think it through the way she did a medical problem. What were the options? What did she have at hand that might help?

It didn't take long to realize she was out

of options, and there was nothing at hand to help, except a horse that was surely every bit as exhausted and hungry as she was. She left the horse to graze on the stubble of grass that surrounded them and walked to a pear cactus nestled in the dry, cracked ground nearby. She broke off a prickly piece and used the pocketknife her father had told her never to be without to slice it open. Then she sucked the liquid from it. She closed her eyes, savoring the moisture, and thought she heard voices. A hallucination or just wishful thinking? She returned to the buggy and scanned the horizon.

There . . . in the distance — riders — three of them. One was singing, and the other two were laughing as if they hadn't a care in the world. Their voices carried across the flat land. She hesitated. They could be friendly — or not. They might work for the Tiptons. On the other hand, they might work for one of the smaller ranches, the Porterfields or Johnsons. And even if they were Tipton cowboys, if she kept her distance but followed them, she would eventually find her way back to familiar ground.

She watched the men carefully, squinting as she tried to determine their purpose. They rode slowly, as if they had no place to be. That was a good sign. If they had been going out to watch the herd overnight, they would have ridden with more urgency. These cowboys were going home, she was sure of it. She urged her horse forward, letting the reins fall slack as she kept a close eye on the distant riders. When they angled off toward the southwest, she did the same. When they stopped to let their horses graze while they lit cigarettes and refilled their canteens, she waited.

An hour passed, and the sun was low enough to have painted the sky with purples and oranges. The men picked up their pace, and the surroundings began to seem familiar. In the distance she saw a cluster of buildings and smoke rising from a fire. She knew that place. As a child she and her family had spent many happy times there. As a young woman she had fallen in love by the creek that ran past the adobe house and outbuildings. This was the Porterfield ranch — home of her dear friend, Amanda.

And Jess.

Jess was at his wit's end. He'd ridden hard out to Lucas's ranch, only to learn that Addie had left there before noon. He tried questioning Millie and the older girls without unduly alarming them, but with disappointing results.

"I'm sure she's fine," Millie assured him. "She said something about speaking to Eliza McNew — maybe the two of you passed without knowing it."

But Jess knew every route Addie and her father took when they went to call on outlying ranchers and their families. If Addie had headed back to town after seeing Millie, he would have seen her. No, something had happened. He didn't want to let himself imagine the worst — that her horse had been spooked, maybe by a sidewinder or rattlesnake, and she was lying in the middle of nowhere, wounded and unable to call for help, even in the unlikely event that someone came riding by. Imagining the best case irritated him because it was a scenario that involved Addie getting caught up in collecting some weed or flower so she could make a newfangled medicine she'd read about. In that case the sun could set and rise again without her paying much attention. And more to the point, she could wander far afield from the usual trails.

He ambled along, trying to figure out his next move. The sun was going down, and he had no idea what to do next. So he did what he often did when he was at his wit's end — Jess went home. His mother would set him off in the right direction, he was

150

sure of it. Besides, he could get the hired hands to join in the search. And who was to say Addie hadn't decided to stop by for a visit with Amanda and lost track of time? He spurred his horse to a gallop and set off for the Clear Springs Ranch.

The first thing he saw was the Wilcox's black buggy pulled up outside the corral. The first thing he heard was Addie's laughter coming from the courtyard, mingling with that of his mother and sisters. Annoyed beyond his ability to enjoy feeling relieved that she was safe, he slid from the saddle, threw the reins toward Javier — their housekeeper's youngest son — and stalked off toward the courtyard.

"Well, this is a pleasant surprise," his mother said as soon as she saw him. "We were just talking about you."

Addie's chair was turned away from him, so she had to glance over her shoulder to see him. She didn't move. Rather, she waited until he walked over to kiss his mother's forehead, and even then she did not look straight at him.

He fixed his stare on her. "Your folks are worried, Addie. They sent me to look for you a couple of hours ago." He kept his voice calm and soft, knowing she would understand how upset he was just by the fact that he wasn't yelling.

"I . . ."

"Addie has suffered a bit of a scare, Jess," Amanda volunteered, coming to her friend's rescue as always.

"Her horse bolted on her, taking her miles out of her way. As soon as she arrived, we sent one of the men to let her parents know she was safe with us," his mother added. "We are just now trying to persuade her to stay the night."

"I really should get back," Addie said, apparently finding her tongue when it came to conversing with Jess's mother. "Papa might need the buggy and . . ."

"Of course. I hadn't thought of that. Well, now that Jess is here, he can see you safely home — after you both have had a proper supper." Constance Porterfield turned her attention back to her son. "Besides, we have something to celebrate. Maria and Chet have set their wedding date."

"Congratulations," Jess said, smiling at his older sister. Then he immediately turned his attention back to Addie. "What happened?"

"Happened?"

"Yeah. Out there on the trail."

"Her horse got spooked and just took off," Amanda explained. "She was wandering around for hours trying to find her way, and then she spotted Chet and Trey and Bunker coming home and followed them."

"What spooked the horse?" He did not take his eyes off Addie. He was well aware that any number of insignificant things could cause a horse to startle and take off. Could have been her skirt flapping in the wind, or maybe she sneezed from the dust the horse was kicking up. But there was something about the way she refused to explain that made him think there was more to the story.

She still would not meet his gaze. The woman was incapable of telling a lie, but clearly she was fighting that now. "Does it matter?" she said finally. "I'm here and no worse for it." She smoothed her palms over her skirt and looked directly at him. "I'm fine, Jess. Thank you for being concerned," she added primly.

Concerned? His heart had been in his throat. He had imagined all sorts of terrible things.

His mother picked up the baby the family had adopted and walked toward the house. "Come along, Son. Juanita has supper ready, and Maria has a special favor to ask of you." She led the family into the house, where the long rectangular dining table had been set for supper. She indicated that he should take his father's place at the head of the table. "It seems only right," she said when he hesitated.

Juanita did not seem surprised to see him as she carried dishes of food to the table. "Hello, Nita," he said as she bent to serve him a large portion of rice and beans.

"*Finalmente!* About time you came home," she grumbled. "Your mother sets this place for you every night." She had long been like a second mother to the Porterfield children, and she had no problem reprimanding them, if she thought her opinion was called for.

"I have a job in town, Nita," Jess protested.
"La familia es primero."

"Don't pick on him, Juanita," Maria protested. "I have an important assignment for him." Jess didn't like the sly grin she gave him.

"What's that?" He shoveled a fork full of beans and rice into his mouth.

"I want you to give me away at my wedding."

He was so surprised that he nearly choked. He and Maria had never exactly been close, and after their father died, they'd had some bitter words. Even after he returned, they had argued about his determination to go after the Tiptons.

"Why?" he finally managed. He glanced at Chet Hunter, who regularly joined the family for dinner rather than taking his meals with the other hired hands.

"Because the role of best man was already taken by this guy," Chet said as he patted Trey's shoulder.

"And because it's what our father would want — and what I want," Maria said.

"I'm to be maid of honor," Amanda announced, "and Addie will be a bridesmaid, so you see, Jess, you just have to do your part."

"Let him decide for himself," Maria said. She fussed with her napkin, not looking at him. "If you'd rather not, Jess, I . . ."

"I'd be honored."

The smile that lit his sister's face told him he had given her a gift she treasured. Finally, he had done something right for Maria. He smiled at her in return. "But don't ask me to dance. You know I've got two left feet."

Maria laughed. "You danced plenty the night you came home to us, and I didn't see anyone complaining. Besides, you'll have a little time to practice," she said. "We're planning a Christmas wedding." She reached over and took hold of Chet's hand.

"Chet's little sister, Kate, is coming from Georgia."

"She's the same age as me," Trey announced, and then turned cayenne pepper red. "I mean, she's old enough to travel on her own."

"And dance with you at the wedding," Amanda teased.

"Ma!"

Jess's mother was feeding little Max. The kid had fat cheeks, a gurgling laugh, and he looked nothing like Chet, who'd been falsely accused of fathering him.

As he looked around the table, listening as his mother and sisters babbled on about the wedding, catching Chet's eye and realizing this guy was probably the best thing that had happened to his sister in years, Jess finally let his attention settle on Addie. She was following the conversation without saying anything herself. Once he saw her look at little Max, and the expression that crossed her face made Jess's heart skip a beat. Was she thinking what he was? That maybe one day, if they ever managed to sort everything out, they might have a kid or two?

He let the conversation flow around him as they finished their meal and protested they had no room for the dessert of cinnamon-and-sugar-glazed churros Juanita set on the table. In the end, though, every piece was eaten.

"You two should get started," his mother said, speaking to Addie.

"You're right. Thank you so much." She pushed her chair back and got to her feet to give Constance a hug.

"Just glad you weren't injured, honey. Jess, you'll make sure she gets safely home." It was not a question.

"Yes, ma'am." He hesitated a minute, then kissed the top of Maria's head. "I'm real happy for you." Then he shook hands with Chet as he passed next to Addie. "I'll go hitch up the buggy and meet you outside." On his way out he kissed his mother's cheek and then repeated the gesture as he passed Juanita on his way through the kitchen.

While he hitched up the buggy, he had the sudden thought that he was responsible for all these women now — his mother, his sisters, Juanita. Well, technically, Juanita had her husband and sons, and now Maria had Chet, but this was his family home and with his father dead, surely that meant he was . . . He thought of the way his mother had indicated he should sit in his father's place, and then what Juanita had said about the place being set for him every night. The message was clear. At least as far as his mother was concerned, he was home to stay.

"I can drive the buggy," Addie said, coming up next to him and startling him out of his thoughts.

"I'll drive the buggy," he said as he tied his horse to the back and held out his hand to help her climb onto the seat. She hesitated, of course. "Come on, Addie. It's late. We're both tired, and who knows what's waiting for me back in town."

To his relief she did not argue, but neither did she accept his help climbing up to the seat. Once there she faced forward and folded her hands primly in her lap. When Jess took his place beside her, she actually scooted away from him a little so there was no chance they would be touching. Irritated, he snapped the reins, and the horse took off at a brisk trot. He had to bite his lip to keep from smiling when Addie's reaction to the sudden movement was to unclasp her hands and grip his forearm to steady herself.

"We don't have to race back," she grumbled.

He made no move to slow the horse. "You gonna tell me the truth about what happened today?"

"I told the truth — the horse bolted and I lost control."

"You never said what caused him to bolt."

She sighed and twisted on the seat so she was actually looking at him. "For heaven's sake, Jess, why does it matter? It happened. I am no more the worse for having gone through it, and now it's over."

They rode in silence for several minutes before Jess said, "Just lucky Chet and the others happened to come your way."

She didn't say anything at first, and then she started to laugh, covering her mouth with her fist.

"What's so gol-darned funny?"

"You just have to have the last word, don't you, Jess Porterfield? 'Just lucky Chet and the others . . .' " she mimicked. She made no attempt to hide her laughter now. "You can't help it, can you?" She nudged him with her elbow.

He grinned. She was right, of course. "Guess you'd rather talk about something else — like the wedding."

"Oh, Jess, have you ever seen Maria looking so radiant? So happy? Chet Hunter is such a good man and the perfect match for Maria. Thank goodness she did not rush into marriage with Roger Turnbull. He certainly turned out to be a disappointment, running off the way he did with that woman and . . ."

Her chatter continued until they were

about a mile from town, with his contributions limited to the occasional grunt of agreement or interest. Then her head began to nod, and there were longer stretches between her sentences. "Long day for you," he ventured.

She yawned and nodded. He stretched out his arm, inviting her to lean on him for the rest of the trip. And to his utter surprise and pleasure, she did.

Addie woke when she heard Jess softly call, "Whoa," and felt the buggy ease to a stop.

"We're home?" She lifted her head from his shoulder.

Jess tightened his hold on her to prevent her from moving away while he looped the reins around the brake handle. Not that he had to do anything to hold her there. She was as reluctant as he apparently was to have their time together come to an end.

"Jess, I've been thinking."

"Well, that's always a cause for concern from where I sit," he said.

"Be serious. You're back to stay, and we're living practically next door to each other, and it seems to me that at the very least we ought to be able to be friends again — I mean like we were as kids."

"And what if I want to be more than just

friends?"

She swallowed hard. "Well, that might be all right too," she whispered as she touched his face.

"Ah, my sweet Addie," he said, his voice a raspy whisper of desire. He pulled her gently into his embrace and hesitated.

This was a new side of Jess — one she had not seen in all the years they had known each other. The old Jess took what he wanted when he wanted it and assumed she would be in agreement. This Jess was asking permission, and that was enough to make her willingly wrap her arms around his neck and tilt her lips to his.

At first they were both almost shy, the kiss sweet and tender. But then Jess let out a growl of frustration and cupped her face in his palms angling her head to give him the access he wanted — needed. His tongue probed her closed lips, and she opened to him without question. It all came back to her then — the excitement and delight of being kissed by Jess, the pure passion of shared need.

She pulled off his hat and buried her fingers in his hair, the softness of it as familiar to her as her own. She heard the roar of their mingled breaths. She inhaled the fragrance of his leather vest and the cool night air. His cheeks and chin — usually clean-shaven — were covered in stubble. Stubble that scratched and tickled and told her she was exactly where she had wanted to be from the moment she'd seen Jess come riding into his mother's courtyard.

When he pulled back a little, she moaned in protest, and he chuckled as he fanned kisses over her eyelids and cheeks and forehead. "I'm not going anywhere, darlin'," he said, and then kissed her on the mouth again. This time there was no preliminary dance. Rather he pulled her hard against him, and everything about the way he kissed her told her he wanted more — much more.

And that was enough to bring her to her senses. Nothing was settled between them. They hadn't really talked about the night he'd left or all those months when she'd heard not a word.

She placed her hands flat against the solid wall of his chest and pushed away from him. "It's too soon. I mean, we can't go back. I mean . . ."

"This is me, Addie. You and me, the way we were."

But it wasn't, no matter how much she wished it were true. They were different now. The dreams she'd thought they shared had been tested and broken. She would always love him, but could she trust him not to break her heart again?

"I have to go in," she said. "It's late, and my folks will be waiting for me. Pa needs his rest." She was babbling, and as she climbed down from the buggy, he slowly let her hand slip from his. She felt like someone cast into a river, clinging to the one hand that reached out to save her, and in the end, not having the strength — or trust — to keep holding on.

Six

Getting Lucas to agree to serve as his deputy had been child's play compared to getting his friend to consider the idea of Millie taking in sewing and the family moving into town.

"No wife of mine is going to work as long as I can provide for her and my children," he'd blustered. "Millie's got plenty of sewing to do just keeping up with a bunch of young'uns who outgrow their clothes every year."

"You make a good point," Jess replied. He tipped his chair back on its hind legs and looked out the open door of the jailhouse. "And with you taking shifts here, I expect that's put even more work on her shoulders."

"It wasn't my choice to take this job. You said it was the only way I could keep from having to stand trial and . . . ."

"If you don't care for the terms . . . ." Jess

paused, but did not look at Lucas. He was well aware that the man relished his new role. Everyone in town had seen him strutting down the street at night, checking businesses to be sure doors were locked and nothing was amiss.

"I didn't say that. It's just that Millie's out there on the ranch alone with the children most nights, and I worry about something happening that she can't handle."

"If she worked for Miz McNew, there would be a place above the store for her and the children to stay. You could see her, tuck the kids in at night, and still work. 'Course that's all tied to her working, and I understand your feelings on that score."

"Emma's been wanting to go to school," Lucas murmured, more to himself than in answer to Jess. He walked to the door, staring out at the street — and the mercantile across the way. "You know, Jess, my girls mean the world to me. Sure, I wanted a boy — a boy can help with the ranching, but the girls . . . Emma is smart — reminds me of Addie. And Sarah is such a beauty. She looks so much like her mama. Remember when I first laid eyes on Millie?"

"Never saw a fella knocked off his feet like that," Jess said. He set his chair back on all four legs and pulled some papers toward him, pretending to study them, giving Lucas the time he needed to work this through and praying that he would come to the right answer.

"I think," Lucas finally said after a long silence, "that I'll go over to Miz McNew's store for a bit, if that's okay with you."

"Be back in half an hour. I need to ride out and check on something." Jess made his voice gruff, like he wasn't all that pleased, but as soon as he saw Lucas cross the street, he grinned. He'd give a lot to be able to tell Addie how he'd handled this business with Lucas.

'Course, Addie was keeping her distance. Ever since the kisses they shared when he brought her home that night, she'd found just about every way she could to avoid being in the same place with him — especially avoiding being in the same place *alone* with him. But he wasn't fooled for a second. Addie Wilcox had been as thrilled by those kisses as he had. She had given as good as he gave, and if it hadn't been for the fact that they were parked just outside her family's front door where anybody might see them, things would have gotten a lot more serious.

He'd pretty much spent the rest of that night imagining what it would be like to undress Addie and make love to her. The idea of doing that in a cramped buggy didn't set well with him. No, he'd have to find someplace more suitable — more romantic. There should be flowers and moonlight and warm breezes to tickle her naked skin and . . .

"You listening, Jess?"

Jess looked up to see that Lucas had returned and was pacing back and forth in front of the desk. "Sorry. What's up?"

"Miz McNew says we can take the rooms over the store as pay for Millie doing the sewing for her customers. She says it would be strictly on a trial basis, and she would have to reevaluate things come spring. I told her come spring I would be back working my land, and Millie and the kids would be there with me, although the older two would be in school still. I told her come spring she'd have to find somebody else to take on her sewing and . . ."

Jess gripped his pencil so hard that it snapped in two. After all his work to get Eliza on board with the idea and to get Lucas thinking he was in charge, the man had gone and ruined everything. "What did Miz McNew say to that?"

"She said it would be best if I stopped talking, and maybe let Millie and her work things out." He removed his hat and scratched his thinning hair. "Seems to me that might be a fair idea, although I'm thinking that Addie Wilcox planted some of those ideas — at least when it came to persuading Miz McNew to be part of this. I don't know, Jess. It don't seem right some-how."

Jess chose his words carefully. "Well now, Luc, seems you're still the one in charge. On the other hand, having your family right here in town where you can watch over them, getting your girls settled in school, and not having to worry about Millie all the way out there alone at night with winter coming on . . . Seems to me like you're starting to put together a plan that's best for your family, and my guess is folks will respect you for it."

Lucas frowned, then squared his shoulders and slapped his hat back in place. "Long as Miz McNew understands that come spring I'll be the one doing the deciding."

"Then it's settled. Why don't you ride out to the ranch and help Millie get packed up? Things are pretty quiet here. I can handle 'round the clock for a couple of days while you take care of your family."

"I know I've done a poor enough job of that up to now, Jess, but things are gonna change."

"I didn't say that, Luc. Truth is, you're a durn sight better man than I've been when it comes to family. I ran away from my responsibilities while you stayed and at least tried to face things head-on."

It worked. Lucas almost smiled at the words of praise. "I'll be going then. You'll let Miz McNew know that I'll be back with Millie and the kids in a couple of days?"

"I'll do that." Jess walked his friend to the door and watched as Lucas mounted his horse and headed out of town. Later he would get word to his mother to send over a cowhand with an empty buckboard to help with the move. Right now, he just wanted to tell Addie the good news.

In the weeks following that late night ride back to town, Addie had to admit that maintaining her determination not to fall for Jess Porterfield again was becoming next to impossible. Even her father was impressed with Jess's dedication to his position as the town's marshal.

"I'm pleased to say I've seen no indication that he still holds a vendetta against the Tipton boys," Doc said one night at dinner. "Of course with Jess, you can never be sure. On the other hand, the way he's taken

Lucas Jennings in hand . . . Never would have thought that young man could get himself straight."

"And Millie as well," Alice said. "Addie, whatever made you think of suggesting the whole family move in above the mercantile?"

"It was Jess's idea," Addie replied, and hoped her parents wouldn't notice the blush that seemed to come with the very mention of the man's name. "I'll never know how he was able to figure out a way to make Luc think it was all his idea and get him to agree to it. And there's the ranch — such as it is."

"That seems to be working out all right," her father said.

"Jess says Luc came around after he realized how much it meant to Trey to be able to help out." Lately, Addie felt as if every sentence out of mouth began with "Jess says" or "Jess thinks."

"Perhaps young Porterfield has finally found a proper way to put his crafty ways to good use," her father said. But the way he said it told Addie that he still had his doubts when it came to Jess — as did she.

Now that Lucas had started to settle into his new duties as deputy, Jess was more determined than ever to find answers about what had really happened the day his father was killed. He'd gotten about as much information as he could from Maria and Chet without raising their suspicions beyond a warning to let it be. He'd handled their concerns by saying that he just needed assurance that the killer had been caught and justice would be done. And when Maria had looked like she didn't quite believe him, he'd ducked his head the way he had as a boy, and told her the truth was he felt guilty for having been gone when she and the rest of the family needed him most.

He was pretty sure she didn't buy that either, and he knew for certain that Chet didn't. So he made a point of not asking any more questions. At the same time, he tried to think of a way he might get to the fort and question his predecessor, Tucker. But every time he'd come up with some excuse to stop by Fort Lowell, the commanding officer, Colonel Ashwood, had intercepted him, grilled him about his business at the fort, and then sent him on his way. And always, after those attempts he'd received a visit — and more paperwork — from Addie's father. It didn't take long for him to realize that the direct approach was not going to work.

Instead he decided to take the long way

round, peppering his conversations with Doc with comments like, "You know there's news that a gang of bank robbers could be headed this way. You and Addie need to be extra careful when you go on a call." The one thing Jess knew for sure was that Doc would rather die than have harm come to his wife or children.

"Bank robbers? Where?"

Jess grabbed for the name of any nearby town. "Tucson."

"They won't come here," Doc replied. "Whitman Falls is too small."

"We've got a bank, don't we? And a big land and cattle company depositing money in that bank on a fairly regular basis, not to mention heading to the bank and back to their ranch every week to dole out the payroll they need."

Doc squinted at him, clearly trying to decide whether or not to trust him. "I'll see that Addie makes calls in town," he said finally. "Now that Millie Jennings is here with that brood of hers and Luc's, I doubt she'll give me much argument."

"How's she coming along with her studies?"

"Smarter than any man I ever met," Doc replied. "Too bad the schools back east won't even give her a chance to get her degree."

"When I was in . . . when I was away, there was a doctor in town who didn't have a degree, leastwise not one that was legitimate. He'd gotten his certificate through the mail, fake as a pyrite rock. But the truth was he was just about the best doctor I've ever been to — not including you, of course."

"Or Addie," Doc challenged.

Jess smiled. "Well now, I've never had the opportunity to serve as one of Addie's patients, sir."

"And let's just keep it that way, all right?" Doc scowled, and while he was a much smaller man than Jess was, Jess saw that challenging him would be dangerous — especially when it came to Addie.

"Yes, sir."

"I'm telling you plain, Jess. Keep your distance. That girl has been all moody and starry-eyed since that night you brought her home from your mother's house a few weeks back. I don't know what happened on that ride to town, but I'm telling you that if you value your job, it won't happen again. Do we understand each other?"

"I'm not gonna hurt her," Jess grumbled, insulted by the older man's implication that he would.

"You won't try to hurt her, but sure as I'm sitting here, you will. So if you care for her at all, keep your distance." Doc plucked his hat from the rack in the corner of Jess's office and left.

"I'm not gonna hurt her," Jess repeated to the closed door.

A few days later, as Addie was studying at her father's desk, she heard a light tapping on the outer door. Her father was out on a call, and her mother had gone shopping. There was something about the sound that caused her to hesitate before going to answer the door. The tapping — more of a scratching sound now — continued. Was it an animal — perhaps one of the wild coyotes people had reported seeing near town scavenging for food?

"Come in," Addie called, and with relief she watched as the doorknob turned. A woman entered and closed the door behind her. She lifted the lace curtain to check the street before pulling back the hood of the cloak she wore. Addie could not have been more surprised to see Jasper Tipton's beautiful young wife Pearl standing hesitantly by the door.

Addie glanced at the scrap of paper where her father had noted his appointments for the day. Pearl's name was not on the list. "Good day to you, Mrs. Tipton. I regret that my father . . ."

"I have no appointment, but I saw your father leave earlier, and then your mother was in Miz McNew's store. I thought this might be the best time."

For what? Addie thought, watching as the woman kept glancing nervously toward the window while she twisted a handkerchief in her hands. Addie indicated the chair across from her, and Pearl perched on the edge of it. "How can I help you, Mrs. Tipton?"

"Call me Pearl, please. I wanted to see you because, well, you being a woman and all, I thought you might understand and . . ." A horse whinnied outside, and Pearl startled, then focused her attention on the window until the rider had passed.

"Understand what, Pearl?"

Pearl released a nervous laugh. "You see, I think I may be with child."

Relieved that it wasn't something dire, Addie smiled. "That would indeed be wonderful news. Mr. Tipton has been wanting a child for so long, and now . . ."

To her shock, Pearl burst into tears, sobs that wracked her slim body and left her incapable of speaking. Addie got a glass of water from a side table and knelt next to the distraught woman. "Come, come. I know it must be a little daunting to think of carrying a child, but . . ."

Pearl grasped the glass with both hands and took a sip, then handed it back to Addie. She got up and started pacing. "Coming here was a mistake. I knew it would be, but I had no other place to turn."

Half a dozen explanations for the young woman's distress raced through Addie's mind. Jasper was ten years Pearl's senior, and perhaps she feared being left to raise the child alone. She was young and pretty enough to be vain about what a pregnancy might do to her appearance, but Addie really had never seen her as being that kind of woman. Perhaps it was because the couple had been trying for the pregnancy for two long years, and Pearl was terrified she would lose the baby. Or . . .

"You see, Addie, I cannot carry this child to term, and my husband can never know."

"But your husband has . . ."

A fresh wave of tears brought Pearl back to the chair where she collapsed and wrapped her arms around her body, hugging herself protectively. "He can never ever know," she repeated, stressing each word.

Feeling her way through the situation, as she had when she'd delivered Millie's baby,

176

Addie sat on the edge of her father's desk. "I would say the first thing you need is confirmation," she said gently. "You may not be pregnant at all." She kept her tone calm, the way she'd seen her father do with dozens of patients who were afraid. "How long since your last menses?"

Pearl looked up, her eyes and face damp with her tears. "What?"

"Your last monthly — when was it?"

"It's been four months." She cupped her stomach, pressing down her garments to display the silhouette. "I can't hide this much longer. And then there's the sickness. Jasper is beginning to suspect."

Addie was at a loss. She wished her mother would return, but she knew that once Alice Wilcox and Eliza McNew got to talking an entire afternoon could come and go before either woman noticed the onset of dusk. Her father was miles away and would not be back until the following day at the earliest. She was on her own.

She took a deep breath. "Tell me about the sickness," she said.

"It comes at all hours. I can't keep anything down. Mr. Tipton has had a terrible cold and cough for the past several weeks. So far, I have convinced him I've caught that and will be better in time. He wanted to fetch your father, but I persuaded him to wait."

"And why do you not want to share this news with him and allow him to care for you? He loves you a great deal, Pearl," she added softly.

Pearl's eyes welled with tears again. She bowed her head, and her next words were barely a whisper. "Because the child is not his."

Addie was struck dumb. What to ask next? Had Pearl been violated? Had she willingly lain with another man? None of this was any of her business. Pearl had come to her for medical help, not advice. Addie tried to assume a more professional demeanor. "Will you let me do an examination, and then we can talk further?" Pearl nodded, and Addie indicated the screen used by patients to disrobe. She waited, going over the steps of the examination in her mind, as Pearl shed her undergarments before lying down on the examining table.

Addie locked the office doors and gently positioned Pearl so she could take full advantage of the light streaming into the office. The two women fell silent — one working while the other waited.

Pearl was pregnant — there was little doubt of it. The news must have been plain to read in Addie's expression as she helped Pearl sit up.

"It's true then? I prayed and prayed that I was wrong, but . . ."

"It's true," Addie confirmed. Without realizing what she was doing, she gently stroked Pearl's back. "Pearl, this life you are carrying . . . however that life came to be . . ." Oh, she was so bad at this. "Jasper will . . ."

"This will kill him. He will know, and it will kill him, and I love my husband far too much to put him through such pain." All evidence of tears was gone as Pearl faced Addie with eyes that blazed with determination. "You see, when he met me, I was working as a dance hall girl in Yuma. I came from nothing, and that work was all I could get. I never thought a gentleman like Jasper would want more from me than just . . ." She paused, swallowed hard, and then focused all her attention on Addie. "I can see no solution. It would be better if I were to just die."

Addie was alarmed at the very idea that Pearl had gotten to the point of thinking of killing herself. "You can't do that, Pearl. Think of how devastated Jasper would be. Think of your child."

Pearl looked at her with glassy eyes. "I

hadn't thought of that," she murmured. "If I . . . I would also be taking the life of my baby. I know I asked you to . . . but I don't know if I *really* want . . ."

Addie's heart broke for Pearl. "There has to be another way."

Pearl cradled her stomach and leaned forward, rocking back and forth. "But what am I to do?"

"We will figure this out. I will help you care for yourself and carry this child to term, and together we will find a way to do it so that your husband will accept the baby as the heir he has waited for. Pearl, this is *your* child — a boy or girl you will love and cherish. I am here, Pearl, and will ask you no questions about how this baby was conceived." She placed her hand flat over Pearl's hand covering the slight bump of her pregnancy. "Think of it, Pearl — the child you and Jasper have longed for is right here waiting for your love. You have a husband who adores you. You have so much to live for."

At first there was resistance — even defiance — in Pearl's expression. But then her gaze drifted to where her hand rested, and after a long moment, she nodded. "Thank you," she said softly as she relaxed, and the tears came.

Addie breathed a sigh of relief. "Now about that morning sickness."

For the first time since she'd entered the office, Pearl smiled. "I think in my case it might better be called any time of the day or night sickness."

Both women laughed, and Addie felt as if she just might have saved Pearl and her unborn child.

Unable to avoid it any longer without slacking in her household chores, Addie walked over to the mercantile to buy flour and salt and sugar. She was both thankful and disappointed that she did not see a sign of Jess.

As Eliza filled the order, she told Addie how well things seemed to be working out with Millie. "The woman is a wonder with a needle and thread," she gushed. "But then there's Luc. That is one proud and stubborn man." Eliza shook her head. "I just hope he doesn't do anything to spoil things for Millie and the children." She handed Addie her purchases and walked with her to the front door.

As she bid Eliza good day and prepared to walk back home, Addie saw Jess cross the streets headed for the mercantile. Apparently, so did Eliza, because when Addie ducked back inside and looked around for another avenue of escape, Eliza laughed.

"If you don't beat all, Addie Wilcox. Why don't you just admit you're head over heels for the guy and get on with it?"

"I don't know what —"

"Now, don't you be lying to me or yourself, missy." She glanced out the window. "He's definitely coming here, and I think I know why."

"You think he saw me come in here?"

"I can't say. What I do know is that here comes Jess with that grin no reasonable female can resist. Something's up." She swung open the door. "Well, Jess Porterfield, imagine seeing you here."

Jess's smile turned to laughter as he entered the store and removed his hat in a gesture of respect to Eliza. But his smile faded when he saw Addie.

"I was just going," she said, edging toward the open door.

"I was going to come find you as soon as . . ." He spoke at the same time she did.

Eliza heaved a sigh of impatience. "Well, here we all are. Now what did you come to say?"

"Is Millie here?"

"Not at the moment. She took the kids and rode out to the ranch — that woman insists on keeping up that place no matter what."

"Well, when she gets back, you and her need to talk to Ma and Maria — seems they've decided they want Millie to make the dresses for the wedding."

Addie squealed with delight. "Truly? That means extra money for the family — and you, Eliza," she added.

"My thought exactly," Jess said.

"You didn't happen to have anything to do with putting this idea in your mother's head, did you?" Eliza asked.

The grin that set female hearts aflutter was back. "Aw shucks, ma'am, it wasn't that hard. Just had to mention I'd seen a new shipment of fabric being delivered, and some of it looked mighty pretty."

Eliza grinned. "Sometimes, Jess Porterfield, you can be the dearest man. Isn't that right, Addie?"

Addie had taken a sudden interest in the bolts of fabric stacked on the shelves behind the counter. "This color would be so nice for Amanda — and this one for Mrs. Porterfield, don't you think?"

"I'm pretty sure they'll have ideas of their own," Eliza replied. "But no reason we can't find something that suits you." She pulled out three bolts of fabric, rejected two, and held up the third, unwinding the soft green fabric.

"This should do," Eliza said.

"Oh, Eliza, it's much too . . ."

Jess cleared his throat to remind them he was still there.

"Well?" Eliza asked. "What do you think?"

"I'm afraid you ladies are on to something that I can't really offer an opinion about."

"And just when have you not had an opinion about something?" Eliza demanded.

To Addie's surprise, Jess pushed himself away from the counter and took the fabric from Eliza. He held it close to Addie' shoulders, as if trying it on her — meaning he was standing awfully close. He kept his eyes on the fabric — and noticed the way her quickening breath made her chest rise and fall. Then he slowly lifted his gaze until he was looking straight at her. "Pretty as a picture," he said softly.

Addie snatched the bolt of material from him and handed it to Eliza. "We'll let Maria decide. It's her wedding." She noticed the bemused way Eliza was looking at her and felt a blush spread over her neck and cheeks. "Now, I almost forgot. I'm in need of a new pair of shoes." The shoes were stored on the other side of the store — as far from Jess as she could get.

To her consternation, Jess followed her, and when she reached for a box on a shelf above her head, he stood close behind her and took the box before she could, handing it to her when she turned. Again, he was standing far too close for comfort. It was rare for Addie to be speechless, but around Jess she seemed incapable of practicing her usual good sense — especially since every time he was this close to her, all she could think about were the kisses they had shared. She forced herself to focus on the shoebox, and in opening it, fumbled and sent the shoes and box flying.

As she scrambled to reclaim the items, so did Jess. Their shoulders bumped, their hands brushed, and when they both straightened, they held the shoes, box, and lid between them. His eyes went to her lips, and hers went to his. This time it was Eliza who cleared her throat.

"I have to go," Addie said, pressing the shoes and box firmly into Jess's hands as she grabbed her packages from the counter and hurried toward the door. "I promised Pearl Tipton I would stop by this morning. She must be wondering what's keeping me. First, I'll take these things home, of course." As tongue-tied as she'd been just moments earlier, Addie could not seem to stop talking now. She tied on her bonnet and hooked the basket that held her purchases over one arm, then fled out the door. As she rushed past the window, she saw Jess handing the shoes to Eliza as he watched her go. He did not look pleased.

The Tiptons' housekeeper Clara — a sour-faced woman of undetermined age whom Jasper had hired from another town — opened the front door and led Addie into the parlor. The mansion Jasper Tipton had built for his young bride was impressive, if not to Addie's taste. Pearl had filled the downstairs rooms with more furniture than necessary, and every surface was cluttered with framed photographs and trinkets. The windows were dressed in three layers of drapery — a sheer lace next to the glass, a silk brocade next to that, and finally, a heavy burgundy velvet drape fringed in gold. Excess seemed to be the style as far as Addie could see.

She sat on a heavily brocaded side chair and waited for Pearl. From somewhere upstairs she could hear the housekeeper announcing her arrival. A moment later, Pearl came down the stairs. "Shall we sit on the porch?" she asked the minute she entered the room.

Addie did not miss the way the young woman kept glancing nervously over her shoulder, and she saw that the housekeeper had started cleaning just outside the parlor door.

"That would be lovely," Addie agreed. "It's turned out to be a fine day."

"Clara, please bring us some tea," Pearl said as they passed the housekeeper on their way to the front door.

Clara scowled as she set her dust rag on a side table and stomped off down a narrow hallway that presumably led to the kitchen.

"She hates me," Pearl whispered, hooking her arm through Addie's. On the porch they sat in two large straight-back armchairs built for men and made small talk about the weather and Addie's family until Clara had brought the tea and gone back inside. Addie did not miss the fact that Pearl had chosen to sit as far away from the front door as possible. "She also listens to everything and reports back to Jasper. How I got away with calling at your father's office last week without her finding out, I will never know."

"Have you told Jasper the news?"

Pearl smiled. "I did it last night. He came to my bedroom, saying he was worried about me. He wanted me to see your father. I told him I already had a physician — you.

He was not happy, but when I told him I preferred to have a woman with me as I went through my pregnancy, he almost fell out of the bed." She laughed happily. "Oh Addie, you were so right. He is beside himself with joy and cannot stop talking about all his plans for this child. He suspects nothing. I am so relieved and so very happy because I had come to care for this baby more than I was willing to admit when I spoke with you. How can I ever thank you for talking sense to me?"

Addie smiled and sipped her tea. "How is the medicine working?"

"The sickness is much improved — perhaps a couple of times this last week I have been ill or dizzy, but it is ever so much better than before."

"Your color is better," Addie noted. "How are you sleeping?"

"The medicine seems to help with that as well. I was so nervous the night before I made up my mind to tell Jasper that I thought I would never get a wink, but I took one of the pills and slept well."

"Be careful that you take them only as prescribed, Pearl. The medicine is strong, and you don't want to risk hurting yourself or the baby." Remembering how distraught Pearl had been just a week earlier, Addie wondered if she had made a mistake in prescribing such a powerful medication. Pearl had come to her intent on ending the pregnancy — surely she was past that now. Surely she would not . . . "Pearl, it is none of my business, but have you considered whether or not the father of your child could become a problem?"

Pearl's smile faded, replaced by a frown as she nervously stirred her tea. "He wouldn't dare." She stared off into the distance for a long moment, her spoon suspended above the teacup. Then as suddenly as the darkness had descended, her smile returned. "I want to go shopping. Will you come with me?"

"Of course."

"Jasper says I must pay no attention to price — he always says that." She giggled. "Do you think Miz McNew will have what's needed, or shall I go to Yuma or Tucson?"

"I think you should find what you need here. Besides, this is not a good time for you to be traveling, and whatever Eliza doesn't have in stock, I'm sure she can order for you."

Pearl laughed. "Jasper says he's going to build the cradle — can you imagine? That man is about as handy with a hammer as I am." She set down her cup and cradled her stomach. "This child is going to be so loved," she said softly.

Addie reached over and covered Pearl's hand with hers. "I am so glad it is all working out for you, Pearl."

Pearl clasped Addie's hand. "It's a double blessing because now I have you as my friend. You are my friend, aren't you, Addie? I mean, you're not just . . ."

"Oh, Pearl, of course. Look at the time we have wasted with you living practically across the street. I could not be more touched that you chose me to confide in."

"Well, I know how hard it is for people around here to trust Jasper — or me. He's a good man, Addie, and he cares about this town and the people in it."

"Some people would question that," Addie replied, wondering if being Pearl's friend could be a problem after all.

"Oh, I know he's all business, but it's for the greater good, you see. If Jasper and his company take charge, then everyone will have a better life — more security and . . ." She went on, clearly parroting the conversation she'd heard from her husband.

"And what is Buck's role in all this?"

Pearl hesitated, then gave a nervous laugh. "Buck is Jasper's younger brother. As such he knows his place."

But did he? Addie had her doubts. She gave Pearl's hand a final squeeze and picked up her teacup. "Have you and Jasper talked about names for the baby?" she asked, turning the conversation away from the Tipton brothers and their determination to build a monopoly in the area.

"We talked about that half the night. He has these horrid family names in mind — like Hezekiah and Hermione. I want something more romantic . . . Rose Marie or Branson." She savored the names she preferred. "Or perhaps, we should name the baby after you. I mean, without you . . ."

Addie laughed. "Do not inflict that on your child. I think the names you like are beautiful, and my guess is that Jasper will not care what the baby is called as long as it is healthy."

"And *his*," Pearl said.

But the child was not Jasper's, and Addie could only hope that he never learned the truth of Pearl's deception.

SEVEN

Maria and Chet's wedding, planned for two days before Christmas, was to be the highlight of the holiday season for everyone within traveling distance of the Clear Springs Ranch. People would arrive from miles away to attend the festivities. With the ceremony scheduled to take place at sundown, Amanda was working practically 'round the clock on the decorations, and she had enlisted Addie's help. Dozens of candles already lined the path that Maria and her wedding party would walk on the way to the altar. The altar would be set in a corner of the living room and festooned with potted red poinsettias set among large agave, aloe, and Spanish dagger plants.

As she stood before the fireplace, it was hard for Addie not to think of the time when she had secretly been planning her wedding to Jess — dreaming of what she would wear and imagining him standing near the priest in his Sunday suit, watching her father walk with her down the aisle. But that dream had ended the day Jess expected her to just leave behind family and friends and follow him on his adventure.

"Looks real nice," she heard Jess tell Amanda as he walked into the room. He slapped his hat against his thigh to rid it of excess dirt.

"Stop that," Amanda ordered. "We have enough dust to worry about without you making more." She took hold of his arm. "Now, Jess, when you walk with Maria, you have to take it really slow. Everyone wants to have a good look at her — especially Chet."

"And here I thought everybody would be looking at me," Jess teased.

"Well, Sybil Sinclair might, but then she's desperate to find a man to marry, and . . ."

Addie saw the color rise on Jess's neck. She wondered if that was because he had feelings for Sybil and his sister had noticed. Or could it possibly be that he was embarrassed to have Addie hear Sybil's name mentioned in connection with his? Either way, it was none of her concern.

"There's nothing between me and Sybil, Amanda," he muttered.

"That's not the way she tells it," his sister

replied, and then she was off, calling out to Juanita's son Javier to help her find more candles.

Addie fiddled with the poinsettias, even though she knew next to nothing about arranging flowers. The task made it possible for her to keep her back to Jess. Ever since their ride back from his mother's and the kisses they had shared that night — and then that business in Eliza's store — she found looking at Jess Porterfield difficult, especially when he was standing not two feet away from her.

"You've been spending a lot of time with Pearl Tipton these last couple of weeks," he said. "How come?"

"That's confidential. She's a patient."

"Of your pa's?"

"No. She came to me." As usual when Jess questioned something she did, her tone was defensive. She risked a look at him. He was studying her closely and stroking his unshaven chin. "I really don't see how this concerns you, Jess."

He shrugged. "Just be careful, Addie. Jasper Tipton can be dangerous, especially when it comes to Pearl. If she's sick and doesn't tell him — if you don't make sure she tells him . . ."

Addie knew he was right. Pearl was Jas-

194

per's pride and joy. On a good day she was pale and angelic-looking with her cascades of blond hair. She'd told Addie that Jasper preferred she wear it down. Her slim figure always highlighted the latest fashion ordered from Kansas City, and her sweet, childlike manner endeared her to everyone she met, no matter what they might think of her husband. But she also knew that Jess would not let this go, and if she wanted to protect Pearl's secret, she was going to have to tell Jess at least some of what was really going on.

"If you must know, she and Jasper are expecting a child. Soon it will be common knowledge. I have been treating her, and in the process we have become friends. The truth is I like her, and I'm enjoying spending time with her. After all, we live practically next door to each other. I don't know why I've waited so long to get to know her. She is truly one of the sweetest people I have ever met."

"I guess," Jess said, drawing out the words as if he weren't at all sure. "Just be careful, all right?" He put his hat on and grinned. "I've got to go try on my good suit. Ma says she won't hear of me walking Maria down the aisle in anything but a suit."

Relieved that he had finally changed the

subject, Addie smiled. "She'll let you wear your boots though?"

Jess looked horrified for a second. "That's not up for discussion," he said firmly as he started toward the kitchen door. Just before he reached it, he turned back. "Addie?"

She allowed herself the pleasure of looking him over from head to toe. He was so incredibly handsome that every time she permitted herself to really look at him, she thought her heart might beat right out of her chest. "I'll be careful," she said, assuming she knew what was coming.

He took a step toward her. "No, not that. Just . . . well, I was wondering if maybe you might save me a dance at the wedding."

Ka-thump. Ka-thump. Addie instinctively covered her left breast with both hands, ready to catch her heart should it actually break through. Somewhere in the thunder of her heart beating, she must have nodded, because Jess grinned the way he used to every time he got something he wanted from her.

On the night of Maria's wedding, Jess was surprised to feel the strong presence of his late father as he slowly walked down the aisle with his sister. Isaac Porterfield had been a force to reckon with all of Jess's life.

They had clashed often, and Jess had felt the pressure to live up to his father's reputation as a man who had singlehandedly built one of the most successful ranches in Arizona. Still, he missed his father and would always have to wonder if he'd ever done anything that made his father proud.

Beside him Maria was trembling a little, but smiling radiantly, as she moved toward Chet Hunter — and her future. Jess and Maria had also had their differences through the years, but on this occasion he felt protective of her and all too aware of the fragility and uncertainty of life. And in that moment, he thought just maybe his father was looking down on them and was pleased with the way Jess was finally meeting his obligations to the family.

As he and Maria passed by their mother — who was standing with the other guests, her eyes dancing with excitement and pride — he realized once again that his family responsibilities now extended to her as well, and to Trey and Amanda. For perhaps the first time in his life, Jess felt the pride and pressure of manhood. He was no longer a boy. The years would go quickly, and he did not have a young boy's luxury of everything being ahead of him.

Addie had taken her place to one side of

the altar. She was a vision in a pale green dress embellished with flowers that reflected the colors of an Arizona sunset. The embroidery wound its way around the square neckline, the hem of the skirt, and on the sleeves that skimmed her elbows. She was holding a bouquet of late-blooming wildflowers he knew Amanda had gathered earlier that morning. Her hair — usually pulled back into a no-nonsense, old-lady bun at the nape of her neck — was unrestrained, lying flat and straight over her shoulders and down her back like a curtain. Seeing it brought back the memory of times when he had held her and kissed her, and the strands of her hair had been like silk between his fingers. For once, she was not wearing the wire-rimmed glasses that were her constant companion, and while every eye in the gathering was on Maria, Addie's gaze had settled on him.

He and Maria had reached the altar. Maria kissed him on the cheek, then turned toward Chet. The man was looking at Jess's sister as if she were the most beautiful thing he had ever seen. Jess understood the feeling as he stepped back to stand next to his mother. He felt the same way about Addie.

It was awfully hard for Addie to concentrate

on the ceremony once she had seen how handsome Jess looked in that Sunday suit, walking Maria down the aisle. She was glad that for much of the ceremony her back would be to him — once he gave Maria's hand to Chet and took his seat in the first row. But she could feel him watching her.

Don't be ridiculous, she chastised herself, and tightened her grip on the bouquet of wildflowers to steady her hand. Determined to concentrate on the service and Chet and Maria, she forced a smile and focused her attention on the priest.

But once Maria and Chet had said their vows, Jess and his mother stepped forward to perform the traditional ceremony. Addie had always loved this part of a wedding. The *el lazo* — an oversized rosary, in this case made of several family rosaries linked together — was placed first on Chet's shoulders and then entwined to form a figure eight before Jess draped it over Maria's shoulders. Having performed the role his father would have handled, Jess stepped away from the couple, meaning he was standing right next to Amanda — and Addie.

In the confines of the space, Addie could smell the soap he'd used that morning, and that had her seeing visions of him shirtless as he washed up and had her shaking so badly her knees threatened to buckle. And that simply would not do. With a frown, she willed herself to stand straighter, locking her knees to sustain her for the remainder of the service. When Jess looked down at her, his expression one of concern, Addie kept her gaze focused on the wedding couple.

"You okay?" Jess whispered.

Addie gave a curt nod without looking at him.

Now that Maria and Chet were linked together, they would wear the rosary lasso for the remainder of the ceremony. The way Chet was looking at Maria, Addie was pretty sure he would gladly be lassoed to her for the rest of his life. And that, of course, brought memories of the time when she had thought that she and Jess would be the ones wearing a similar rosary. Why was it that every detail of this wedding — someone else's wedding — reminded her of Jess?

She bowed her head and closed her eyes as the priest completed his blessing of the symbolic binding of Maria and Chet. ". . . the holiness that will preserve your union and that of your new family is to be found in the vows of sacrifice and love that you have given and received today."

Sacrifice. What had Jess been willing to sacrifice for her? Of course, she had been every bit as stubborn, refusing to even consider giving up her dream of serving the people of Whitman Falls as their doctor. She may as well face the truth — both she and Jess were set in their ways, and the idea that they might find middle ground was ludicrous.

We can be friends, she decided. After all, they had been friends long before they became romantically involved. And having come to a decision that held the possibility that she might be able to live in the same town as Jess Porterfield and maintain her sanity, she looked up at Jess and gave him a huge smile.

Jess's initial reaction was one of confusion. But then he smiled back, and as the ceremony came to a close, he offered her his arm, then stopped to offer his free arm to his mother as they followed the newlyweds back up the aisle to the applause of all the guests.

Confident she could convince Jess to come to the same conclusion about their future, Addie relaxed. Everything was going to work out just fine.

Jess was happier than he'd been in years.

Maria had found a fine man in Chet Hunter — a man fully capable of taming her impulsiveness. Then there was the fact that his mother truly appeared to have recovered from the malaise she had suffered in the months immediately after his father's death. And there were his younger siblings. Amanda was a beauty all right, but she was every bit as smart as Maria was — and as caring. Trey clearly loved ranching, and one day Jess could see him taking charge, or maybe, having a little spread of his own.

But what gave him the greatest happiness on this December night was that Addie Wilcox had danced every dance with him, laughed at his jokes, let him bring her punch, and once she had even brushed his hair back from his forehead, a gesture he permitted to only two women — his mother and Addie.

So when Addie suggested that he should dance with Sybil Sinclair, Jess was stunned. He had led her just outside the barn door where the guests had gathered for the dancing after the ceremony. They were standing in the shadows so he couldn't see her face. "I thought you didn't care for Sybil," he said.

"Well, we're not the best of friends, but that doesn't mean I don't like her and wish her well."

"I guess I thought what you didn't like was her with me."

Addie looked away. "There was a time when that was true, but now I realize you have every right to be with any woman you choose."

"I choose to be with you, Addie Wilcox. I thought I'd made that pretty clear."

She bristled, and he knew he had made her mad — again. Things had been going so well. What was happening? He felt his own temper flare. "Of course, if you've got somebody else lined up . . ."

"Oh, stop that," she snapped. "We both know well and good that we are no match for each other, romantically speaking. But why spoil a lifelong friendship in the bargain?"

"You sure did kiss me like we were more than just friends," Jess argued.

"You kissed me," she replied primly.

"And you kissed me back. So what the devil is going on here?"

She sighed heavily and sank down onto a bale of hay. "I want to marry and have a family, Jess. I want to live out my days here in Whitman Falls. I want to practice my medicine here. You want your freedom to pick up and go. You want romance but not commitment. I'm not blaming you for that. But . . ."

"Do not say another word, Addie. Just stop talking. You don't know the first thing about me and what I want. You're determined to blame me for taking off like I did. Well, I made a mistake. I'm not perfect. You're the one . . ." He shook off the accusation. "Look, I'm back now and have settled into the job of marshal and . . ."

"And you're looking for every opportunity to find something you can use against the Tipton brothers to prove they ordered the murder of your father. You're playing with fire when it comes to crossing them. You don't seem to care if it gets you killed, and all of that comes before me, or any feelings you might have for me."

Jess dumped the dregs of his punch on the ground and stalked away. If he stood there one more minute, he was either going to grab Addie and shake her until she talked sense again, or he was going to kiss her in front of everybody just to shut her up. She wanted him to dance with Sybil? So be it.

He stalked across the barn to Sybil, who was gossiping with a bunch of other girls, held out his hand to her, and without a word led her to where several guests were dancing a reel. Thankfully, the dance was intricate and lively enough that he was not expected to make conversation. They came together and parted and changed partners as the dance required. And when the music finally stopped, Jess was sure that he was still hearing the beat of it in his brain, until he realized what he was hearing was the thunder of horses racing full out toward the yard.

"Something's up," he told Sybil. "Stay with your folks."

Everyone had gone silent as the horses came closer. Jess and Chet and all the hired hands from the Clear Springs Ranch formed a barrier between the path leading up to the house and the festivities in the barn. "Go be with your bride," Jess ordered Chet. "We've got this covered."

"It's Jasper Tipton and his men," Chet replied. "Best let me stay."

The riders pulled up just shy of the standing line of men. Most stayed on horseback, but Jasper Tipton slid from his saddle and stalked toward Jess, his face mottled with fury. "Where is she?" he demanded, scanning the gathering behind Jess and the others. "Where is that woman who calls herself a doctor?"

"You need to calm down, Mr. Tipton," Jess said, keeping his voice firm but quiet.

"And you need to do your job and arrest that woman."

"If you'll tell me what the trouble is, sir . . ."

For the first time since dismounting, Jasper Tipton turned the full force of his gaze onto Jess. His eyes were wild and bloodshot, and Jess wondered if the man was drunk. His lips worked as if he could not find the words he wanted. A dribble of slobber ran from the corners of his mouth. He looked like a mad dog.

"The trouble?" he finally managed. "You ask me what the trouble is?" And then to Jess's utter astonishment, the man burst into tears — sobs that racked his entire body and left him falling to his knees, pounding the ground with his fists.

Jess tried in vain to help the man up, but he was dead weight. He glanced at the men who had ridden in with him, and finally, saw Jasper's brother, Buck, lurking at the back of the group. "What's this about, Buck?"

"That woman murdered my brother's wife and his unborn child, so either you do your duty and arrest her, or me and the boys here will take matters into our own hands."

"Pearl's dead?" Jess asked.

"Her and the baby. Found her just lying

there on her bed."

Nothing made sense. Sure, Addie had been spending a good deal of time with Pearl Tipton over the last several weeks, but, according to Addie, once Jasper had realized his young wife was finally pregnant, he'd been the one to insist that Addie call on Pearl at least once a week. True, he would have preferred that Addie's father make the calls, but Pearl had told him that she would allow only Addie to examine her. And, by all accounts, Pearl and the baby had been doing just fine. So how could they be dead? And why would Jasper call it murder and blame Addie?

"I'm not gonna wait all night, Marshal Porterfield," Buck snarled.

The buzz of conversation behind him told Jess that everyone had heard why the Tiptons had come and what they were demanding. He did some quick calculations. Tipton's men were armed and spoiling for a fight. The guests at the wedding were mostly unarmed and were standing in harm's way if they tried to protect Addie.

"I don't like your attitude, Tipton. Seems to me now would be the time to be consoling your brother here, not throwing around threats."

"Is that an answer?"

"No, here's your answer. I will be taking Miss Wilcox into protective custody until I have had the opportunity to investigate Mrs. Tipton's untimely death. I'm going to ask Doc Wilcox to come with me."

Buck snorted. "Oh, that's fair — like bringing a fox along to examine a henhouse."

To Jess's surprise his mother stepped forward. "That's just about enough out of you, Buck Tipton. Your grieving brother needs to be all you concern yourself with at the moment. Now you and one of your men help me get him to his feet and into the house. We'll all wait here while the marshal and Doc get Addie back to town and sort this out." She bent and placed her hand on Jasper's rounded shoulders. "Come along, Jasper."

When neither Buck nor his men made a move to help, Trey and one of the hired hands stepped forward, lifted Jasper to his feet, and half-carried, half-dragged him across the courtyard and into the house.

"I'll go hitch up Doc's buggy," Chet said as he headed for the stable.

Jess nodded and turned to his deputy. "Luc, you go ahead and ride back to town. I expect you'll find Mrs. Tipton's body in the house. Make sure no one goes in or out until Doc and I get there. Is that clear?"

Lucas took off for the corral, and two minutes later, he was riding hard and fast toward town. Jess was a little surprised that neither Buck nor any of the other Tipton men tried to follow. "Buck, you ought to stay here with your brother while your men go back to the ranch. I expect they've got chores that need doing."

"I want to see her," Buck said. "Bring her forward."

"No."

But Jess might have known better than to speak for Addie. The woman had a mind of her own, and even when she was making a huge mistake, like she was right at this moment, nobody Jess knew could stop her.

"I'm right here," she said, and the crowd parted to let her through. She spoke in a voice loud enough for all to hear. "The last time I saw your sister-in-law, Buck, she was just fine and so was her baby. Her death was not due to anything I did or did not do."

Buck grinned and fumbled in his pocket for something. "Oh, no? Who gave her these pills then? Who gave her the very poison here that killed her?"

Jess was surprised when Addie's posture of self-confidence and certainty visibly faltered. "She took them?"

"Every blasted one," Buck confirmed.

Jess stepped forward as Addie's knees gave way. "He's right, Jess," she said softly. "I killed her as sure as if I had fed her those pills."

"What's that, girlie?" Buck shouted. "Sounds like maybe a confession to me, Marshal, so you gonna do your job, or you gonna leave it to me?"

Jess scooped Addie up into his arms just as her tears came. "Oh Jess, he's right. What have I done?"

"Shut up, Addie. Not another word."

Addie sat between her parents as her father drove the buggy back to town. Jess rode his horse, keeping pace with the buggy, while he and Doc Wilcox discussed what steps Jess needed to take next. All of them were well aware that Buck Tipton and at least two of his men were following them, although, blessedly, they were keeping their distance.

"Probably best you keep her at the jail," her father was saying.

"No," her mother protested.

"Now, Alice, it's for her own safety. And we can't allow the marshal here to be accused of showing favoritism."

Addie realized that this was the first time

she'd heard her father refer to Jess by his title. It was a mark of respect — and progress. "Papa's right," she said, her throat still raw from all the crying she'd been doing. "The truth is I prescribed those pills for Pearl to help manage her morning sickness. They also helped her get a good night's sleep. I thought she was no longer thinking about . . ."

"Stop talking, Addie," Jess growled. "Just stop talking."

Addie's father patted her hand. "He's right, darling girl. The less you say the better until we can get the full story in the matter."

But she needed to talk. She needed to understand how the unthinkable could have happened. She was certain that Pearl had come to love the baby she carried and was no longer desperate enough to take her own life. She remembered how excited Pearl had been when they had gone shopping for the layette at Eliza's store. Eliza had fussed over her and spoken glowingly of how radiant Pearl looked and what a wonderful mother she was going to be. Pearl had lapped up every compliment like a kitten offered its first bowl of cream.

That day Pearl had blushed and laughed and cradled her stomach as if already imagining the child in her arms. She had giggled with Eliza and Addie as she revealed Jasper Tipton's decision to talk to the child, even read and sing to it, although it was known by anyone who attended local church services that Jasper was no singer. "But he loves me so," Pearl had said softly when the laughter subsided. "And this baby is going to be so loved and cared for."

She had insisted that Eliza close the store for an hour and allow her to treat them all to lunch at the hotel's restaurant. She had even invited Millie Jennings along and spent the entire hour seeking Millie's counsel on parenting.

Once they returned to the store, she proceeded to buy just about anything that Eliza offered in the way of clothing for the child, as well as toys and furnishings for the nursery. As Clara supervised the loading of all the purchases onto the buckboard that arrived to collect them, Pearl had actually hugged Addie and whispered, "Thank you, dear friend. I see now that everything will work out in the end."

That had been less than a week ago. That woman was not planning to take her life and that of her unborn child, Addie thought as they entered the outskirts of town. What had changed? What had Addie missed?

She'd been so busy with the preparations for the wedding that she hadn't seen Pearl for days. She should have made time.

"You're shaking, dear girl," her father said as he pulled the buggy to a stop just outside the jail. "Let's get you inside out of this wind."

But Addie knew her shaking was not weather-related. Her shaking was born of regret and shame and guilt — and the certainty that nothing could ever be the same again.

Jess followed Addie and her parents into the jailhouse. Her father led her to a chair and stood next to her, patting her shoulder while her mother filled a glass from a pitcher of day-old water and offered it to her.

"I suspect our girl could use something stronger, Alice," Doc said, nodding toward the pint of whiskey Lucas had placed on the shelf to remind himself of what drink had nearly done to his family. Alice Wilcox offered no objection, but twisted open the cap on the bottle, dumped the water out the open window, and splashed a generous amount of the amber liquid into the glass.

Doc took the glass his wife passed to him, took a swig of the whiskey himself, and then offered it to Addie. She clutched the glass with both hands and still the liquid sloshed against the sides of the glass because she was shaking so badly. It frightened Jess to see Addie this way. Her eyes were dull and without expression. Her posture, normally so proper and upright, was that of someone who had endured a beating and feared more blows to come. She was wearing the dress she'd worn for the wedding — the same pretty green thing with matching satin ribbons entwined in her hair.

She finally managed a gulp of the drink. Jess expected her to spit it out at once, but instead she took another swallow, and then a third.

"I think that's enough," her mother said, easing the glass from her daughter's grip. "You two men should get over to the Tipton place. No telling what Buck Tipton has done to destroy whatever evidence there might have been."

"He says she swallowed all the pills. If she did . . ." Doc began.

To everyone's surprise, Addie spoke up. "Pearl Tipton did not kill herself or her baby. She loved that child too much to do it any harm. If she was planning to kill herself, she would have first made sure the baby was safe." She managed to get to her feet, weaving a little as she made her way to one of

214

the two cells, where she collapsed onto the cot and turned her face to the wall.

"Go on, you two," her mother instructed, shooing them to the door. "She'll sleep now, and you can interrogate her later."

Reluctant to leave Addie for even a moment, Jess nevertheless had a job to do, and he knew Addie would never be safe — or free — if he didn't uncover the truth behind Pearl's death.

"Come on, son," Doc Wilcox said as he held the door to the street open and waited for Jess. And as Jess headed out he felt Doc touch his shoulder in a way that told him Addie's father understood his hesitation to leave Addie.

Together they crossed the street. The Tipton mansion was ablaze with light. Every window glowed, and the front door stood wide open, giving passersby a view of the foyer and the massive curved stairway that wound its way to the second floor. If Jess hadn't known better, he would have thought Jasper and Pearl were giving a party. They often entertained, usually business associates from the area or dignitaries who saw the importance of currying favor with the territory's largest landholder. But as he and Doc mounted the steps to the open door, the only sounds they heard were the low rumble of men's voices and the clink of glasses.

"Where's the body?" Doc asked Lucas, who was standing guard in the front hallway, keeping an eye on Buck and his men. They were enjoying their drinks as they sprawled on furniture in the lavish parlor — furniture that seemed far too dainty for them.

"Bodies," Buck corrected. "That bitch killed my brother's baby."

Doc stiffened. "Are you referring to my daughter?"

"Well now, let's see. Your daughter would be the one handing out pills to my sister-in-law? Then yes, I am speaking of your precious, high-and-mighty daughter."

Jess saw Doc take a step toward Buck, who was lounging on a sofa, his dirty boots propped on the fancy fabric. He stepped in front of the older man. "We'll be upstairs examining the scene and the body. After that, I'll have some questions."

Buck frowned. "You got no cause to question me or my men here, Porterfield."

"Don't rightly believe I said who I was going to question, Buck, but now that you mention it, since you found the body, I imagine you've got information I'm gonna need." He turned to Lucas. "Deputy Jennings, please let me know if any of these

216

men tries to leave the premises."

He followed Doc up the winding staircase and down the hall to the single open door on the second floor. Pearl Tipton lay on the high sleigh bed, her golden hair fanned over the pillows, her face peaceful, and her folded hands resting on the mound of her pregnancy. She might have been asleep, Jess thought, and realized he was practically tiptoeing into the room in an effort not to disturb her.

Doc, on the other hand, was all business. He went straight to the bedside, set his black bag on a side table, and removed his coat and hat. He started his exam by gently opening Pearl's eyelids.

Jess took this opportunity to look around the room. Everything seemed to be in order, no signs of a struggle. In some ways, the room was too orderly. Nothing was out of place — no drawers or wardrobe doors left partially open, and every item on the dressing table lined up perfectly. Had Pearl been that kind of woman? One who was so precise in her daily habits?

"You might want to look at this, Jess," Doc said. He had two fingers inside Pearl's mouth, and when he withdrew them his fingers were white with powder.

"The pills she took?"

217

"Maybe. I can test the residue to be sure. But there's something else." He turned Pearl's head to one side, exposing a small but deep cut at the base of her scalp, one that had bled enough to stain the pillow. "She might have fallen — the pills would make her groggy and disoriented — but . . ."

"But you don't think that's how she got that wound."

"Seems unlikely, given the location. And if she fell and struck her head, how did she get in the bed?"

"Maybe she had help," Jess said. He took a closer look at the position of Pearl's body. Her skirt was bunched against her legs in a way that was in keeping with somebody having lifted her onto the bed. Of course, that was just pure conjecture on his part and hardly evidence that would take the blame off Addie.

"Any sign of a note?" Doc asked as he continued his examination.

"Not that I've found so far." Jess stopped at the door and allowed his gaze to slowly roam the room. Again, he was struck by the pristine condition of his surroundings. He recalled that the rooms downstairs had been in more disarray. Surely a woman who was this particular about her bedroom would have been just as particular about the condition of the formal parlor where she entertained guests. Of course, Buck and his men might be responsible for any untidiness in that room. He recalled how Buck had lounged on the sofa, his feet propped on a damask pillow.

He looked at the floor. A small hand-braided rug was slightly askew next to the bed — the only thing out of order in the room.

He moved closer and saw pellets of dirt embedded in the rug. He studied Doc's boots — polished and clean, then his own. Doc was standing on the opposite side of the bed. Jess knelt down and plucked a glob of the debris from the fibers. And all he could think about was Buck Tipton's dirty boots.

"You finish up here, Doc. I'm going downstairs to question Buck."

"You're wasting your time," Doc said.

"Maybe. But something tells me he's got a part in this."

As he walked downstairs, he could hear Buck and his men laughing. They were well on their way to being drunk. Might not be a bad idea to question them when their guard was down. But when Jess reached the parlor, Buck got up and faced him, and he seemed to be stone cold sober. "You satisfied, Marshal? That woman murdered my sister-in-law and her baby. She'll hang for this."

"Who found the body?" Jess asked, ignoring Buck's rant.

"Who do you think found her? Her husband — my brother. Broke his heart."

"And you were in the house at the time?"

"I live here."

"So your brother found the body and then what?"

Buck glared at Jess. "You're questioning me? You've got your killer locked up over at the jailhouse."

"Just answer the question."

"I heard my brother's cries for help, and I ran up the stairs. Pearl hadn't come down for supper, and Jasper went to check on her."

Jess was disappointed. Buck had just offered a plausible explanation for the dirt from his boots on the rug next to Pearl's bed. "And then what?"

"Jasper went crazy. He ran into the street shouting for Doc. I told him Doc and most everybody else was out at your ma's place for the wedding. He mounted up and took off. Me and the boys followed." He took a step closer to Jess. "Is that it?"

"So if Jasper was calling for the doctor,

Pearl wasn't yet dead?"

"She was dead all right. My brother just refused to believe it."

"You found her just as she was when Doc and I saw her?"

"Nothing was moved, if that's what you're saying."

"Then how did you come by the empty pill bottle?"

For the first time all evening, Buck seemed to falter. "I . . . it was right there. I just grabbed it."

"Right where? On the side table? On the bed? In the deceased's hand?"

"It was on the floor. I nearly stepped on it when Jasper cried out, and I went running to see what had him so upset." His confidence was returning.

Jess held out his hand. "I'm going to need that pill bottle, Buck. It's evidence — unfortunately, it's contaminated, but it's still evidence."

Buck pulled the bottle from his pocket and studied it then tossed it to Jess. "I didn't do anything you wouldn't have done in the same circumstances."

Jess turned to Lucas. "Stay here, and make sure nothing else is disturbed or tampered with, including the body. Buck, you and your boys should leave."

"I live here," Buck reminded him.

"Not tonight you don't. Both you and your brother need to find other accommodations."

"My brother needs to make arrangements for burying his wife and baby."

"First thing tomorrow," Jess said. "For now, you need to leave."

The two men with Buck staggered to their feet in a show of support for their boss. "He ain't leaving 'til he's good and ready," one of them slurred.

Jess kept his focus on Buck. "Your brother needs you, Buck. There's nothing you can accomplish by being here."

Buck's eyes were glassy with the effects of his drinking. He frowned, then slapped his hat onto his head and turned. "Come on, boys. We got work to do." The two men followed his orders without question. As he reached the door, Buck turned back to face Jess. "I know you're gonna try and clear the name of that woman, Porterfield, but the facts don't lie. She as good as killed Pearl. She might as well have forced those pills down her throat herself."

"That woman has a name, Buck — one you know all too well, since you've been trying to get her to let you come calling for some time now. Seems to me you're mighty set on teaching her a lesson."

To Jess's surprise, Buck grinned. "Well, she's learning hard times now, ain't she?"

When Addie realized she was alone — her mother having gone to their house to collect some blankets and a change of clothes for her — she pushed herself off the cot and approached the door to the cell. It wasn't locked. She gave it a tap, and it swung back on its hinges, giving a screeching sound that made Addie cover her ears as she stepped into Jess's office and looked around.

Jail was the last place she'd ever imagined that she'd be. But here she was, and from everything she knew so far about Pearl's death, this was probably where she belonged. What could she have been thinking giving Pearl that sleeping potion?

She felt tears of remorse well in her throat and sat down in Jess's chair, her legs too weak to keep standing. On his desk sat the bottle of whiskey and the glass. She'd never in her life been drunk, but people said it helped one forget. Maybe, just for tonight, it was the best possible remedy. Given what she had consumed earlier, she wondered why she wasn't already drunk.

She filled the glass halfway and gulped a bitter mouthful of liquor. She heard men's voices outside, the horses riding away, and then footsteps on the boardwalk approaching the jail. She finished off the whiskey and was refilling the glass when Jess walked in.

"That's about enough of that," he said as he gently pried the glass from her fingers and set it and the bottle on a shelf.

She focused on his badge — a tin star that had given him the power to arrest her. "Not enough," she muttered, and realized she was having trouble forming words. Her tongue suddenly seemed way too large to fit inside her mouth, much less speak around.

"We're gonna figure this out, Addie. Nobody believes you murdered Pearl Tipton."

"Nobody except her husband." She looked up at the whiskey bottle and wondered if she was drunk yet. She wondered how men thought drinking this poison was pleasant. Frankly, she'd rather have a nice, cold sarsaparilla.

"It's not really murder, you know," Jess continued. "I mean, prescribing the pills."

She really wished he would stop calling Pearl's death "murder." She'd truly had no inkling that the woman might take her own life. Or had she? Hadn't she hesitated just a moment before giving her the sleeping potion? She shook off the thought.

"After all, even if you might have given Pearl the idea of how to do it, she killed herself."

"I gave her the sleeping potion — to help her *sleep,* and that was it." She realized she was having trouble finding the words she wanted to speak, but one thought was front and center in her mind. "Jess," she slurred, then shook her head in an attempt to speak more clearly. "This is Jasper Tipton's wife. We both know — the whole town knows — that if he decides I did this, then there's not a lot we can do about it."

One more big gulp should do it. One more river of scalding alcohol coating her throat, and with any luck she'd pass out. She got up and reached for the bottle.

"You've had enough," he said, intercepting her reach. He wrapped his arm around her waist and half-carried her to a cell. "I'll see if I can find you a pillow," he said as he eased her down to sit on the cot.

"Don't treat me any different than you would Luc or some other prisoner." She curled onto her side, facing the wall, and the world went black.

Hours — maybe an entire day — later, Addie was awakened by the screech of the cell door. She opened one eye and saw Eliza

McNew dipping a ladle into a steaming pot and emptying the contents into a bowl. "You need to eat something."

Addie took one whiff of the stuff in the bowl. She knew it was Eliza's famous pot-roast stew, but frankly, it smelled like manure. She slid to her knees and doubled over the slop bucket next to the cot. It felt like her guts were coming up. Nope, she was definitely not a drinker.

Eliza sat on the side of the cot and pulled Addie's lank hair away from her face. "Get it all out," she counseled. "Don't know what Jess was thinking, letting you drink like that."

Addie pushed herself to her feet and immediately sat on the low wooden table next to the cell bars. She leaned her head back, feeling the coolness of the metal against her neck. "Not his fault," she said hoarsely. She looked at the cell door, remembering the loud clank of its opening earlier — and closing, last night. Tears welled as she turned her gaze to the small window above the cot. "Looks like rain," she said.

"Yep, a storm's coming, that's for sure." Eliza placed the cover on the pot of stew, blessedly extinguishing the sickening smell. "I want you to keep one thing in mind, Addie Wilcox. You are presumed innocent.

Got that?"

Addie nodded, trying hard to keep her composure. "You should get back to the store."

"Millie's minding the store."

"I'll bet I know what the topic of conversation is this morning," Addie said with a brittle little laugh. "It's me, right?"

"Don't concern yourself with such foolishness. Talk will die down once Jess proves you had nothing to do with this."

"Where is everybody?"

"You mean Jess?"

"I mean Jess, Luc, my parents . . ."

"Your father is preparing Pearl's body for burial." That made sense. In a town the size of Whitman Falls, the doctor often pulled double duty as undertaker. "Your mother insisted on staying here all night while you slept, so I sent her home to get some rest. Luc is standing guard over at the Tipton place, and I sent Jess over to the hotel to get some breakfast. That man hasn't slept or eaten since this all started. He'll be back directly."

From outside Addie heard a wagon pass and the jingle of bells. "Today is Christmas Eve," she whispered.

"That it is," Eliza confirmed.

"Did Maria and Chet leave for their wed-

227

ding trip?"

"Of course not. You can't think anyone who cares for you would be anywhere but close by until this entire mess is cleared up."

Christmas Eve. She had made gifts for her parents, her friends, and even one for Jess. But she doubted anyone was going to feel much like exchanging gifts and singing carols now.

Eliza shook out a housedress she'd plucked from a stack of clothing set on a bench outside the cell. "Now, why don't you wash up and change into something more practical for . . ."

She paused, fumbling for words to complete that statement.

"Thank you," Addie said. She took the dress and spread it on the cot. "Maybe I could wash my face and hands?"

"Of course." Eliza hurried out the back door and returned with a basin of water, a bar of lye soap, and a towel. "You get yourself freshened up. I'll stand guard to be sure nobody comes in."

Addie opened the gown she'd worn for the wedding and let it fall to her waist. She washed, then spotted her hairbrush on a shelf with her glasses and brushed out her tangled hair. There were no hairpins, only the ribbon she'd worn for the wedding, so instead of her usual bun she braided her hair and tied it with the ribbon. Then she stepped out of the gown and into the cotton dress. She was just fastening the last button when she heard Eliza talking to someone.

Jess.

In spite of her decision to encourage his pursuit of Sybil and to base the future on friendship rather than romance, her heart raced at the sound of his voice. She couldn't hear what he was saying, but from the tone she knew he was exhausted and disheartened, all of which only added to her own misery.

"She's freshening up a bit," Addie heard Eliza say.

"I'm fine," Addie called out, and a moment later, Jess entered the small office and came directly to her cell. He took hold of her hands and allowed his eyes to rake over her, as if to reassure himself that she was truly all right.

"Well, I'll just be getting back to the store," Eliza said as she picked up the pot of stew. "If you need anything, Addie, anything at all . . ."

Addie could not seem to drag her eyes away from Jess's haggard face. "We'll be fine," she said. "Thank you."

Jess framed Addie's face with his large

palms and drew her closer. She wrapped her arms around his waist and pressed her cheek to his chest.

Eight

Addie's parents and brother Brian made the best they could of Christmas Eve. Her mother and Brian's wife prepared a special dinner and invited Eliza, the Jennings family and, of course, Jess to join them. Everything was laid out on Jess's desk and a side table that was usually cluttered with files. The small tables — stools, really — that sat next to the cots in each cell were pressed into service as extra seating. When it started to rain, Brian's children and the Jennings girls played tag, racing from one cell to the next and squealing with delight.

"Hard to believe tomorrow is Christmas," Addie's mother said as she unwrapped a basket of rolls and set them on the desk.

"When is Pearl's funeral?" Addie asked.

"Day after tomorrow."

Addie froze. "So soon?" Her first thought was whether or not her father would have the time he needed to fully examine the body and determine for certain the cause of death. "I mean, my heart goes out to Jasper, but still, what about family that may want to come for the service?"

"Pearl had no family — at least not that anyone ever knew of," Eliza said.

Addie recalled a day when she had called on Pearl. During the examination, she had made a comment about proud grandparents. Pearl's response had been that this child would not be blessed with grandparents — Jasper's parents were both dead. It had seemed odd at the time that she had not mentioned her own parents, but that had been early in their friendship, and Addie had not wanted to pry.

Brian's wife, Ruth, joined the conversation. "I heard that when Jasper met her, Pearl was working as a dance hall girl over in Yuma. Rumor has it that he took her to a high society friend of his and had her instruct Pearl on how to be a proper lady." Ruth was a bit of a gossip, and Addie realized she felt protective of Pearl.

"I think Pearl had a difficult life before she met Jasper." Addie turned her attention to her father and Jess, who seemed oblivious to others as they sat in a corner of the room, talking quietly. The minute her father saw her moving their way, he motioned to

Jess to stop talking, and turned to her.

"How are you holding up, child?"

"You tell me," she replied. "What were the two of you looking so worried about?"

Jess and her father exchanged a look.

"I've had a wire from the district judge," Jess told her. "You're to be held over for trial."

Addie felt as if she'd been struck in the chest. Her breath seemed to leave her in a rush. "When?" she managed.

"It'll take weeks for the man to make his way here," her father assured her. "And that gives us the time we need to build a case to prove your innocence in the matter." He didn't sound all that sure.

"And in the meantime?"

"I can't let you go, Addie," Jess explained. "I'm under orders to keep you in custody."

"It's all right, Jess. I understand." She drew in a long breath, steeling herself for what lay ahead. "So how do we prove my innocence?"

"You don't," her father said. "It's up to your accusers to prove your guilt."

Addie smiled. "In theory, that's probably true, Papa. In reality?"

"We're going to find the truth," Jess said, his voice tight but determined. He glanced up at her. "Something's not right here,

233

Addie, and if it's the last thing I do, I'm going to uncover what really happened to Pearl."

Behind them, they heard Ruth call for the children to settle down and wash their hands.

"Looks like it's time for supper," Doc said. He wrapped his arm around Addie's shoulders and escorted her to the table where the local Catholic priest, Father Francis, had joined the group and asked that they all bow their heads in prayer.

Addie had never been much for organized religion, but she believed in the power of a higher being to influence what came next. On this occasion, she closed her eyes and prayed hard for Jess to make good on his promise to find the truth about Pearl's death, and to give her back an opportunity she had so cavalierly set aside — that perhaps one day she and Jess might build a future together.

Thanks to the children, the Christmas Eve dinner Addie's mother had prepared was a lively event, punctuated by laughter and spills and some tears, as well as memories of past Christmases. For a short time everyone seemed to forget that they were sharing this meal in a jailhouse and that one among them had been accused of murder.

Jess spent the better part of the meal watching Addie and marveling at her ability to put aside her troubles as she enjoyed the gathering. She laughed along with the others when Brian told of the time she had decided to make gifts for her parents.

"She was determined to knit Father a sweater," Brian said. "Trouble was, she didn't know the first thing about how to knit, and she made this decision just four days before Christmas."

Everyone laughed, even Addie, but Jess did not miss the way her eyes sparkled with unshed tears. She was fighting to hide her fear. He'd seen that look before. It was the way she had looked at him the night he left. It was a look of disbelief at having found herself in these circumstances and the foreboding that came with the realization that she might not have the power to change the situation.

The truth was that things were looking bad for Addie. Anything Jess had been able to find that might work as evidence in her favor was easily explained away. He was sure that Buck was somehow involved in Pearl's death, and yet he could find nothing that tied the man to the deed. And besides, what motive would he have?

From what Doc had told him about the district judge, the man was a political appointee who would rule based not on evidence, but rather on who might prove most useful to him in the future. When Jess compared what Addie and her family might have to offer the judge to what the Tipton brothers might offer, his heart sank.

"I do not see why Addie cannot attend midnight services with the rest of us," Alice Wilcox was saying.

"Now, Alice, I've explained the need to counter any idea that our daughter is receiving special treatment," Doc replied. "Down the road that could hurt her if this thing goes to trial."

"When it goes to trial," Addie said. She laid a shawl around her mother's shoulders. "You go on, Ma. I'll be fine. Actually, I would probably fall asleep right in the middle of services, and you know how that embarrasses you." She kissed her mother's cheek. "You go pray for us all, and I'll get everything here cleared away and packed up."

Alice Wilcox cupped her daughter's cheek. "Get some rest," she said softly. "We'll see you in the morning."

"Merry Christmas, Mama."

It was the first time her voice had cracked,

and Jess saw that she was barely holding on to any semblance of composure. He moved to her side. "I'll make sure she gets some rest, Miz Wilcox."

The church bell chimed, calling the faithful to services. Reluctantly, the Wilcoxes followed Eliza and the Jennings family down the street, where Father Francis waited at the entrance to the adobe chapel, welcoming those who had come to worship. Jess leaned against the open doorway of the jailhouse watching them, and when he turned around, Addie was busy wrapping leftover food and clearing away dirty dishes.

"If you'll get me a pan of water," she said, "I'll wash these up, and you can take them back to the house and . . ." Her hands shook, and a plate clattered to the floor and broke into three pieces. As if she'd lost something precious, Addie bent to gather the pieces and burst into tears.

Gently, Jess relieved her of the broken crockery and helped her stand. "I'll take care of this. You've had about all you can take for today. Come on. Lie down." She did not resist as he led her to the cell and helped her settle on the edge of the cot. "Close your eyes and sleep, Addie. You need your strength."

She swiped at her tears and nodded. With

a weary sigh, she lay back and watched him as he covered her with the quilt her mother had brought. "Jess, I really thought that Pearl . . ."

"Shhh," he whispered as he traced the outline of her lips with his finger. "We're going to figure this out together, okay?"

She nodded. "Promise?"

Jess chuckled. "Well now, seems to me in the past, you've had some trouble trusting any promise I might make." He was deliberately baiting her, teasing her, doing whatever it might take to fan the flame of Addie, the fighter.

She clasped his hand. "I trust you now," she said softly. She sniffed back fresh tears.

Jess settled himself next to her on the narrow cot, their backs against the wall. He pulled her into his arms. "Hey, we are going to beat this thing. Tipton has a weak case. You didn't force Pearl to swallow those pills, and you had every reason to believe you were helping her when you prescribed them and . . ."

"Can we please talk about something else?" she begged.

"Well, we could talk about how pretty you looked at my sister's wedding," he said. "We could talk about how when I held you in my arms for the dancing, I didn't ever want to let you go. We could talk about how much I want to kiss you right now. Any of that strike your fancy?"

"The kissing part sounds good," she whispered.

Jess grinned. "More than happy to oblige, ma'am."

Kissing Addie was like coming home after a hard day. Her lips on his washed away everything ugly about his world. In her kiss he found peace and solace and strength. Kissing her gave him hope for the future and the courage he needed to face whatever lay before them.

As they cuddled together, kissing, holding, touching, no words were necessary. Later, when they heard the congregation leaving the church, singing carols as they made their way home, Jess got up and locked the front door. When he turned around, Addie was standing in the doorway that led to his sleeping quarters.

"I don't want our first time to be in a jail cell," she said as she slowly unbuttoned the bodice of her dress.

He could hardly believe what was happening. "Are you saying . . ."

She hesitated, then buttoned her dress again. "I thought . . . forgive me for believing that . . ." She stumbled past him and back to her cell, where she lay down on the cot and pulled the quilt around her.

Jess could not believe his luck. Every time he thought they were on the same path, something happened to spoil it. "Addie, don't be that way. Of course I want you. Of course I hoped. Why do you think I locked the door?"

"You want me, but that's not the same, is it?"

"As what?" The woman could confound a professor with her riddles.

"As loving me. I love you, Jess Porterfield. Can you say the same?"

He hesitated. If he said it back to her, she was bound to think the only reason was because he wanted to take her to bed. If he didn't . . .

"Thought as much. Well, at least we've cleared that up. Good night, Jess." She pulled the quilt more tightly around her and turned her face to the wall.

"Addie . . ."

She actually gave a snore, pretending to be asleep already. Jess wasn't fooled. "You know something, Addie Wilcox, you are one of the world's most stubborn and impossible females, and why I have loved you from the first time I saw you is a mystery to me, but that's my cross to bear. One of these days, you are going to realize that we were meant to be together, and maybe it won't be too late for us to make that happen. In the meantime, I am going to do whatever it takes to get you out of this mess you've gotten yourself into and . . ."

That did it. She threw back the quilt and reached the bars of the cell in three quick steps. "I did not get myself into a mess," she countered. "I practiced good medicine and tried to help a woman in need. If you and Jasper Tipton can't understand that, then I guess I'll hang, but do not accuse me of making trouble for myself."

"That's not what I meant, and you know it. Honestly, Addie, will you stop and look at the situation and try to help me help you before it's too late?"

She was struck speechless for once. He watched as she tried to come up with something to hurl back at him. Instead, he saw her face crumble as the reality of her circumstances hit her again. She started to tremble, and her eyes were huge and round — and defeated — when she looked up at him. "Help me, Jess," she said softly. "I am so very afraid. What if . . ." She could not bring herself to give words to her fears.

Jess opened his arms to her, and she came willingly to his embrace. Outside all was silent. Inside the only sound was their breathing in tandem as Jess lifted her in his arms and carried her to his room. He laid her on the bed and sat beside her. "Sleep now," he said. "It's not home, but it's not jail either. So get some rest, and tomorrow . . ."

It was her turn to hold out her arms to him. "Lie with me," she said huskily. "Hold me."

Fully dressed, he stretched out beside her and pulled her into the curve of his body. "Better?" he asked.

She turned to face him. "What if this is the only chance we get?"

He didn't have to ask what she meant. "We'll have time," he assured her.

"You can't know that. You said you love me — prove it."

Addie could not believe she was being so brazen. On the other hand, she was in jail and, if not yet charged, certainly under suspicion for contributing to Pearl's death. What did she have to lose? Certainly not her reputation — that had flown out the window the minute the Tipton brothers had arrived at Maria and Chet's wedding to accuse her. At the moment, the empty pill bottle seemed the only evidence of Pearl's demise, and it was true that Addie had prescribed those pills and trusted Pearl with a full bottle, instead of doling them out herself, so she would know for sure that Pearl wasn't abusing them.

"You don't know what you're saying, Addie." Jess had already pulled back, and while he was still lying next to her on the narrow bed, so close she could feel his breath on her face, he had put what distance he could between them.

"I know exactly what I'm saying, but if you . . ."

With a growl of frustration, he gathered her in his arms. "You drive me crazy, woman. Think what you are asking of me. Think how you will regret this tomorrow, or certainly, once all this mess is laid to rest. Think, Addie." He stroked her hair back from her temple.

"I do not wish to think. I wish to live. I want to experience the life I've always dreamed of — a life where you and I love each other and talk of the future we will build and the children we will have and . . ." She felt tears trickling down her cheeks and brushed them away. "Jess, we don't know what tomorrow will bring, and we've wasted so much time already. You say you love me but . . ."

"I love you, Addie. Can't you see that's exactly why I don't want to risk doing anything you might regret later?"

"I'm a grown woman, Jess. I take full responsibility for my decisions and actions. And what I have decided is that I do not want to leave my future to chance. Whatever tomorrow or next week or next month may bring, I know that if I go forward having fully experienced the love you and I share, I can face whatever comes." She stroked his cheek, shadowed by stubble. "It's Christmas, Jess, and the gift I most want to give and receive is *us* — you and me together as one."

That did it. He kissed her with all the passion of the first kisses they had shared as teenagers — those magical kisses that come with the discovery of what exactly creates excitement, and a level of passion that is nearly impossible to resist. He covered the length of her body with his. He probed her mouth with his tongue, pushing hers aside to give him greater access. She could feel their hearts beating in unison. He pulled free after a long moment, his breath ragged and coming in gasps, as if he'd run a race. He watched her breasts heave with her own breathlessness, then he covered them with his large hands, his eyes riveted on hers as he kneaded and massaged until she thought she could stand no more.

She reached to pull him back to kiss her again, but he resisted and began to unbutton her dress, push the fabric open, untie the laces of her corset, and spread it open to reveal her breasts pressed against the thin linen of her chemise.

"Addie?" His voice was hoarse with desire.

"I'm sure," she whispered, and reached up to unbutton his shirt, pulling it free of his waistband to finish the job. While he shrugged out of it, she went to work on his belt and the buttons of his trousers, her fingers fumbling around the fullness of him pressed against the garment. He rolled away from her and sat on the side of the bed while he pulled off his boots and socks. Then he removed her shoes, her stockings, her pantaloons. He slowly ran his flat palms over her calves, thighs, and then gently touched the private space between her legs.

She knew what was happening. She knew what came next. After all, she had studied this. But studying a manual and actually experiencing Jess touching her so intimately were two entirely different matters. And when he got up to finish undressing and turned to her, she gasped.

He actually chuckled — the arrogant devil.

"Pretty proud of yourself, I see," she managed, trying to retain some semblance of influence over a situation she was clearly about to lose all control over.

As usual, she faced her uncertainty head on. She pushed herself higher onto the bed and wiggled out of the rest of her clothes — and immediately regretted her shamelessness. What if he didn't like what he saw? She was hardly as buxom as Sybil Sinclair, and she certainly did not have Amanda's glorious hair that would have fanned over her shoulders becomingly.

"Holy . . ." He did not finish that thought as he crawled back into the bed and pulled her to him. As he kissed her tenderly, he guided her to straddle him. She could feel his manhood pressing against her, and her body assumed a will of its own as she adjusted herself to receive him. Her scientific side told her it was going to be an impossible fit, but her passion demanded she make it work — and when it did, she thought she had just discovered a wonder that had surely been left out of all the medical texts she'd ever studied.

"Easy," Jess whispered, and rolled with her until he was the one on top. He placed his hands under her hips, lifting her to receive each slow, deep thrust. She was aware of sounds — his breathing and hers, followed by little shrieks of surprise and delight that she realized were coming from her. But although she fought hard to keep up as Jess gradually increased the pace of their mating, Jess suddenly cried out and rolled away from her. She was certain she had done something to hurt him.

"What is it?" she said as she sat up and turned to him. "Are you in pain? Did I . . ."

To her shock, he started to laugh.

"What is it?" Was the man hysterical with pain? What was going on? "Jess, I can't help you, if you don't tell me what hurts."

He sobered and clasped her face. "Nothing hurts, you beautiful woman. What could possibly hurt when I just made love to the woman I have wanted for most of my life?"

"But you stopped and pulled away and cried out and . . ." She scooted around to face him. Neither seemed to notice they were both naked.

"I did that for you," he protested.

"Jess Porterfield, if we are going to have any chance at a future together, you have got to stop thinking you need to make decisions for me. I am perfectly capable of —"

"Even if you had ended up . . . you know . . . in the family way? Pregnant?"

They were both shouting. It was nothing

new for them. It seemed to Addie as if somehow they always ended up raising their voices, each of them trying to make a point before the other one could speak. But the word "pregnant" stopped Addie cold. She'd been so caught up in the moment of re-alizing that Jess wanted her, all rational thought had flown away. What if Jess hadn't stopped? What if she'd ended up with child? Would Jess have married her? Yes, but would it have been for love, or out of a sense of obligation?

She shuddered, realized she was naked, and pulled the blanket on Jess's bed around her shoulders. "I know better than to get pregnant," she grumbled.

Jess stood and put on his pants. "I know you do, but dabnabit, Addie, even you can get carried away sometimes, and you have to admit that . . ."

"Don't you dare judge me, Jess. You were the one grunting like a hog in heat."

"Maybe that's because I was in heat, and so were you. Talk about taking the romance out of things." He picked up his boots and looked around the bed, rummaging for something in the covers.

"What are you looking for?" Addie scooted closer to the foot of the bed.

"My shirt." He tossed aside her undergarments and finally peeled his shirt from the tangle of her dress. He shook it out, shoved his arms into the sleeves, and with it hanging unbuttoned and untucked, headed for the outer office.

"It's the middle of the night," Addie protested. "Where on earth are you going?" She got off the bed to follow him, but her bare feet got tangled in the blanket, and she was forced to stop.

"I plan on getting at least an hour of sleep, and then I'm going to try and keep you from getting hanged."

He slammed the door.

Addie threw one of her shoes at the door. "Merry Christmas to you as well, Jess Porterfield," she shouted.

From beyond the door she heard the squeal of the old swivel chair Jess used when he sat at his desk and the thud of his boots hitting the warped and scarred top of that desk. A moment later, all was silent. With a growl she pulled the blanket free and began putting on her clothes. If Jess thought for one minute that she was going to sit back and wait while he tried to prove her innocence, he had another think coming.

Unable to sleep, she stared out the small window at the deserted town. She saw lights still blazing at the Tipton mansion and

wondered why Lucas didn't extinguish
them. The deputy had been given the assignment of keeping watch, but neither Jasper nor Buck was in residence. Once Pearl's
body had been moved, both men had
headed for their ranch.

Poor Pearl.

Addie reviewed every time they had been
together since that day Pearl had first come
to her for confirmation of her pregnancy.

"Jasper can never know," she had said.
"It's not his child."

So if Jasper wasn't the father, who was?
Addie had believed it didn't matter, and she
had given it little thought. She was not one
to enjoy gossip and speculation. But if Pearl
had taken those pills, Addie needed to know
why. What had changed?

Suddenly, she had an idea. If Jasper wasn't
the father, the most likely candidate, the
person who would be the most likely to have
the opportunity, was Buck. If she played
things right, maybe she could get him talking. If he thought she was coming around
to liking him, he would want her to understand, and if she could make him believe he
had a chance with her . . .

She tiptoed to the door and opened it a
crack. Jess was sitting there, his feet on the
desk, the chair reared back, and his hat

covering his face. He was breathing evenly. She crept past him and had reached the door to the street when he gave a snort, muttered an oath, and apparently, went back to sleep. Slowly, she turned the knob and eased the door open. She checked the street and, as expected, found it deserted. Every shop window was dark, and the only light came from the Tipton mansion across the way. She suspected that whatever might save her was inside that house — in the room where Pearl and her baby had met their tragic end.

Jess woke with a crick in his neck and an ache in his heart. He and Addie had fought — again. It was as if he could never do right by that woman. How could she not appreciate the fact that he'd chosen to protect her rather than risk having her end up pregnant? Did she have any idea what it had cost him to pull away? He'd been — no, they had both been on the ride of their lives, and because he didn't want to take any chance she might regret it, he had deliberately denied himself the full measure of pleasure their lovemaking had promised.

He pushed back the chair and got up, stretching and yawning as he did. Outside, the street was unusually deserted, and it took a minute for him to remember this was Christmas Day. Other than the Dandy Doodle, all businesses in town would remain closed, and folks would spend the day with family. Come to think of it, he would need to make some time to ride out to the ranch — maybe around noon. His mother wouldn't be expecting him with all that was going on with Pearl's death. He'd have to make sure Lucas was around to watch over Addie. He'd surprise Ma and the others. Maybe that would make up for the fact that he hadn't exactly gotten around to buying gifts for the family.

He glanced toward his bedroom. The door was closed. He imagined Addie sleeping. Was she still naked under the covers? The idea made him want her, and he opened the door. The bed was a jumble of tangled bedclothes, the lone pillow on the floor. There was no sign of Addie or her clothes. He shut the door and strode down the narrow hallway to the cells.

Both unoccupied.

The woman had escaped.

"Yoo-hoo!"

Jess spun around to see Eliza McNew coming through the back door carrying a basket. "Brought you two a little Christmas breakfast," she announced as she handed him the basket. Then she glanced around. "Where's Addie?"

"Gone," Jess admitted glumly, setting the basket aside.

"Gone?" Eliza glanced at the unlocked door she'd entered, the two unlocked cells, and the front door that stood slightly ajar. "Well, you didn't exactly take precautions to keep her here, did you?"

"I never thought she would do anything so foolhardy," Jess grumbled. "Sometimes she can be so . . ."

"Well, she can't have gotten far. When did you last see her?"

"I don't know — sometime after midnight."

"Maybe she went home to be with her family for Christmas Day."

That was, of course, a logical guess. But surely, if she'd just come waltzing into the house, her father would have been on Jess like flies on honey, berating him for shirking his duties. "I don't think she went home." He glanced out the window and saw Lucas coming toward the jail. "I'll have Luc stay here in case she turns up while I go look for her. I'd appreciate it if you could . . ."

"Won't say a word," Eliza promised just as the surprisingly well-rested deputy entered the office.

"Merry Christmas, Jess — Miz McNew," he said.

Jess was all business. "The prisoner has escaped, Luc. I need you to stay here in case she turns up. I'm going out to . . ."

"You mean Addie?"

"Of course he means Addie," Eliza said. "Are there other prisoners you're holding here?"

"Addie's over yonder," Lucas said, jerking his thumb toward the street. "At the Tipton place. She told me you said it was fine. Something about you wanting her to look at Miz Tipton's bedroom with a woman's eye and such." Lucas's face was growing red with embarrassment, as he understood that he'd been duped.

"And you just walked off and left her there?" Jess didn't wait for an answer. He slapped his hat in place and stormed across the street. He took the steps leading up to the double front door of the Tipton house two at a time and was surprised to find the door locked. "Sure, Luc," he muttered to himself, "lock the door after the damage is done."

He used his fist to pound on the thick wood. "Open up, Addie. I know you're in there." Truth was, he didn't know any such thing. She might have taken off by now.

Still, he kept pounding.

Suddenly, the door flew open, and Addie grabbed his hand and pulled him inside. "Stop making such a ruckus," she instructed. "Do you want the whole town to know we're over here snooping around?"

"Correction, Miss Wilcox. *You* are snooping around. I have a legal right to search these premises."

"Well, la-de-da," Addie shot back as Jess stepped past the door, and she hurried to close it. "And in your oh-so-thorough search of the premises, what did you find? Because I found the one thing that might be able to clear my name and point you to the real killer."

Without another word, she started up the lavish stairway. "Coming?"

Of course he was coming. He had to see what she'd found, and more to the point, he had to get her out of here before the Tiptons returned or someone noticed she was missing from her cell.

He followed her down the wide hallway to the room where Pearl had died. He was pleased to notice that nothing appeared any different from the way the room was left once Pearl's body was removed. At least Lucas had done that right. But if Addie had searched this room, surely she had touched things and moved things and . . .

She walked straight to the bedside table, slid open the single drawer, and removed it. She dumped the contents on the bed and turned it over. There, taped to the bottom, was an envelope. "What do you suppose this is?" she asked.

"I'm sure you're going to tell me."

Her eyes widened in surprise. "I haven't read it, Jess. I just found it, and I was going to come tell you about it, so I didn't run the risk of destroying evidence that might prove who killed Pearl."

Jess had to find a way to keep her from trying to solve the mystery of Pearl's death. "Pearl died of a self-inflicted overdose of medication," he reminded her. "That's the official charge until I can come up with . . ."

"Pearl was murdered," Addie replied firmly, "and not by me or anything I did."

Jess took the drawer from her. "Look, Addie, Jasper Tipton is beside himself with grief. I can't imagine what he must be going through, and even though he and his brother have caused my family and neighbors untold heartache . . ."

"The Tiptons murdered your father, Jess — isn't that what you and Maria believe? If that's the case, why can't you believe them capable of killing Pearl?"

"What would be the motive?" Jess argued. "Say what you will about Jasper, but he loved that woman, and once he found out she was pregnant . . ."

"What if I told you the child was not his? What if the real father found out and killed Pearl and the baby? What if Jasper found out and killed her? What if . . ."

Jess's head was spinning. "Why didn't you tell me any of this before?"

"It was not my secret to tell. It was Pearl's. I'll admit that when she first came to me she wasn't thinking clearly — talking about how she might be better off dead and all. But last night I kept going over and over the times I spent with her, and I know beyond the shadow of any doubt that she would not have harmed that baby."

"Anybody who contemplates suicide is not right in the head, Addie. Whatever Pearl might have felt for her baby, she was not thinking of that the night she took those pills."

"No, she was fighting for her life."

"So you think Jasper . . ."

"I think it was Buck. I think Buck was the real father, and when he found out, he figured it was only a matter of time until Jasper learned the truth, and then where would Buck be? If Jasper didn't shoot him

257

on the spot, for sure he'd be out of the business. Jasper loved Pearl. If she told him that Buck had forced himself on her, who do you think he would believe?"

It was true. Jasper had spent a good deal of his adult life reining in his hotheaded younger brother. Jess fingered the envelope secured to the bottom of the drawer with brown paper tape. He slid his thumbnail under the tape and heard Addie release a breath of approval. She moved closer as he freed the envelope and opened the seal.

He removed a single folded sheet of paper and handed it to her. "You found it. You read it."

My beloved Jasper,
If you are reading this, it can only be because the truth has come out, and you know that the child you have called your own is in fact born of the seed of another man. I will understand if you can never forgive me, but I am begging you to remember that in all of this, the baby bears no blame. Our child is our child — yours and mine.
If you must know more, talk to Addie Wilcox, but I beg you not to try to determine the man who did this to me. It can only bring you more pain. I pray

you will know in your heart that I did not lie willingly with this man. How could I so much as look at another man when I had your love? Please forgive me, my darling. You are my life, and without you, I have no reason to live.

Your devoted wife, Pearl

Jess and Addie were both silent once she had finished reading the letter aloud. It was Jess who spoke first.

"It could be seen as a suicide note, Addie. If Jasper found out . . ."

"Jasper has no idea. I'm certain of that. His grief is real. And what about this part where she pleads with him not to try to determine the true father? 'It can only bring you more pain.' If that isn't a dead giveaway that the culprit is Buck, I don't know what is."

"Still, there's no real proof. And what about the fact that she mentions you by name? Some might think that would be cause for you to cover up your part in this."

"The letter was hidden," Addie pointed out. "How would I know?"

"She might have confided in you, told you she was leaving the letter . . ."

"But she didn't."

"I'm just thinking out loud here, Addie.

This note could either save or condemn you. Either way, I have to take it as evidence. And I have to get you out of here and back to your cell before someone knows you're gone." He inserted the note in its envelope and stuck it in his vest pocket. Then he put the contents back in place and slid the drawer closed. He checked the room for anything out of place and pointed to the door. "Let's go."

They walked in silence back to the jail. Because of the holiday, no one was out and about to see them, although Jess nervously glanced around to be sure nobody happened to be looking out a window as he escorted Addie.

Lucas was sitting at Jess's desk when they entered through the back door. He sprang to his feet. "Sorry, Jess. I didn't know . . ." He glared at Addie for getting him in trouble.

"No harm done," Jess said as he waited for Addie to enter the cell before he locked the door for the first time since he'd brought her there. "But let's just keep this between the three of us, okay?"

"And Miz McNew," Lucas reminded him.

"Right. I'll go take care of that now, and then I've got some business to handle." He handed Lucas the note. "Lock this up in the safe."

While Lucas hurried to do as he asked, Jess turned to Addie. She was sitting on the edge of the cot, looking as if she were ready to spring into action. "You stay put," he instructed. "Let me handle this."

She focused on the locked door. "I don't have a lot of choice, do I?"

Jess shook the cell door lightly to test its security. "Nope. Looks like you might have to trust that I might know what I'm doing for once." The unresolved remnants of their argument the night before hung in the air between them, and they both understood they were talking about more than Pearl Tipton's untimely death.

NINE

This had to be the worst Christmas Addie had ever known. Surprisingly, she was less concerned with being held in jail for killing Pearl than the fact that what should have been the most magical night of her young life had turned to slush before dawn. As usual, she had ruined everything. How could she not have learned that trusting Jess to love her without stamping that love with his unreasonable conditions was an impossible task?

Months earlier she had thought if she refused to go with him on his grand adventure into city life, he would abandon the idea and come back to her. Instead, every time she tried to talk to him about it, he mumbled something about not being ready and changed the subject. Most people thought that the only reason he had returned was because his plans had been thwarted, he'd run out of money, and he had nowhere else to go. She didn't believe that. Jess Porterfield had come back to care for his family, and even after finding his family doing just fine, she liked to think that maybe she had been part of the reason he had decided to stay.

And what could she have hoped to accomplish when she'd so boldly thrown herself at him the night before? That she would make him love her? That he would assure her that once her name was cleared they would be married and finally begin the life that had been on hold for so long? On the other hand, did she want him to choose to be with her out of some sense of duty?

No.

Even as she sat alone in her locked cell, she felt her cheeks flame with shame. What had she been thinking?

Clearly, she hadn't been thinking at all. Instead she had acted purely on emotional panic. What if she couldn't prove her innocence? What if she were sent to prison? What if she never saw Jess again? What if they never . . .

"Stop this!" She got up and paced the dirt floor of the cell that allowed her exactly three steps from cot to door and a mere six steps from wall to wall. If she worked things right, she could stretch her walk to fifteen steps or more by walking to one wall, turning and walking down the center of the space to the other, turning again, and walking along the cool metal bars that separated the cell from the rest of the jail. If she walked toe to heel, she could add even more steps. The challenge of solving the problem kept her from thinking about her situation.

But after she had exhausted all possible combinations for traversing the cell, she slumped back down on the cot. Her stomach growled — the only sound in the deserted building. Jess had been gone for hours. At her assurance that she was no escape threat now that the cell was locked, Lucas had gone to share Christmas dinner with his family and Eliza. Addie had insisted her parents maintain the tradition of having their dinner at Brian's house. Ever since the births of Ruth and Brian's three children, the family had always shared dinner and gifts at her brother's. Her mother had promised to stop by later so they could bring her gifts. Opening presents in jail was not exactly high on Addie's list, but she saw that it would make her mother happy, so she agreed.

And Jess? She hoped the business he'd mentioned had to do with stopping by the ranch for Christmas with his family. His mother would be so tickled to see him, and with Maria and Chet refusing to leave on their wedding trip, having Jess at home with the whole family there would be even more special.

Addie pressed her hands over the skirt of her dress. Eliza had brought her a basin and lavender soap to clean herself up with and had — to Lucas's great relief — stopped by to escort her to and from the outhouse to relieve herself. There, she had allowed herself to explore the aftermath of Jess's lovemaking. There was nothing really tangible, just a feeling of having been changed. Her breasts felt fuller and heavier. She had closed her eyes, recalling his mouth covering hers, the dance of their tongues, his hands moving over her bare legs. She had touched herself the way he had and been unable to silence the low groan of pleasure that came with the memory of him inside her.

Eliza had called out to ask if she was all right. She'd assured her she was and made quick work of her business before joining Eliza for the walk back to her cell.

On Jess's orders, Lucas had once again locked the door before he and Eliza left. "Jess should be back soon," Eliza had assured her.

But he hadn't come back, and soon what sun there was would disappear, and it would once again be night. Suddenly, her heart began to race as she realized going to the ranch might not be all Jess had intended when he rode out of town. Had he confronted Buck and Jasper? Did Jasper now know that the child he was mourning was not his own? How would he react to such news, and if — as Addie suspected — Buck was the real father, what would he do?

"Oh, Jess," she whispered, "please, don't do anything foolish. Please come back to me."

Jess could not stop thinking about the note Pearl had left behind. He wondered at her writing it and then hiding it so it might never have been found at all. Maybe she had planned to tell Addie about it just in case something should happen to her. Or maybe, after she'd written it, she'd been so distraught that she'd decided she could not face Jasper learning the truth. He had hoped to get Chet Hunter's thoughts on the matter since he'd had some dealings with the Tiptons, but his mother had persuaded the newlyweds to spend their first Christmas together away from the ranch. They had left the day before for a cabin the family kept in the high country.

"You seem distracted, Son," his mother said, keeping her voice low so the others gathered around the table would not hear her. "I know you're worried about Addie, but . . ."

He patted his mother's hand and smiled. "Sorry, Ma. Bet you never thought you'd see the day when my mind was on my job rather than on food."

"I'll admit there were days like that." She clapped her hands to gain everyone's attention. The gathering included Jess's sister and brother as well as Max. Juanita and her family, and all of the hired hands who weren't on duty watching the herd, were also enjoying the lavish spread of food. "Who would like to open gifts?" Constance exclaimed, directing her attention to little Max.

"Me!" The kid was a charmer. Jess would give him that. He'd clearly won the hearts of everyone around the table, and Jess had to admit that when the little fella had stuck out his small hand for a manly handshake when Jess had arrived, he'd been won over as well. Trouble was, being around the kid brought back memories of his night with Addie and drummed up all sorts of images of the two of them with their own little family.

Max toddled off with Juanita's younger son, Javier, and the two soon returned pulling a cart loaded with gift-wrapped packages in all sizes and shapes. Trey and Amanda took charge of distributing the presents — tobacco and new kerchiefs for all the hired hands, a lovely shawl for Juanita, a new hat for her husband Eduardo, and for the children, toys that Jess recognized from the shelves of Eliza McNew's store. After thanking the family, the cowboys excused themselves to return to the bunkhouse, and Juanita herded her family into the kitchen to help with the dishes. This too was part of the ritual, because it left the Porterfield family to exchange their more personal gifts in private.

Jess had never gotten around to shopping, and for the first time all day, he turned his thoughts from Addie and her problems to focus on his family. His mind raced as he unwrapped a new pair of socks from Amanda, a crudely carved wooden star from Trey, and a leather vest that had been his father's from his mother. Even little Max had a present for him — a stick of peppermint candy.

"Try on your vest," Trey said.

Jess did as he asked and accepted the compliments of the others, taking note of the tears in his mother's eyes as he turned to show her how well the garment fit. "Your father would be so proud. *Is* proud," she corrected.

"I'm sorry, but I . . ."

"We know, Jess," Amanda said. "Ma warned us that with everything going on with Addie, you wouldn't have time to shop. The way I see it, we'll just have to extend the celebration for a bit, so you'll have time to shop and get Addie's situation straightened out and . . ." She smiled. "We could have another party."

His sister did love planning parties. Jess laughed. "That's a promise," he said. "Now, if you'll all excuse me, I do need to get back to town."

His mother hooked her arm through his as they walked out to the corral, and she peppered him with questions about the status of things in town. While he saddled his horse, he told her what he could without mentioning the note Pearl had left, then mounted up. "Good to be home, Ma," he said, "and I want you to know that I understand why you gave me Pa's vest. I won't let him — or you — down again."

He thought his mother was fumbling in her apron pocket for a handkerchief, but instead she brought out a small gift-wrapped box. "I assume you also had no time to shop for Addie," she explained as she tucked the package into his saddlebag. "This is the pendant your father gave me when he asked me to marry him."

"Ma, we aren't . . . I mean, right now, Addie's got . . . I mean . . ."

"Now you listen to me, Son. You and that young woman are wasting precious time — have already squandered time you should have been together. It is plain to anyone who knows you that you love her, and she loves you in return. Stop dillydallying, and get on with it."

"Ma, Addie's being charged with a crime. She might go to prison."

"Poppycock. You are not going to allow that to happen, Jess Porterfield. So stop making excuses for doing the one thing you should have done months ago. It's Christmas Day — make it one that neither of you will ever forget."

"Yes, ma'am." Suddenly, Jess felt a lightness that he hadn't felt since the night of his sister's wedding and the sudden arrival of the Tipton brothers to accuse Addie. He could do this — he *would* do this. He leaned down and kissed his mother's weathered cheek, then took off at a gallop toward town.

But when he left his horse at the livery

and, clutching the box, practically ran the short distance to the jailhouse, nothing was what he had expected. Once again, Addie was gone, and this time her parents, her brother, Eliza, and Lucas were all waiting for him to bring her back.

Addie's family had come to the jail with a picnic basket filled with food and another basket filled with gifts. Her mother had found the keys and insisted that her husband unlock the cell in spite of his protests. He had hesitated until Brian assured him that as his sister's legal representative, he would take full responsibility.

For a little while, Addie had almost forgotten her circumstances. She had laughed and shared memories of Christmases past. She had eaten with gusto and opened her gifts. But as the shadows deepened into night, the cheerful atmosphere of the evening had disappeared. There had been long silences punctuated by the sounds of weary children.

"You should go," Addie had told them and, obviously relieved, her sister-in-law had taken the opportunity to herd the children toward the door with promises to stop by to visit in a day or so.

Brian had given her a hug and whispered,

"Stay strong, Addie. This will all be over soon."

When her mother seemed inclined to dawdle, Addie had given her father a pleading look, and he had announced that he had an early call the following morning, and Addie needed her rest as well. Her mother had hesitated, but when Addie stifled a yawn, she agreed that perhaps it was time to go. They were on their way out the back door when Addie called her father back.

"You should lock the cell, Papa. I don't want Luc to get into trouble, and when Jess returns, if he sees me here alone with the cell . . ."

Her father frowned, then nodded and did as she asked. He hung the keys back on the hook by Jess's desk.

After everyone had gone, Addie tried to get some sleep, but her mind was racing with thoughts and questions, so she reached for the medical text her parents had given her, one she had been wanting for some time. It was a newer text — one her father did not have in his library — and Addie was soon engrossed in reading about the strides that had been made in medicine just in the last decade. So caught up was she in reading about new findings that she barely paid attention to the sound of horses and a wagon stopping just outside the jail.

But when the door swung open and three men entered the office, she laid the book aside and tried to make out their faces. It was dark except for the single kerosene lamp her father had lit and placed on the table just outside her cell before leaving. She had been sitting next to that lamp to read.

"Who's there?" she asked, her voice quavering with fear.

Buck Tipton stepped into the light. "It's me, sweetheart. Me and the county sheriff and the district attorney from Tucson." He jangled the keys he had removed from the hook by the front door. "Gentlemen, this here is the woman who murdered my sister-in-law and my brother's child. Do your duty."

Addie did not have to be told that the Tiptons' land and influence encompassed most of the district served by these two men. The entire Arizona Territory had been divided into three districts, each presided over by a judge appointed by the president. The two men with Buck had been elected to their positions, but everyone knew they had been handpicked by the Tiptons.

"Looks like you've been having a party in here," Buck said, picking up a ribbon from one of Addie's gifts and a scarf her brother's family had given her and showing them to the other men. "It's like my brother and I said, Sheriff. There's those in town here who would stand in the way of real justice."

Buck unlocked the cell. Addie stepped closer to the back wall but realized there was no escape. "I thought the judge was coming here, and we would . . ."

"Well, you thought wrong," Buck growled.

He stepped back, and the sheriff entered the cell. "Adeline Wilcox, I am arresting you and charging you with contributing to the death of Mrs. Jasper Tipton and her unborn child. You are to be removed immediately to the county jail in Tucson."

Addie had lost all sense of time. Was it late? Where was Jess? Would anyone know she had been taken? And how did she know these two men with Buck weren't just two of his hired hands posing as the sheriff and district attorney?

"How do I know you are who you say?" she demanded, finding her nerve at last.

"Told you she would be a handful," Buck muttered.

The district attorney stepped forward. "You are in no position to be asking questions or making demands, Miss Wilcox. Now come along peacefully."

"Or what?" Addie regretted the taunt as

soon as the words left her lips.

The sheriff smiled and stepped forward, grasping her upper arm so tightly that Addie had no doubt there would be a bruise. "Or we'll have to do this my way," he said, his mouth close to her face, his breath foul with whiskey.

"I have . . . my brother is a lawyer and . . ."

The sheriff tightened his grip.

"And once the trial is scheduled, he'll have ample time to prepare your defense," the district attorney replied. "Now it's late, and we have some distance to go. Please do not make this any more difficult than it has to be, Miss Wilcox." He nodded to the sheriff, who pushed Addie out of the jail to an enclosed wagon hitched to a pair of waiting horses. She did not miss the fact that there were bars on the small openings on either side of the vehicle.

Buck chuckled as he helped the sheriff push Addie aboard. The door swung shut, and she heard a lock being clamped into place. "Have a nice ride, sweetheart," Buck called as he mounted his horse.

The district attorney watched, then he passed the medical text she'd been reading through the bars of the narrow opening. "I'll leave word for Marshal Porterfield," he told her.

"And my family," she bargained. "They live just there." She pointed to the house, dark now, her parents no doubt asleep and unaware of the drama playing out just yards from their front door. "My father is the head of the town council — and the local doctor."

"Yes," the man said, and she realized that perhaps he was a reluctant partner in this entire business.

"What's your name?"

"Collins," he replied. "Hector Collins."

"And you are truly the attorney for the district?"

"Yes, ma'am."

She wasn't sure she could trust him. He could be putting on an act, but she didn't think so. "Thank you for your kindness, Mr. Collins."

The wagon suddenly moved forward with a jerk and Addie was thrown off balance. She toppled to the floor, banging her head on one of the two narrow benches, and heard Buck and the sheriff talking as the driver followed them out of town. She struggled to her feet, felt blood trickle down her cheek, and grabbed onto the bars as the wagon made the turn that took them from Main Street into the open country that lay between Whitman Falls and Tucson.

When Jess entered the jailhouse, everyone was talking at once. Mrs. Wilcox was grilling Lucas, while Addie's father tried to explain to Brian what had happened. Eliza was talking to a stranger and was the first to see Jess.

"Marshal Porterfield," she said, "this is District Attorney Hector Collins. Earlier tonight he and the sheriff and Buck Tipton came here to take Addie into their custody and move her to Tucson where she's to be held for trial."

Collins extended his hand, and Jess shook it automatically as his eyes settled on the open door of the deserted cell where he'd last seen Addie. "Why?" The single word was an explosion of all the frustration and worry Jess had stuffed inside since the moment that Addie had first been accused.

All conversation around him stopped as every eye was riveted on the attorney.

"Mr. Tipton asked Judge Ellis to intervene," Collins replied, as if that explained everything.

The occupants of the office allowed these words to register, and then all began speaking at once, this time making their points to

Collins. Jess couldn't help feeling a little sorry for the man as he held up his hands, asking for quiet. "How do we get her back here?"

"You don't," Collins replied. "Formal charges have been filed. The judge agreed that there was probable cause to believe that assembling a jury from the citizens of this community would give Miss Wilcox an unfair advantage."

Eliza turned away in disgust. "Just because she's innocent, that's no cause to think we wouldn't hear things fairly," she huffed.

"I wish to see my daughter," Doc added.

"That can be arranged," Collins assured him. "But, sir, you have my word that no harm will come to her while she is in custody."

Mrs. Wilcox snorted. "It is my understanding that Mr. Buck Tipton was present when the transfer of custody was made?"

"Yes, ma'am."

"Then, sir, our daughter is in danger, and you'll forgive me for saying so, but if you believe she will get a fair hearing in Tucson, you are the fool here."

Jess had always thought of Addie's mother as a quiet, accommodating woman, one who avoided conflict at all costs. But she had just insulted the district attorney — the man who would be prosecuting Addie. There was more of Alice Wilcox in her daughter than Jess had imagined.

"Now, Alice," Doc said quietly, stepping up to place his hand on his wife's shoulder, "the man is simply doing his job. You go home and pack, and we'll head for Tucson as soon as it gets light."

"You have patients," she reminded him. "Lottie Daniels is due to deliver within the week and . . ."

"I can go with Miz Wilcox," Jess offered. "Luc can handle things here."

"Yes, ma'am," Lucas assured her before turning to Doc. "I can do this. I owe that much to Addie. If it hadn't been for her and Jess, I might never have found a way to care for my family. And besides . . ."

"Very well," Doc agreed. "Alice, go get ready."

"I'll help you pack," Eliza said. She placed her arm around Alice's shoulders as they left the jail.

"I'm not sure this is wise," Collins said, studying Jess intently. "It is my understanding that you and the prisoner . . ."

"The prisoner has a name," Jess said.

"You and Miss Wilcox are involved in a romantic relationship, are you not?"

"That is none of your business. Miss Wilcox is a lifelong friend, as is her family. I would do anything I could for any one of them, not to mention pretty much everyone in this town."

Collins smiled. "You make my point, sir."

"Which is?"

"The case before the court is unlikely to receive an unbiased hearing in this community."

Jess was pretty sure that he'd never in his life wanted to punch a man more than he did this smart-mouthed lawyer standing before him. He clenched and unclenched his fists, then turned to Lucas before he could act on his impulse. "You sure I can count on you?" He understood that he was taking out his frustration with the lawyer on Lucas and was pretty sure Lucas understood that as well.

"I won't let you down. Give Addie our best," he added.

"I will." He turned back to face Collins. "Ready?"

"We can leave any time, but I have to remind you, Marshal, you have no authority once we leave Whitman Falls."

"And I'll remind you that if anything happens to Miss Wilcox, you and I are going to have a problem." Jess didn't wait for the lawyer's reply. Instead he strode out the back door and over to the Wilcox house. Eliza was just coming outside. "She ready?" Jess asked.

Eliza nodded. "Brian says you should take the wagon. He's decided to come with you."

"Then he can drive the wagon, and I'll ride." Jess was anxious to get started. It would take over two hours of hard riding to reach Tucson. The wagon would slow them down considerably. He tried not to think what the ride must have been like for Addie and realized it had only been a couple of hours since the sheriff had taken her. They would still be on their way. If he rode hard, he could maybe catch them.

"Tell Brian and Miz Wilcox that I'm going on ahead," he said, already retracing his steps to where he'd tied up his horse earlier.

"Jess . . ." Eliza was warning him.

"I won't make trouble," he promised as he mounted up. "Tell the Wilcoxes that I'll make sure she's safe and see them in Tucson." He spurred his horse to a gallop and took off.

The rhythm of the wagon had finally lulled Addie to sleep. She was huddled into a corner, her head leaning against the back wall of the enclosure, the blood from her fall now dried, and the bruise on her arm painful whenever the rocking wagon caused it to bump against a hard surface. She had opened the top two buttons of her dress, trying without success to take advantage of the slight breeze. The trouble was that any breeze emphasized the horrid smell of urine and sweat that permeated the boards surrounding her. There was some dirty straw on the floor, and the benches meant for prisoners were pocked with splinters and scuffs. The walls were marked with iron rings, where evidently, prisoners could be anchored. She supposed she should be grateful that the sheriff had not tied her to one of the rings. At least she was the only passenger and free to move around.

She had done plenty of that when the trip began, realizing early on that Buck and the sheriff were riding alongside the wagon's driver and the team of horses. If she could open the door without them realizing it, she could escape. It was a dark night, and it could be hours before they noticed that she was gone. But the rear entrance was solid wood with no opening where she might reach out and try to pick the lock.

"How are you doing, sweetheart?" Buck shouted, giving the side of the wagon a sharp rap with his fist. "Oh, forgot to allow you time for the necessary before we started

out. But then, that's what the straw is for."
He was joined in his laughter by the sheriff
and driver.

She never acknowledged these taunts,
although she was fairly certain that her
silence only irritated Buck more.

For the first hour or so, Addie was certain
this was a ruse and that Buck was in fact
kidnapping her for his own purposes. She
wondered if he knew she suspected that
Pearl's baby was his. If he did, he would go
to any length to keep her from telling others. At first, this idea kept her in a state of
terror of what her fate might be, if left to
Buck. But then the chill of the night and
the long hours of no sleep had caught up
with her, and she had curled into the corner
of the wagon and closed her eyes.

So when she heard a new voice and a new
tone of animosity added to the male conversation, at first she wondered if the district
attorney had finally caught up with them.
She felt she might be in better hands if he
was with them. On the other hand, she
knew nothing about him, and it had become
clear to her that Buck, the sheriff, and the
driver were in agreement when it came to
her. Maybe he was one of them as well.

She moved closer to the opening, taking
note of the rising sun in the distance and

realizing they must be well on their way to Tucson by now. She tried to listen in on the conversation that floated back to her from the front of the wagon and gasped when she saw Jess keeping pace with the others. Her heart beat more rapidly. She was filled with relief that here at last was help she trusted and could count on to keep her safe.

"Just making sure my prisoner gets to where she needs to be," she heard Jess say in answer to some muttered comment from Buck.

"No longer your prisoner," the sheriff blustered. He was slurring his words, and Addie suspected that some time earlier, when the wagon had come to an abrupt stop and the three men had gone off, leaving her to shiver in the confined space, part of their little break had included the consumption of alcohol. Certainly when they had returned, Buck had taken a lot of pleasure in riding around the wagon, whooping like a wild animal, and firing his pistol in the air. The other two men had not so much laughed as they giggled like schoolboys getting away with some prank.

"She's my prisoner until she reaches Tucson," Jess bluffed, and his tone fairly shouted that he would not back down.

Suddenly, instead of relief, what Addie felt

was fear. There were three of them, and only one of Jess. What if they decided to shoot him? What if they decided to fight him, beat him up, and leave him for the buzzards? What if they decided to tie him up and throw him in the wagon with her? What if they decided to make an example of her — pull her from the wagon and have their way with her, while Jess was helpless to save her?

Her mind ran amuck with all the possibilities — none of them good. Oh, why had Jess come at all? There was no way this could turn out well for either of them. The man seemed determined to drive her crazy with worry. She had to find a way to talk some sense into him.

"I need some water," she croaked, her face close to the bars. She coughed for effect, although the truth was, she was indeed quite parched.

The wagon came to an abrupt halt, and she realized Jess had grabbed the team's harness. "You left her back there with no water?" he demanded.

"Guess we overlooked that little detail," Buck said. He untied his canteen, opened the lid, and took a long swallow before holding it up to the bars. "Here you go, little lady. Just stick out your tongue there."

She heard the sheriff snicker, but noticed

the driver was quiet. "Boss," she heard him say, his voice shaking.

Buck pulled the canteen away and glanced toward the front of the wagon. Addie strained to see what was happening.

"You're not planning to shoot an innocent animal," Buck challenged, and Addie guessed that Jess was holding a gun on one of the team of horses.

"Two of them, if I have to. Just a little persuasion to get you fellas to do what's right. Now, Sheriff, if you'd be so kind as to give the prisoner a chance to stretch her legs, get some water, and maybe take care of some personal business, we can all be on our way. Of course, it's coming on daylight, and we might just sit here a spell until that lawyer fella catches up with us. See what he has to say about the situation."

Buck reached for his gun, and Addie gasped and shut her eyes.

"I wouldn't do that, Buck."

"Go ahead, shoot me," Buck blustered. He raised his hands. "Here I am. 'Course, there's two witnesses you'll need to shoot as well — if they don't get you first."

"The driver's not armed, and the sheriff there seems to be too drunk to even find his weapon, much less use it. So let's all just settle down here, open the wagon, and give

Miss Wilcox the same rights due any prisoner — water, a chance to relieve herself . . ."

"Do I look like an idiot, Porterfield?" Buck lowered his hands and leaned forward, his forearm resting on his saddle horn. "As soon as we open that door, you're gonna swoop in, grab the girl, and go riding off."

"And spend the rest of my life and hers on the run when she's innocent? Not a chance, Buck. Tell you what I'll do — I'll stay right here while the driver there lets her out, walks with her down to the creek where she gets some water and a chance to cool herself off a bit, and he fills this here canteen for her to keep for the rest of the trip. Once she's back inside, I'll drop back and just follow along until we all get to Tucson."

Buck's grin was slow to come, but there it was. "You always were an arrogant son of a gun, Jess Porterfield. You think she's gonna beat this thing, and you're so sure that you're willing to let us take her in. If she was my woman, I'd . . ."

"She's not anybody's woman, Buck." Jess's voice was a low, feral growl, and once again, Addie's heart sprang to her throat.

"The judge won't like hearing we didn't treat her fair," she heard the driver say. "If

Collins is on his way . . ."

"All right, Porterfield, we'll do it your way this once. Sheriff, keys," Buck instructed.

Addie heard the jangle of metal and saw Buck catch a ring of keys one-handed. He saw her watching him and frowned. "Don't think you've won, missy," he grumbled. "Enjoy your little moment of freedom while you can, 'cause once we get to Tucson . . ."

"Stop threatening her and let her out," Jess said.

Once the door creaked open and the shadowy confines of her moveable cell were flooded with the gray morning light, Addie stumbled down, shielding her eyes with her hand.

"She's hurt," Jess exclaimed. "You hurt her, you . . ."

"Jess, no!" Addie stepped between Buck's horse and Jess's. "I fell. It's nothing. You'll see once I wash it off."

Hoping he would believe her, she started walking toward the creek. To her surprise, none of the men followed her. A couple of lizards and a jackrabbit she startled along the way scurried out of range. Once she reached the banks of the shallow creek, she knelt and bathed her face and neck in the cool water, then cupped her hands to gather water she could drink. She heard a rustling

288

sound behind her and turned to see the driver coming toward her. He held out the canteen, and when she took it, he turned and walked back to where the others waited. She filled the canteen, then headed for the stand of shrubbery she'd noticed as she walked down to the creek. The bushes would afford her enough privacy to relieve herself.

She took her time, and once she'd finished she knelt again by the creek, splashing water onto her face and neck.

"She's stalling," she heard Buck complain.

"I'm coming," she shouted as she picked up the canteen and walked back to the wagon. On her way she spied a single marsh aster, still vibrant in spite of the late season. She carefully plucked it by its stem and worked it into her hair. "How much farther?" she asked as she climbed back into the wagon, as if she were simply rejoining friends on a trip.

"Less than an hour," the driver replied, offering her a hand up before he shut and locked the door, leaving her once again in mostly darkness with slender shafts of light forming the pattern of the bars on the walls of the wagon.

"Satisfied, Porterfield?" she heard Buck ask.

Jess ignored the question. "Addie," he said, coming alongside the wagon so he could see her face pressed close to the bars. He studied her forehead for a long moment.

"See? It's just a scratch," she said. "Keep your word and drop back," she added in a lower voice meant just for him.

I'm sorry, he mouthed, even as Buck ordered the driver to move out.

TEN

Once they reached Tucson, Addie was taken inside a building larger than anything in Whitman Falls. From the signs she read above closed doors, as the sheriff guided her through the corridors, the building housed the jail, the sheriff's office, the judge's chambers, and the courtroom where her trial would take place. The sheriff took special pleasure in pointing that out to her.

Blessedly, Buck and the driver had headed for the nearest saloon. But to her despair, the sheriff had thwarted Jess's attempt to accompany her inside. "She's my prisoner now, Marshal Porterfield. You'd best head on back to Whitman Falls."

Jess had kept his eyes on her when he said, "I'm not going anywhere, Sheriff."

"Suit yourself, but you let this girl's ma and brother know that in my jail folks just don't come wandering in and out at their pleasure." He had taken hold of Addie's bruised arm then, and she had tried not to wince because she didn't want Jess to know she was hurt. "Let's go," the sheriff growled, and Addie realized that he no longer seemed as inebriated as he had on the trail. Somehow, that made him a far more intimidating foe.

She did not look back as he guided her inside and down the corridor to a stairway that led to a dank and shadowy cellar. The first thing she realized was that she was not to be the only prisoner. The cells she passed housed several others — all men. Men whose curiosity brought them close to the bars where they stared and smirked and whistled as she passed by. She realized that the sheriff was deliberately parading her past these men.

Finally, they came to the last cell, and the sheriff unlocked the door and shoved her inside. The space was larger than the cell in Whitman Falls. It was also occupied by two women who looked her over from head to toe. One of them came close and touched her hair, then cackled as she scurried back to one of four cots that lined the space. The other woman, big-boned and powerfully built, stared from her place next to the cot near the high window.

"Fresh meat for you, Minnie," the sheriff

said, and laughed as he slammed the door shut and turned the key. Addie heard him making the return trip to the stairway, barking out orders to the male prisoners as he went. Once he'd climbed the stairs and closed the door at the top, all was silent.

Far too silent.

"Hello." Addie focused her attention on the woman by the window.

"Get this straight, honey. This is my space." She marked out a perimeter. "Cross into it at your own risk."

Addie nodded and selected one of the two empty cots. "Is this all right then?"

"Suit yourself." The woman returned to her cot and stared out the window.

"My name is Addie Wilcox," Addie ventured after a few minutes of watching the big woman stare out the window. The other prisoner picked at a sore on her arm and mumbled to herself.

"Did I ask?" The big woman did not turn around.

"No, ma'am, you didn't."

Addie sat on the edge of her cot and took inventory of her surroundings — the sounds, the smells, the sights. The men down the way had gone back to whatever they'd been doing when she arrived. She heard the slap of playing cards. She heard two men murmuring in low voices. She heard coughing that sounded like more than a simple cold and wheezing she was sure was the result of the damp and chill of the place. She smelled sweat and urine and stale food. She saw a rat race along the bars, moving from cell to cell, and thought to herself that at least somebody in this place was free to do as he liked.

Time passed, and the door at the top of the stairs opened again. As one, the prisoners rushed to the bars. Addie stayed where she was.

"You want to eat?" the big woman said, glancing back at her. "Then line up like the rest of us. Get your cup there." She nodded toward a cubbyhole in the wall where Addie found a battered tin cup that looked and smelled as if it hadn't had a good washing in some time.

A man in uniform moved down the line, starting with the men. He scooped up gray soup from a pot loaded onto a cart and splashed the contents into the proffered tin cups. Half the time a good deal of the soup missed the cup and went onto the floor.

"Stop wasting that slop," her cell mate barked. "You'll be out before you get down this way."

The guard gave her a toothless grin.

"Keep your knickers on, Minnie. Better yet, take them off, and maybe I'll be moved to give you extra."

"That's enough," Addie protested. "We may be prisoners, but we are not animals, and we have rights, so . . ."

The guard had reached her now. He glared at her, dipped the ladle into the pot and brought up a full measure of soup mixed with potatoes and onions and scraps of an undefinable meat. "That your cup, is it?" he asked with a smile.

Addie held the cup beneath the ladle. The guard grinned, then moved the ladle so all of her soup splattered onto the dirt floor. "Oops," he said, and all down the way, Addie heard laughter.

She returned to her cot and turned her face to the wall, so neither the guard nor the woman called Minnie would see her tears.

After she heard the door at the top of the stairs close and things had gone quiet once more, she wondered when she might see food again. It had been hours since she'd eaten. When she felt someone sit on the end of her cot, she pulled herself into a tighter ball.

"Here," Minnie said.

Addie ventured a look and saw the woman

holding out her tin cup.

"You too proud to take my food?" she challenged when Addie hesitated.

"No. Thank you. I just . . . thank you."

"There's water in that bucket over there," Minnie said as she watched Addie devour the soup. She seemed to be studying Addie as if she wanted to ask her something. "You crazy like Fanny there, or just too dumb to know you can't pull stuff like that when you're on this side of them bars?"

"I didn't think," Addie admitted. She handed the cup back to Minnie. "It won't happen again."

"Good, because that guard is pure mean, and as it is you're gonna pay a price for opening your mouth. Lucky for you, he don't work every day." Minnie did not seem inclined to move back to her own cot, so Addie waited for her to say more.

Only she didn't. She just sat on the end of the cot watching the other woman — Fanny — pick at the scabs on her arms and legs. Addie watched as well, and then her medical training would not allow her to simply sit and watch. She got up and crossed the cell for a closer look. Fanny scuttled back against the wall, her eyes wild with fear — and fever.

"She don't like to be touched," Minnie said.

"Those sores are infected. And I think she has a fever. How long has she been like this?"

Minnie shrugged. "She was down here when they brought me in last week. You a midwife or something?"

"My father's a doctor. I help him out." For reasons she didn't fully understand, Addie thought it best to underplay her medical knowledge. "If I can get word to my brother, he could maybe bring me a salve that might help heal Fanny's sores."

Minnie laughed. "Better get enough for the whole gang," she said as she pulled up her skirt to show her legs covered in spots as well. "Better make sure he brings some for you too. If you're down here overnight, you're bound to get bit."

"By what?" Addie was pretty sure she knew, but she wanted to keep Minnie talking.

"Bugs, rats, scorpions — you name it, it's down here somewhere just waiting for dark."

Addie shuddered, and this time it wasn't because of the dank chill of the cell. This time it was because she realized that in the late afternoon and evening, they likely would not have a lantern or even a candle.

On top of that, it hit her that Minnie had been here for days already, and Fanny even longer.

"Hey," she shouted to the other occupants of the cells. "Anybody down there sick? Running a fever?"

At first there was silence, then from the cell at the far end came a hacking cough and a reedy voice. "I got a cough I can't get shed of."

She waited.

"What's it to you, girlie?" another male voice called out.

"Her pa's a doctor," Minnie bellowed.

"Is her pa in jail here?" the man shot back.

"No," Addie replied before Minnie could further agitate the man, "but there are a few good patent medicines my brother may be able to purchase, and they might prove helpful."

"Your brother's a doctor too?" another voice called out.

"He's a lawyer," Addie replied.

"She's not like the rest of us," Minnie snapped. "This one's got class and connections."

The door leading to the offices and courtroom opened, sending a shaft of light down the stairway and into the gloomy corridor outside the cells. Addie heard footsteps and

298

knew that this time there were at least two, and perhaps three, men coming their way.

"Well, well, well," Minnie said softly, and she started primping her hair as Jess stepped forward into the light. She sidled up to the bars. "Aren't you a good-looking cowboy," she said in a sultry voice.

Jess ignored her. "I brought Brian," he said, and stepped away to allow Addie's brother room.

"Five minutes," the third man instructed. Judging by his uniform, he was a deputy, and Addie was relieved that it wasn't the guard that had deliberately dumped her food on the floor. As if to make his point, the deputy pulled out a watch from his pocket and leaned against the wall.

"Are you all right?" Brian asked.

"I need you to write down some things, and bring them to me as soon as possible."

Brian took out the small notebook he always carried and a pencil. "What things?"

Addie started rattling off a list of medications that to the best of her knowledge could be used to treat the others. "And heavy socks and stockings," she added, after naming the medicines. "And twine and . . ." Her brother had stopped writing. "Take this down —"

"Addie," Jess whispered, moving closer so

299

the deputy did not hear. "They are not going to allow you to have any of this, especially not twine."

"Why on earth not?" Addie whispered back. "These people are ill. There are rats and bugs and scorpions, and the bites have become infected, and there's a man down there who could be well on his way to . . ."

"Addie." Jess and Brian spoke at the same moment.

Then Jess stepped away. "You try talking some sense into her."

"Two minutes," the deputy announced.

"Addie," Brian said in a low voice. "We can't be worrying about others. You're in a mess of trouble here, and I need you to focus on your situation."

"Did you show Brian Pearl's letter?" she asked Jess.

"The letter only makes matters worse," Brian said. "It reads like she was planning to take her life, and you knew that. It doesn't help you, Sis."

"Time's up," the deputy said, and started moving toward them.

"Get the medicine," Addie pleaded as Jess and Brian started backing away.

"Ma sends her love," Brian called, but Addie's eyes were on Jess.

He started to say something, but in the

end, just raised his hand in a gesture of farewell. The gathering darkness made it impossible for her to read his expression, so she stuck her hand through the bars and sent him the signal they had once developed as children. She crossed her ring finger over her little finger and held up her hand, palm out. When they were children, it had meant, "See you soon." Now Addie gave it a new meaning — one she hoped Jess would understand.

Now — at least for her — that signal said, "I love you."

ELEVEN

Jess was beside himself with worry. While the courthouse and offices were impressive with their wood paneling and brass door-knobs and busts of important people placed on stands outside the closed doors, below that marble floor was the jail. The place was dank and dark, and it held the stench of hundreds of prisoners coming and going. Addie had looked so small and fragile, and his heart went out to her. The cell was three times the size of the one back in Whitman Falls, and the cots were canvas with a threadbare blanket and no pillow. A dish of some sort of watery soup sat near the cell door, and the place reeked.

But had any of that bothered Addie? Not a bit. She was focused on getting medicines for her fellow inmates. Come to think of it, she had not pushed for information about when she might get out of this hellhole. As they walked back to the hotel across from the courthouse, Brian handed Jess the list Addie had dictated.

"There's the apothecary down the block there. If it's not already closed for the night, maybe you can get some of this stuff while I check on Ma."

Jess started to protest, but Brian stopped him. "I know my sister, Jess. If we want her to listen to what we say, first we need to attend to the others."

He was right, of course. Addie always had been one to put everyone else's needs before her own. It was one of the things that frustrated Jess the most and also one of the reasons he loved her.

The apothecary was deserted except for a woman sipping a cup of hot chocolate as she sat at one end of the long soda counter. She was visiting with a man Jess assumed was the owner.

"We're just getting ready to close. Can I help you, sir?" The man stepped around the counter, and Jess handed him the list.

"I need these medicines if you've got them."

The druggist read the list, then looked up at Jess. "That's quite a list. Mind telling me who the patient is?"

Jess noticed that the woman at the counter was listening intently to their conversation.

He lowered his voice. "It's for a friend who is trying to treat some people over there at the jailhouse. She's a doctor and . . ."

The woman — more a girl, really, since she couldn't be much older than Trey — slid off her stool and offered him her hand. "I'm Ginny Matthews, reporter. I'm working on a story about conditions in the jail."

The druggist rolled his eyes. "This is my daughter, sir, who fancies herself a news reporter."

"Jess Porterfield. I'm the marshal over in Whitman Falls."

"You're a long way from home," Ginny said, eyeing him closely. "Your friend is local to Tucson?"

Jess really didn't want to go into detail about the situation. "Can you help with the medicines?" he asked the druggist.

"I may not have these exact items, but I can probably come up with a close approximation." He went behind the pass-through, where Jess could see shelves filled with bottles and boxes. A large mortar and pestle sat on a desk. "May have to mix some of it," the druggist called as he began selecting items from the shelves. "Ginny, leave the man be."

But Ginny was not to be discouraged. She went behind the soda counter and prepared a second cup of cocoa, set it down next to Jess, and said, "It'll take Daddy awhile to mix everything and get it ready, so you might as well sit."

The steaming beverage looked and smelled mighty tempting. Jess reached for a coin to pay.

"Your money's no good here, Marshal," Ginny said as she slid back onto the stool next to him and spun it so she was looking directly at him. "This friend of yours — how did she get down there? Word has it the sheriff won't allow anyone to see his prisoners unless they are family or a lawyer."

"Her brother qualifies on both counts — he's family and a lawyer." Jess hesitated, but when he saw that the druggist was listening as he filled the order, he decided perhaps telling Addie's story might just be exactly what was needed to get help. So he gave them the short version. "She's innocent, of course, but right now, there's not a lot we can do to prove that, and the sheriff is making it mighty difficult for her brother to see her so they can build a case."

"Sheriff Richter's up for re-election next year," the druggist said. "Maybe if you and the lawyer make enough noise, he'll give you more leeway."

"What if you told him that getting medicine and letting your friend treat the other prisoners could be a first step toward improving conditions in the jail, and he could take the credit?" Ginny's eyes sparkled with excitement. "Daddy, you can talk to the editor over at the paper. Maybe if he told the sheriff that he'd heard about this man coming in for the medicine . . ."

For the first time since arriving in Tucson, Jess felt a glimmer of hope. He turned to the druggist. "Anything you could do to help would be more than welcome, Mr. Matthews."

The druggist wrapped the medicines and handed the package to Jess. "I'll talk to the newspaper editor," he said. "Not sure what good it will do, but . . ."

"Thank you, sir." Once again he dug into his pocket for money. "How much?"

"Let's put it on a tab. Chances are once your friend gets started, she's going to find she needs more." He walked Jess to the door. "Good luck to you — and your friend."

"Thank you, sir." Jess tipped his hat to Ginny. "And my guess is that you're going to be a fine reporter one day, miss."

Ginny grinned. "It's me who should thank you, mister. You just gave me an idea for the story that's going to be my big break."

"She's something else," Jess said to the druggist.

He shook his head. "My daughter, the muckraker," he said with a sigh.

Jess laughed as he left the store — the first time he'd felt like laughing in days.

Back at the hotel he found Doc Wilcox and his wife waiting for him in the lobby. "Oh, Jess," Alice Wilcox said. "Wait until you hear the news."

Jess turned to Doc. "You found something that will help Addie?"

"Pearl did not swallow those pills — at least not all of them."

"But . . ."

"Remember that night when I showed you the powdery residue from her mouth?"

Jess nodded. "You said that was from the pills."

"It was, but there was something about the amount of it that just didn't add up. If she had ingested the pills, there simply would not have been that amount of residue left in her mouth."

"Then how did she die?"

"My best guess is she died from the wound we saw on the back of her head. It was small, but its location was such that it could have caused death. My guess is that she was already dead when someone forced those pills into her mouth."

"That's incredible," Jess said, trying to take in all the details.

"Brian says this still doesn't clear Addie completely. Jasper's housekeeper is claiming Addie called on Pearl that afternoon and was the last to see her alive."

"She was at the ranch," Jess protested. "Half a dozen people saw her there."

"But the housekeeper swears she came to the mansion before leaving for the wedding, and what reason would she have to lie?"

"I can think of half a dozen. She didn't like Addie or Pearl. She works for the Tiptons and will do whatever they say. She could have killed Pearl herself . . ."

"But we can't prove any of that, and right now, it's the housekeeper's word against Addie's," Doc reminded him.

"Where's Brian?"

"He went over to the courthouse to try to get Addie released on bail."

Jess shifted the package of medicines from one hand to the other. "I should take her these," he said. "She wants to treat some of the other prisoners."

"I'll take them," Doc said. "More likely the sheriff will allow me down there than you, and he's certainly not about to let Addie out of that cell, even to help the others, unless his hand is forced." He leaned down and kissed his wife's cheek. "Have faith, my dear," he said, leaving Jess and Mrs. Wilcox standing in the lobby.

"It appears we will be dining late this evening. I think I'll have some tea, Jess. Will you join me?" She nodded toward the tearoom attached to the hotel.

"No, thank you, ma'am. I need to . . ."

Addie's mother placed her hand on his forearm. "I know you love her, Jess, but don't allow that love to make you take action you might later regret — action that could make matters worse for our dear Addie."

"I won't, but we both know who's likely behind all this, and maybe it's time somebody started asking some hard questions."

"On what basis?"

"On the basis that according to Addie and the note we found in Pearl's room, Jasper Tipton was not the father of that baby. On the basis that the next most likely candidate is Buck."

If Jess had thought to shock Addie's mother, he had underestimated her. In that moment, he saw that Mrs. Wilcox — like her daughter — was not easily taken aback.

"You may be right," she said, "but if you truly believe that, Jess, then stop and think.

If you go throwing around accusations you can't yet prove, you give Buck the advantage. I am pleading with you to be patient and let Brian see what he can do to free Addie."

Jess hesitated, but Mrs. Wilcox's grip on his arm had tightened considerably. "All right," he said finally. "I'll see how Brian does getting her out of that place, but once she is . . ."

Mrs. Wilcox loosened her grip and patted his arm. "That's fine, but first things first. Now, let's have tea."

Jess saw no other option than to escort the woman he hoped would one day be his mother-in-law to the tearoom. After all, once this was all over, it would be good to have her as an ally when he went to ask Doc for permission to ask Addie to marry him.

"Something's up," Minnie said, shaking Addie awake.

Addie sat up and rubbed her eyes, trying to adjust to the darkness.

A single light glowed from the far end of the corridor, and she heard men talking — among them her brother and her father. She hurried to the bars, straining to see. "Papa?"

"Give me a minute, child," he called. He was holding a package, one he kept pointing to as he spoke to the sheriff.

"That man never comes down here," Minnie said, and Addie understood she meant the sheriff. "Your pa must have something on him."

"We're from a town miles away and never even met the sheriff before I came here."

They turned as they heard the jangle of keys, and a cell door at the far end of the hall swung open. "Gentlemen," her father said as he and the light disappeared into the cell.

It must have been an hour later when her father reached Addie's cell. "Hello, my dear," her father said as if he had been off running errands and just returned. "Will you introduce me to your friends?"

Addie made the introductions, noticing how shy Minnie suddenly became and how Fanny not only willingly allowed her father's touch, but also babbled on to him about this and that. None of it made any sense, but her father smiled and nodded as he examined Fanny's sores.

The sheriff and Brian waited outside the cell, watching.

"I understand how difficult your job is, Sheriff Richter," Doc said as he applied a salve to Fanny's wounds. "If I may, I have some suggestions that could make life easier for you."

"I take a helluva lot of crap from the newspaper about the way I run this place," the sheriff growled. "Those do-gooders don't seem to understand that these people are criminals — some of them dangerous."

"And yet should they appear in court in less than their best condition, I expect they win some sympathy from the jury?"

"You got it, Doc." It occurred to Addie that the man seemed to have forgotten he was speaking to the father of one of his dangerous criminals. "I do the best I can," he whined, "but every month there's more to do."

"A few simple steps, Sheriff. For example, place lanterns all along the hallway here once it is dark. That will discourage those critters that like to attack in the night. And perhaps one of the women's groups from a church would provide extra blankets to the prisoners to ward off the chill and prevent chest congestion and such."

"I don't know, Doc. Not much for mollycoddling these people — word gets out, and voters see me as weak and . . ."

"On the contrary," Addie said, unable to hold her tongue a minute longer. "I believe people will see you as someone who is fair and compassionate — someone who stands for the very principle on which the law in this territory was founded."

The sheriff turned his attention to her. "And that would be?"

"Innocent until proven guilty," she said, aware that by speaking up she might just have ruined everything. Certainly Brian looked alarmed, and her father had paused in his treatment of Fanny, as if waiting for an explosion.

"You need to shut up, girlie," the sheriff growled.

"Yes, sir," she murmured, and retreated to her cot as Brian let out a breath.

"My daughter here is also a trained physician," her father continued, as if there had been no interruption in his conversation with the sheriff. "She is capable of checking these prisoners and administering the medications necessary to get them well enough to appear in court. That would reflect well on you, sir."

The sheriff ignored the suggestion. "You about done?" he asked, his voice once again that of someone in charge.

"I am. May I leave the balance of these medicines with my daughter?"

"I'll take them," the sheriff said, holding out his hand. "Can't have her poisoning anybody else with her 'treatments,' now can we?"

Addie's heart sank. She had thought that her father had made some connection with the sheriff, but clearly not. On the other hand, as one accused of using medicine to cause a death, perhaps she could see the sheriff's point.

Brian stepped forward as the sheriff closed and locked the cell door. "Sheriff Richter, on the matter of this new evidence . . ."

"That has nothing to do with me. You need to talk to Hector Collins and the judge on that business. Judge Ellis is out riding the circuit. He'll be back tomorrow or the next day."

Addie was on her feet and once again gripping the bars of the cell. "What new evidence?"

"We'll be back," Brian promised as he followed the sheriff and their father back up the stairs.

Addie did not sleep a wink as she tried to think through what possible evidence there could be. There was Pearl's note, but how would that help anything? There had to be something else.

She paced the cell while Minnie and Fanny slept. Would this nightmare never end? At least her movement seemed to keep the rats and other critters at bay, so she supposed she should be thankful for that. But the possibility of weeks, or even years, spent locked up under such conditions made her skin crawl, and in her fear, she searched for some other train of thought — anything to take her mind off her situation. Seeing Fanny sleeping peacefully, she began to focus on what she might do to provide better conditions for prisoners should the day come when she was lucky enough to be free again.

And as she imagined the things she might do in her quest, she came to understand how Jess had been captivated by his dream of making a success of himself in the city. She realized that, in his own way, he had been thinking of their future. He had dreamed a better life for them — and why not? At the time his father died, and he left for the city, things in Whitman Falls had been dire indeed. There had been no real future for Jess — not on the ranch and not in town. She wished she could see him, tell him she understood, tell him she loved him, hold him — and be held in return.

"You gonna ever stop that infernal pacing?" Minnie grumbled.

"I'm thinking."

"You think with your feet, do you?" Minnie shot back. Then she sat up, her back against the cold wall of the cell, and waited. "Well, you gonna tell me what's got you all stirred up, or do I get to guess?"

"I'm thinking about when I get out of here."

Minnie snickered. "You mean *if* you get out."

"I prefer to dwell on the positive," Addie said, her patience wearing as thin as her nerves.

"Well, here's a positive thought you might want to consider, honey. I am positive that from what you've told me about your case, the chances of you leaving here any time soon are about as good as mine or Fanny's. Is that positive enough for you?"

"We can't just give up hope."

"Watch me." Minnie pulled the threadbare wool that passed for a blanket around her shoulders. "On a more *positive* subject, why don't you tell me about you and that good-looking cowboy who showed up here before? Believe me, sweetie, I would not kick that man out of my bed, and I wouldn't even charge him."

"Minnie!" Addie felt her cheeks flame red and was glad for the darkness.

"Oh, do not tell me you haven't thought about it — what doing it with that man

316

would be like."

"I love him," Addie admitted.

Minnie chuckled. "That's about the worst kept secret I ever heard. You shoulda seen your face when you saw him coming this way. I thought you might bend those bars open with your bare hands just to get at him."

"Stop it," Addie said, but she couldn't help but smile. "He is handsome, isn't he?"

"Honey, I wouldn't let that man get within three steps of me before I tore that shirt right off him and ran my hands over those muscles. Hard-packed that one is — and I bet he's packed in other places as well."

"Minnie!" Her exclamation gave way to laughter, and once she started, and Minnie joined in, neither of them could stop.

"You two hens gonna cackle all night?" one of the men yelled.

"Not much you can do to stop us, now is there?" Minnie shot back.

The man swore at her but then was quiet.

"Like us laughing is any worse than them snoring," Minnie muttered. "So you and that cowboy planning on hitching up together?"

"We were once."

"And now?"

Addie shrugged. "Not sure."

Minnie stifled a yawn. "Well, if he's still on the market, then here's my plan. I'm gonna lay down here, pretend I'm in a bed with fancy sheets and all, and he's there with me. And with that on my mind, I figure I'll sleep through your pacing and the snoring from down there and anything else that might come up before sunrise. Good night, Addie."

Addie realized it was the first time that Minnie had referred to her by her given name. "Good night, Minnie," she replied softly, as she curled onto her cot and pulled the thin blanket over her shoulders.

Minnie's plan wasn't half bad, she thought. Dreaming of sharing a bed with Jess might just be what she needed to steady her nerves and calm her fears about the future.

It was during the night that Jess realized the following day was when Pearl's funeral was scheduled. If they buried her, then how was anybody going to prove that she'd died not from an overdose, but from the injury to her head? He was up, dressed, and standing outside the courthouse when Hector Collins came to work.

"If the funeral's scheduled for today, you can't stop it," Collins explained. "By the time you or anyone else rode back there, it would be over."

"We could send a wire," Jess argued.

"And who has the authority to stop the service?"

"What about my deputy? If I could get word to him . . ."

"Look, if it comes to it, we can get a court order to exhume the body for further examination. That's the best I can offer."

"Tipton will never stand for that," Jess argued.

"Look, Marshal Porterfield, I understand that this woman is your friend — maybe she's more than that to you. But the fact is that you should be talking to her lawyer," Collins said. "After all, I'm the prosecutor in this case. I'm sorry, but there's nothing I can do."

"Do you want to prosecute an innocent woman?"

"Prove her innocence, and I'll be happy to lose this one. Now, if you'll excuse me . . ." He walked past Jess and into the courthouse.

Jess hadn't noticed the sheriff standing just inside the door and eavesdropping on their conversation. "What's this new evidence you and that girlie's family keep talking about?"

"That's my business," Jess said as he brushed past the man.

"You don't want to be disrespecting me, Marshal," the sheriff shouted. "Not while that girl's in my jail."

Jess froze and spun around. He grabbed the sheriff's shirtfront and backed the man up against the wall of the courthouse. "If any harm, no matter how minor, comes to that woman — if she so much as catches a cold from being locked up in that hole you call a jail — I will personally make it my business to hunt you down and . . ."

"You itching to get locked up too?" the sheriff sneered. " 'Cause I can sure make that happen, boy. Now let go of me, and get out of town within the hour."

Aware that several passersby had stopped to observe the altercation, Jess released the sheriff and headed back to the hotel. As he crossed the street, he heard the sheriff call out, "Nothing to see here, folks. Just a little misunderstanding. Move along now."

He did not look back.

Ten minutes later, he answered a knock at his door to find Brian standing there. Addie's brother pushed past him to enter the room, and Jess closed the door. "Have you got news?" he asked, hoping that maybe the lawyer had finally gotten someone to listen.

"Are you crazy or just stupid?" Brian yelled. "You attack an officer of the law in front of half a dozen witnesses? How is that supposed to help Addie?"

"I need to . . ."

"You need to leave," Brian said firmly. "You need to head back to Whitman Falls and do your job there. You can't help her, Jess, and if you can't keep hold on that temper of yours, you're sure gonna end up hurting her."

Jess knew he was right. He was so frustrated with not having any power to help Addie. "It's my fault she's here," he said.

"Look, the Tiptons pulled strings the way they always do. Jasper Tipton wasn't about to let you handle this." Brian put his hand gently on Jess's shoulder. "Go home, Jess. I'll keep you informed. I'm asking my parents to leave as well. Pa has patients, and they won't let Ma see her, so what's the point?"

Jess looked at Addie's brother, perhaps seeing him for the first time. The man was every bit as upset as Jess was. He saw the unfairness of it all. He understood what could and could not be done because he knew the law. If anybody could save Addie,

321

it was probably her brother. "Okay, I'll go. But first, do you think you can get a letter to Addie? I wouldn't want her to think I'd just up and left her — like last time."

Brian smiled. "I'll get her your letter, if you'll promise me something."

"What?" Jess didn't like where this was headed.

"Stay out of it. Back in Whitman Falls you are bound to run into Jasper and Buck. If you don't hold your temper, then the real culprit in Pearl's death is gonna walk away."

Jess hesitated.

"I need your word, Jess."

"All right," he agreed. "You think it was Buck that killed Pearl?"

Brian frowned. "If I was a betting man, I'd bet my house on it."

Jess smiled. At least he could leave knowing Brian believed as he did. "I'll write that letter. Tell Doc and Miz Wilcox I'll meet them down in the lobby in a half hour."

"Twenty minutes," Brian corrected, looking at the pocket watch he carried. "Do not think for one minute that Sheriff Richter won't be looking for an excuse to make good on his promise to lock you up."

"Twenty minutes," Jess agreed. "Now leave me to it."

He stared at the blank paper for half of

the time he had left. In the end, he scrawled a short note.

Addie,
It's not like last time. This time I'll be back for you. I love you.

J

He folded the paper, thrust it inside an envelope with the hotel's return address stamped on it, added the locket his mother had given him, and sealed the envelope. Then he threw his belongings into his saddlebags and headed downstairs. Brian took the note and escorted his parents to their wagon. He hugged his mother, shook hands with his father, and then turned to Jess. "Look across the street," he murmured.

Jess did and saw the sheriff and two deputies standing on the courthouse steps. The sheriff was holding a pocket watch, making Brian's point that he would just love to have a reason to arrest Jess.

"I'm trusting you to keep your word," Brian said as he watched Jess mount up.

"And I'm trusting you to make sure Addie is safe and gets my letter," he replied before kneeing his horse to a lively trot and leading the Wilcoxes out of Tucson.

■ ■ ■ ■

Once Addie learned of Jess's departure, her anxiety only increased. It was as if while he was nearby, she would be all right. Together they would find a way to beat the charges against her, and she would once again be free to get on with her life. When Brian had handed her the envelope, she had hesitated.

"Open it," her brother advised. "I think there's more than just words on paper in there."

Sure enough, she could feel something more — something hard. She tore open the envelope, and a small locket on a thin gold chain fell into her hand. She turned it over and saw the inscription on the back — *Forever my love.*

She knew this locket — had seen Constance Porterfield wearing it more than once. And now, it had been passed to her. The love that Jess's parents had shared was near legendary to those who knew them. Now Jess was passing the symbol of that love to her, and she felt her heart swell with the fullness of the message. He loved her, and this was his promise of a future where that love would blossom and flourish.

She dropped the envelope and note and

fastened the locket around her neck. It lay flat against the bare skin of her throat. Jess might not be there in person, but he was there with her nonetheless.

To her surprise, the district attorney, Hector Collins, approved visits and medical supplies from the local druggist, Mr. Matthews. He came with his daughter, Ginny, and the three of them were allowed to examine and treat other prisoners who lined up in the hallway. Addie noticed that Ginny made copious notes about the conditions of the men and women, as well as about the conditions under which they were being held.

Once a day Brian was allowed five minutes with her. On the fifth day of her jail time, Brian told her a date had been set for her trial. "It's tomorrow morning," he said.

Addie felt as if she might be sick. "Tomorrow? But that's too soon. Can Papa get here in time to testify about the pills and how Pearl couldn't have swallowed them? And what about . . ."

"It's tomorrow, Addie. There's been some new evidence according to Hector Collins. He hasn't said what — just that someone has come forward with new information."

"That can't be good for me," Addie replied. She and Brian were sitting on her cot and speaking in low tones, but she could see Minnie was listening and knew by the woman's posture that she, too, felt this was not good news.

"Time's up," the guard shouted as he came down the hall and unlocked the cell.

Brian hugged her. "I'll bring you a clean dress to wear in court," he said.

"And a comb and some hairpins — and bring something nice for Minnie and Fanny as well," she whispered as she hugged him back.

"Get some rest," he replied, and then he was gone, and she faced another long night — this one longer than most as she contemplated her fate.

Jess could not have been more astonished when Jasper Tipton came walking into the jail just two days after Pearl's funeral. The man had aged at least a decade. His full head of hair had gone white seemingly overnight, and his face was lined with sagging jowls and wrinkles that Jess was certain had not been there before.

"Mr. Tipton," he said, standing out of respect for the man's grief. "How can I help you?"

"I need you to find my brother."

Jess took his time, pouring a glass of water

for the older man, and then wondering if perhaps he should have offered whiskey. If ever there was a man who looked like he could use a stiff drink, it was Jasper Tipton. His eyes were rheumy with lack of sleep, and something more — something that Jess recognized from his days in Kansas City. There had come a time when Jess had been so low that when he looked in the mirror, he did not know the face staring back because he did not know that man's life. His life — like Jasper's — had always been something he controlled. But in those days, before he finally decided to return home, Jess had been lost — the way Jasper was now.

"Buck is missing?"

"My brother is on the run. He needs to be found and arrested."

Jess could not believe what he was hearing. He studied Jasper closely for any sign that the man was delusional.

Jasper met his stare with an unwavering glare of his own. "Have I not made myself clear, Marshal Porterfield?"

"Perhaps this is a matter for Colonel Ashwood," Jess suggested.

"My brother resides in town, as do I. As did . . ." His voice broke. "Do your duty, Marshal."

"I'll need to know what the charge would be."

"He betrayed me."

Jess relaxed slightly. "I'm afraid that's not a crime, sir. At least not one I have the authority to detain him for."

Jasper's twisted smile held no warmth — only malice. "He murdered my wife and child, Marshal. Do you think that is enough for you to detain him?"

Jess's mind was instantly flooded with all the possible ramifications of that statement. Addie would go free. But how did Jasper know this? Perhaps he was so distraught over Pearl's death that he was casting about for anyone to blame — unable to accept that she might have chosen to end her life.

Suddenly, Jasper spotted the whiskey bottle on the shelf. Without asking permission, he ignored the water and filled another glass two fingers full of the amber liquid. He tossed that back as if he were downing a cold glass of lemonade on a hot summer's day. He set the glass on Jess's desk and leaned back in the chair, folding his hands across his stomach. "Do you need the particulars?"

"That would be helpful," Jess said, and pulled a pad of paper and pencil out of the desk drawer. "Did Buck tell you he . . ."

"Of course not. He tried to deny the whole thing. But once it was out, he could hardly put it back in the box, could he?" His eyes filled with tears. "My own brother . . ." he said in a raspy whisper.

"Tell me what happened," Jess said, and realized that for the first time in his life, he was feeling sorry for one of the Tiptons. It occurred to him that the broken man sitting across from him might well have given the order to kill his father, but seeing him now, Jess was no longer so sure. "Start with the funeral," he suggested.

"Buck showed up late and so drunk he could barely walk. I wasn't in much better shape myself, but as the service wore on, I realized Buck was agitated, as if something was eating at him. I thought it was his temper and his fury at Miss Wilcox. I understood that, or thought I did."

"But something else happened?"

"We went back to the house following the service. There were very few mourners at the cemetery, but I thought that was because of the raw weather — the drizzle and cold. At my instruction, our housekeeper, Clara, had prepared food for fifty. We waited an hour, then two, but no one came. Buck blamed the Wilcox woman — said everyone in town was taking her side against us. I knew the truth."

"Which was?"

"My wife was . . . I met Pearl at a brothel, Marshal. She worked there. I know the rumors of her past followed her here. She often spoke of not having any friends. I told her it was because of the business Buck and I are in. I told her it had nothing to do with her. The way we did business made people our enemies or associates, but never friends. And then she met Miss Wilcox, and she was so very happy — changed in a way I had only hoped to see. Why would she take her own life? Why would she murder her own child?" He paused and looked down at his hands, which were shaking. "Why?"

"She wouldn't," Jess said. "She didn't."

Jasper looked at him, his eyes narrowed into a squint. "You knew?"

"I knew that blaming Addie for this was wrong." He considered telling Jasper about Pearl's note but rejected the idea. "You haven't told me why you now think that . . ."

"I *know* that my brother murdered my wife and child, Marshal. Buck is as guilty as Miss Wilcox is innocent. That's why he ran — and she didn't." He got up abruptly and put on his bowler hat as he turned toward the door. "Go find my brother, Marshal, and you will have your killer."

"I need hard evidence, sir. What makes you so sure that your brother —"

"Because he admitted it. He didn't mean to, but that night after the funeral, when it was just the two of us in that big house, he started rambling on about how he'd finally fixed Addie Wilcox, and she wouldn't be so high-and-mighty with him. Then he moved on to women in general — how they all thought they were too good for him, even the . . ."

Again, his voice broke, and this time he could not go on.

"He was talking about Pearl?"

Jasper nodded. "All of a sudden, it was clear to me — the way Pearl changed whenever Buck was around."

"Changed how?"

"She'd go quiet, and most times she would make some excuse to leave the room. Why couldn't I see that she was afraid of him?" He buried his whiskered face in his hands. "I am a fool. Pearl would be alive today if . . ."

"You couldn't have known. I mean, you had no reason to believe that Buck was capable of murder, did you?" Jess didn't realize what he was really asking until he saw Jasper's face. The businessman looked up at him, shook his head as if trying to clear a muddled mind, and then sighed.

"I'm tired, Jess. Tired of trying to do what I thought would be best for this territory. I love this land, and I am still convinced my plan to form a huge land and cattle company by acquiring small ranches is the best for all concerned. People like your family and the Johnsons haven't a chance. We're coming to the end of an era, son, and . . ."

"Don't call me 'son,' " Jess growled. "My father is dead — he was murdered. Did you or your brother have anything to do with that?"

"I came here because of Pearl — Buck killed Pearl. He says it was an accident, and maybe it was, but he's a dangerous man, Jess."

"I'm gonna ask you one more time, Mr. Tipton — did Buck kill my father?"

"I don't know. What I do know is that if you arrest him for killing my wife, you'll get justice for both Pearl and your father." And with that, he left the office.

Jess watched as Jasper walked slowly across the street and up the steps leading to his mansion. Later that night, as he met with Lucas and Chet and Bunker to deputize them and plan their strategy for hunting down Buck Tipton, Jess glanced out the window and saw that only one light burned

in the Tipton house — the light in Pearl's
bedroom.

TWELVE

"You are free to go, Miss Wilcox." Those were the last words Addie had expected to hear that morning.

Hector Collins faced her and smiled broadly. She was pretty sure this was the dream she'd been having when the jailer came to get her and bring her to the court-room. Surely she had only imagined that she'd entered the wood-paneled room to see the district attorney, the sheriff, and Brian all standing before the judge, waiting while he rifled through a stack of papers.

Meanwhile, the jailer had ushered her to the table where she saw her brother's briefcase and more papers. She sat down and tried to hear what the men who would determine her future were saying.

"And Mr. Tipton is quite certain of his facts?" the judge asked.

"His brother confessed to him," Hector Collins replied.

His brother confessed. Buck? Were they speaking of Buck?

The judge cleared his throat and went back to scanning the documents.

"Your Honor," Sheriff Richter said, "I mean, the folks in Whitman Falls are determined to get the prisoner off. They would do . . ."

The judge glared at him. "Are you suggesting, Sheriff Richter, that a man who has recently buried his wife and unborn child who died under unusual, if not criminal, circumstances would care one whit about your prisoner?"

"No, Your Honor, but . . ."

The judge held up one hand to forestall any further comment from the sheriff. Then his eyes settled on Addie. "Miss Wilcox?"

Instinct brought her to her feet. "Yes, sir."

"It would appear that the real culprit in this case has confessed, and while he is not yet in custody, there is no reason for this court to detain you further. You have our apologies for the inconvenience."

Inconvenience? Now Addie was pretty sure she was dreaming. Who in their right mind would call holding an innocent person in that dungeon a mere inconvenience? She felt her temper flare and was about to give the judge a piece of her mind when Mr.

335

Collins stepped between her and the judge's high bench. "You are free to go, Miss Wilcox."

Brian had returned to his place at the table and gripped her hand. It was hard to say whether the gesture was one of relief, congratulations, or — more likely — intended to keep her from saying anything that might cause the judge to change his mind.

The judge slammed down his gavel three times. Brian hugged her tight.

"It's over, Sis. Buck confessed to Jasper." He shook hands with Hector Collins then wrapped his arm around Addie as he picked up his briefcase and started to lead her from the courtroom.

"Miss Wilcox," the judge called.

Addie froze, as did Brian.

"Yes, sir," she replied, turning to face him.

"I understand that you have some thoughts on improving conditions in our jail here."

She saw the sheriff smirk.

She squared her shoulders as she stepped away from her brother and approached the bench. She lowered her voice to a level meant for the judge's ears only. "Your jail, sir, is not fit for human inhabitation. Your prisoners are being bitten by rats and other

336

assorted critters — critters that may carry disease. The food is abominable. There are insufficient provisions for warmth and exercise and —"

"Perhaps, Miss Wilcox, you would be so generous as to prepare me a full report with your suggestions for improvements — keeping in mind that not everyone housed there is innocent, as you are."

"Yet everyone down there is presumed innocent until this court determines otherwise, is that not so?" Since Judge Ellis was speaking in a normal volume, Addie saw no reason to continue to modulate hers.

It was as if every male in the courtroom gasped in unison. The only other female — the stenographer — glanced at Addie and smiled.

The judge cleared his throat, and as the men in the courtroom recovered and began talking among themselves, whispering as they looked nervously at Addie, the judge banged his gavel.

"I see your point, Miss Wilcox. Would you be willing to prepare the report I have requested?"

"I would if you will permit me to continue to call on the prisoners and treat their afflictions."

She did not have to look back at her

brother to know that he had rolled his eyes heavenward and was silently praying for her to hold her tongue.

"That seems a fair bargain, Miss Wilcox." The judge nodded.

Addie smiled and nodded in return. Then as she turned to go, she thought of one more thing. "I wonder, Your Honor, if it might be all right if I appoint a surrogate to see to the health of the prisoners." It was obvious that the judge was running low on patience, so she hurried to explain. "You see, sir, Whitman Falls is a good distance from here — Sheriff Richter can attest to that."

"Your point, Miss Wilcox?"

"Well, sir, your local druggist, Mr. Matthews, is well-qualified to examine and treat those in need. Of course, if there were something dire, I would make the journey, however . . ."

Judge Ellis released a sigh of pure exasperation. "Miss Wilcox, make the arrangements, add them to your report and recommendations, and I will consider them. Are we quite done now?"

"Yes, Your Honor," Brian replied, stepping forward to take Addie firmly by the arm and lead her away. "Thank you, sir."

Addie gave the judge a little wave — one

that he returned — as she allowed her brother to escort her from the courtroom. Once they stepped outside and into the sunlight, she realized for the first time that she was indeed free. Free to come and go as she pleased. Free of the stigma of friends and neighbors believing she had assisted Pearl in taking her life. Free of her doubts about whether she had missed signs of Pearl's intent.

"Tell me what happened, Brian."

Brian still had hold of her elbow and was guiding her down the courthouse steps and across the street. "Why don't you let Jess tell you?" he said with a grin.

Addie looked up and saw Jess leaning against a hitching post. His arms were folded across his chest. His badge glinted in the sun, but that was nothing compared to the brilliance of his smile. When she saw him, he opened his arms to her, and she ran to fill them.

The second the courthouse door swung open, Jess felt his heart freeze. Would she be there or had the judge rejected the new evidence and ordered a trial? For a second, the sun reflecting off the flagpole distorted his view — but then he saw her.

She was thinner, her dress loose on her

shoulders and at her waist. Her hair had no shine, and Brian held tight to her as they crossed the street. But there was no mistaking his Addie. She was talking to her brother, gesturing with her free hand, and clearly peppering him with questions. But she paused mid-sentence once she realized that he was there. She walked toward him, and as he opened his arms to her and felt her pressed against his chest, he vowed that he would not risk another day without at least the promise of Addie Wilcox as his wife.

"Marry me," he whispered as they clung to each other and filled their embrace with the release of all the fear and stress the last days had brought. "Marry me today," he said when she pulled back and looked up at him.

She traced the outline of his jaw, ran her thumb over his lips, and said, "Shush. You don't have to . . ."

He tightened his hold on her. "This is not a case of *have* to. It's a case of *want* to. Marry me, Addie. Let's go right now and tell the judge that we want —"

"You are not getting off that easily, Jess Porterfield. I want the down-on-one-knee proposal, along with a big ceremony with the whole town in attendance, food and dancing the likes of which the folks in Whitman Falls have never seen before . . ."

She was smiling, and then she was crying, and then she was laughing as he held her close. "I don't want to wait another hour," he said, his own voice cracking with emotion. "If I were to lose you . . ."

"Shhh," she whispered, and he could feel her tears dampening his shirt. "We're safe. We're going to be fine. We have our whole lives ahead of us." She choked out the words, and he understood the reality of all that she had suffered.

"Big wedding, huh?" he said as he brushed her tears away with his thumbs. "No way 'round that?"

She shook her head and sniffed back her tears.

"She drives a hard bargain, Porterfield," Brian said. "Just ask the judge."

"Well, then maybe we ought to put my sister Amanda in charge. That girl knows how to throw a party."

"Oh, Jess, it's going to be so much fun," Addie exclaimed as she hooked arms with Jess and her brother and headed into the hotel. "You'll see."

Jess understood that Addie was thinking of the wedding, but he was thinking far beyond that. He was thinking of the marriage, and all the good times — and some bad — they would face together.

When Addie first returned to Whitman Falls, she felt a sense of foreboding every time she looked at the Tipton mansion. Jasper had closed the place up and moved out to his ranch. No one had seen any sign of Buck, and most people thought that by now, he would be miles away, never to be heard from again. But Addie had a feeling that he would not go away so easily. After all, he had a huge investment in the company he had built with his brother.

But as the weeks passed and Amanda filled her head with elaborate plans for the wedding, Addie had little time for worrying about Buck Tipton. She and Jess spent every moment they could spare together. Unfortunately, her rounds with her father — delivering babies, seeing three people through the end of their lives, and treating various stomach ailments and accidents — rarely seemed to coordinate with Jess's duties as marshal. They were both frustrated that there never seemed time for more than some serious kissing and cuddling. There was no doubt in either of their minds that a repeat of the night they had spent together in Jess's bed was out of the question.

"I'm not sure I can hold out much longer," Jess whispered one night as they sat together on the porch of the Wilcox house. They had just shared a kiss that had left them both breathless. His shirt was untucked and unbuttoned, and her cheek was pressed to his bare chest. She could feel the life pulse of his heart beating and knew that being in his arms, cradled against him, would always feel like home.

"Two weeks," she promised.

He groaned. "Feels like forever."

"I know, but the time will fly by. You have your rounds to make collecting taxes, and I have to go to Tucson to present my report to the judge on improving conditions at the jail. That takes care of the first week. Then the week of the wedding . . ."

"Our wedding," he said, and tweaked her nose. "Have to say there was many a time when I thought the day would never come."

She laughed. "Well, don't go trying to get out of it now, Marshal Porterfield. A promise is a promise, and I have friends in high places who will hold you to it."

"Like the judge?"

"The judge and the district attorney — I even think Sheriff Richter is starting to like me a little."

It was Jess's turn to laugh. "Don't bet on

it. That man is only interested in one thing
— holding onto his job. The fact that the
newspaper there has written those articles
about you and the work you're doing is
what keeps the sheriff on his toes." He
kicked the swing into motion and pulled
her closer. "Two weeks." He sighed. "And
then you'll be all mine."

Addie frowned. "You make me sound like
a horse you're buying, or a piece of property."

"No, that's not . . . I mean . . ."

"Because let's be clear on one matter, Jess
Porterfield — I am, and always will be,
exactly as I am. Do not go trying to change
me."

They were both sitting up and apart now.
The rocking of the swing mirrored the
change in their mood.

"Who said anything about changing you?
I'm the one who has done the changing
here. I came back. I got a job here in town
so I could be near you. I —"

"I . . . I . . . I . . . You made all those decisions. I didn't ask you to do anything. If
you have regrets, well, that's your fault, not
mine."

"I never said I had regrets," he protested.
"You have a way of putting words in my
mouth, Addie Wilcox, and it always ends

bad for us when you do."

"Lower your voice before you wake the whole town."

Jess set his feet firmly on the floor, stopping the swing with a jolt. He pushed himself off the swing, setting it in motion again.

"You're going?" she asked as he buttoned his shirt and tucked in the tails.

He reached for the hat he'd placed on the side chair her father preferred when sitting on the porch. "I don't want to fight with you, Addie, and we've got a full day tomorrow. I'll see you when you get back from Tucson." He kissed the top of her head and then stroked her cheek. "I know you still have doubts, but the way I figure things, if I tell you how much I love you umpty-eleven times, maybe one day you'll believe it."

He was halfway back to his room at the jail before Addie caught up to him. "I love you, Jess Porterfield — always have and always will — but sometimes . . ."

Jess hesitated for half a second but kept on walking. "And I love you, Addie Wilcox," he called out to her, "always have and always will — but sometimes . . ." He left the sentence hanging there in the cold night air as she stopped trying to keep up with his long-legged stride and watched him walk away.

Two weeks, she thought. It was a long time — time enough for everything to change.

Jess was so stirred up that getting any sleep was about as likely as mulish Addie Wilcox yielding to anything he might suggest. The woman drove him batty, and yet all he had to do was remember the feel of her cuddled up next to him, the taste of her, the little sounds of pleasure she made whenever he kissed her, and he was lost. The fact was that if their wedding day — or rather their wedding night — didn't come soon, he wasn't sure what he was going to do.

Lately, it seemed like all he could think about was making love for as long and as often as they pleased. He pictured them in bed, naked and entwined. He pictured her face, those incredible brown eyes wide with surprise as he taught her all the ways they could love each other. Oh, it was going to take some time — years — a lifetime.

And the thing was that when he got to thinking that way, it made him smile, and inside he felt a kind of peacefulness and certainty he'd never known before. Of course, then he would try to tell her — as he had earlier — how much he was looking forward to the day when they were finally married, and she'd take his words the wrong way, and then she'd be upset, and he'd be upset and . . .

Well, there was one thing he was pretty sure they could both count on — life together would never be dull. Neither was likely to back down from a difference of opinion. On the other hand, making up could be mighty sweet. He grinned as he imagined meeting the stage when Addie returned from Tucson. He'd bring her flowers — no, a single, perfect flower — as a peace offering, and she would pretend to still be upset with him for about a minute. Then she would laugh and tuck the flower in her hair and hold out her arms to him. She wouldn't care who might be passing by. Addie put no stock in the opinions of others when it came to ideas about the proper behavior for an engaged couple.

"We're in love," she'd say reasonably. "Why on earth would we hide that?" And she would stand on tiptoe and kiss him right there on the street in front of the busybodies and those who would simply grin and shake their heads. For that was Addie, and everybody in Whitman Falls knew it.

Two weeks, Jess thought. Time enough to

finish fixing up the little house he'd bought with his savings and a loan from his ma — the little house with an anteroom he figured would be just perfect for Addie to set up her doctoring office.

The morning after their disagreement, Addie stopped by the jail. Jess was talking to Lucas about handling his duties for a few days before and after the wedding. When he saw her coming through the back door, he stopped talking, and she could tell he was trying to gauge her mood.

"So, should I assume the wedding is still on?" she asked, grinning up at him. "Or maybe you were talking about marrying somebody else?" They both knew that teasing him was her way of apologizing, and his was to play along.

"Funny you should think that. I was just about to tell Luc here that I've been asking around, and it seems like most folks think the only woman crazy enough to have me is you."

Addie let out an exaggerated sigh. "Oh, very well, if you're that desperate to find a wife, I'll do it."

Jess took a step closer, his eyes blazing with wanting her. She reached up and smoothed his hair back from his forehead.

Lucas cleared his throat.

"Leave," Jess growled without looking at his friend and deputy. "Now," he added.

Lucas headed for the door. "Good seeing you, Addie. Millie and I . . ."

"Now!" Jess repeated, and the door had barely closed when he lifted Addie in his arms and strode with her toward his bedroom.

"Put me down, Jess Porterfield. It's the middle of the day."

He grinned. "Oh, we're going to be on some kind of a schedule, are we?" He kissed her, his tongue parting her lips as he kept moving toward the bed. As he cleared the door, he kicked it shut.

"Jess, we . . ."

He tossed her onto the bed and began unbuttoning his shirt. "What? Can't? Shouldn't? Absolutely must not?" The shirt was off. The grin was devilish. "The Addie Wilcox I know never cared about rules like that." He sat on the edge of the bed and opened the top three buttons of her shirtwaist. He spread the neckline open and leaned in to kiss her throat. "That Addie Wilcox once asked me point-blank to kiss her like this and touch her like this . . ." He cupped her breasts.

Addie groaned with sheer pleasure. This

was getting completely out of hand. She ran her nails over his bare chest and smiled when he shuddered. Two could definitely play this game.

She pulled his ear to her lips and whispered, "But if I let you have your way with me now, will you still marry me?"

She traced the outline of his ear with her tongue. He shuddered violently and pressed her back against the iron headboard. Straddling her, he finished opening her bodice and pushed the garment off her shoulders while he bathed her throat and face with kisses.

"I'll marry you, Addie, because the idea that any other man might be with you like this would surely kill me. Now shut up, and help me get this skirt and your petticoats out of our way."

Addie giggled, then froze.

From the outer office, she heard someone calling. "Yoo-hoo! Marshal?"

"That's Miss Lillian," Addie whispered, instinctively pulling her dress closed and pushing Jess away.

"Well, if anybody would understand, it's Miss Lillian."

A knock on the bedroom door made Addie go scarlet with embarrassment. "Marshal Porterfield? Are you in there?"

"Go see what she wants," Addie hissed.

"Coming," Jess called as he shrugged into his shirt and headed for the door.

"Don't let her see me," Addie whispered.

Jess rolled his eyes. "Stay put," he instructed.

But the minute Addie heard Jess and Miss Lillian leave — something about her needing him to take a look at a stranger who'd come into the saloon, a man who bore a striking resemblance to a wanted poster she'd seen at the bank — she got dressed and left the building by the rear door. Thankfully, everything was fine between Jess and her, and she had work to do.

Addie was working on a surprise of her own — one she hoped would please both Jess and her parents. She'd received a letter from a doctor in Tucson offering to sponsor her application for medical school, one she could attend by taking classes via the mail, and where her prior experience would count. It seemed almost too good to be true, but the name was valid, according to her father. She hadn't told him why she was asking, but she had inquired if he knew of a Dr. Boyle in Tucson.

"He's respected," her father assured her. "How did you come to think of him?"

"His name was mentioned the last time I

was in Tucson to meet with the judge and the reform committee." It was a lie, as was the story that she was going to Tucson the following day to meet with the committee. But to tell her father the real reason she was asking would spoil the surprise.

THIRTEEN

But when Addie rang the bell at Dr. Boyle's home on the evening of her appointment, the house was strangely dark and silent. Perhaps she had gotten the date wrong, or the time. Perhaps Dr. Boyle had gone out on an emergency call. She had checked the address with the hotel desk clerk to be sure.

"Hello, Addie."

She whirled around to face Buck Tipton's evil grin just before he pulled a smelly sack over her head, tied it round her neck, and threw her over his shoulder.

She kicked and screamed as well as she could, but he had her in a hold like a vise, and her cries were muffled by the sack. Buck smelled of sweat and liquor, and she thought she heard him chuckle.

The journey was far shorter than she might have expected. They could not have gone more than a few yards when she heard Buck grunting as he struggled to keep hold of her and, apparently, open a door. Once again, she set up a ruckus — kicking and freeing one hand from his grip to try to remove the sack. To her shock he dropped her, and then he slugged her with what felt like all his might.

"I don't want to seriously hurt you, but if you push me . . ." He gave a grunt, and she heard a protesting screech from whatever he'd been trying to open. Again he heaved her over his shoulder. So stunned had she been by his assault, she had failed to remove the sack when she had the chance. Now she was aware they were going down some stairs. The air was rank and damp, and most of all it was pitch-black.

Think.

Her medical training had taught her to be observant — the smallest detail could lead to a proper diagnosis. It could save a life. In this case . . . perhaps hers.

She heard the flare of a match and saw the flicker of a candle through the loose weave of the burlap. She heard the door slam shut, and then the ties were cut with a knife that came much too close to her jugular for comfort, and Buck jerked the sack from her head. She gulped in air, trying to catch her breath.

"What do you think of big ol' dumb Buck

now, girlie?" Buck was standing over her, the sack and knife in one hand, and a half-filled bottle of whiskey in the other. He took a long drink, wiped his mouth with the sack, and offered the bottle to her.

She shook her head.

"Too good for a little cheap whiskey, are you now?" Blessedly, he moved away and slumped down on a bedroll, giving her the first real look at her surroundings.

He had brought her to a cellar — the doctor's cellar, judging by the short distance he'd carried her. She was sitting on sacks of potatoes and onions. The smell, not to mention the lumps, were enough to tell her that. The door had been one that led outside. A quick glance around told her there were no other ways in or out. No door leading into the house. No windows. Once again, she was a prisoner.

She thought about the strangely dark and silent house and shivered. "Where is the doctor, Buck?"

"I ain't hurt him if that's what you're asking."

"Like you hurt Pearl?" *Shut up, Addie. Try for once not to say the first thing that comes to mind.*

Silence filled the room like a cloak of fog. She knew Buck was staring at her, although she could not see his features. "You sent me the letter?" she asked, hoping that changing the subject might keep Buck from striking her again.

It worked. He chortled and took another swallow of the whiskey. "I did. I got a girl I was poking at the saloon out there on the edge of town to steal the stationery when she went to get treated at Doc Boyle's. I told her what to write, like she was the good doctor's secretary, you know. Then I signed it and sent it off. Told her it was a joke I was playing on my little sister. We laughed a good deal about that." He sighed. "Too bad she won't be doing much laughing where she's gone, I expect."

"She left town?"

"You might say that. She met with an accident — poor thing got run over by a stagecoach. 'Course, she didn't suffer. She was dead when I laid her in the road." He threw the now empty bottle against a rock wall, and it shattered, sending glass shards flying.

Addie covered her face to shield her eyes. When she looked up, Buck was watching her. "You see, Addie, once you kill one girl, the next is easy, and I expect the third will be even easier. But if you come to your senses and accept that you and me were meant to be together, then everything will be just fine." He struggled to his feet, staggered a little, and then advanced on her, a rope in one hand.

"Lie down," he ordered, indicating a bare patch of the dirt floor.

"Buck, I . . ."

"Oh, you're gonna play nice, are you? Gonna beg a little, are you? Believe me, that'll come." He grabbed her by the arm and flung her to the floor face down. He was on her before she could react, wrapping the rope around her arms, which he twisted behind her back. Then he tied the rope so tight around her ankles that she could feel the fibers cutting into her skin.

"Ever have to hog-tie a patient, Addie? This here is how you go about that." He gave a pull on the rope, and Addie could not swallow the yelp of pain. "I gotta go out for a while. Got some business to take care of." He pulled a bandana from his back pocket and knelt next to where her cheek was pressed against the dirt floor. "You gonna be a good girl?"

She opened her mouth to answer, and he stuffed the bandana inside. When he left, he was laughing, and she hated him more than she thought possible to despise another human being.

■ ■ ■ ■

Once again Addie was missing. Only this time it hadn't been a matter of hours. This time she'd been gone for three days. If her family and friends could be described as distraught, Jess could only describe what he was feeling as scared out of his wits. He turned the daily duties of town marshal over to Lucas and spent every waking hour searching for Addie, following a trail that led him to Tucson and then went cold.

Neither the judge, nor the pharmacist, had seen or heard from Addie, and no, there had been no meeting scheduled as she had told Jess and her parents. The clerk at the hotel did recall her asking directions to a local doctor's home.

"Seemed right excited about meeting up with Doc Boyle," the clerk reported. "I tried to tell her I was pretty sure he and the missus had left for a trip to visit his sister in Phoenix, but she'd already headed out. I figured she would come back, and I could tell her then."

Jess went to the doctor's home, but as the clerk had told him, no one was there. It didn't look as if anyone had been there for days. A layer of sandy dirt covered the porch, but on closer examination he saw there were footprints — two sets — going toward the door, but only one leaving. He took a closer look. The footprints approaching the door but not leaving were smaller — a woman's? Addie's?

He banged the heavy brass door knocker repeatedly with no results. He peered in the windows and saw furniture covered in dust cloths, as if the occupants planned to be away for some time. More certain with every passing minute that Addie had been lured here, he searched around the house looking for any sign that someone had broken in.

Everything was secured, even the lock on the double doors that led down to a root cellar.

He returned to the hotel and got the clerk to open the room where Addie had been staying. Tears filled his eyes as he stopped just inside the door and saw a medical text on the table next to the bed. What if she had been taken, and he never found her? He was pretty sure Buck Tipton had a hand in this, and that being the case, Addie could be anywhere. He swiped at his eyes with the back of one hand as he packed the medical book and the rest of her belongings in the small carpetbag she'd brought with her.

That's when he saw the letter.

It was handwritten on stationery that carried Dr. Boyle's name and address — a feminine script, but the signature was a masculine scrawl. He left the carpetbag with the desk clerk and hurried to the courthouse and the office of Hector Collins.

"That's Doc's stationery all right, but not his signature," the district attorney confirmed. "You think Miss Wilcox was lured here and taken captive?"

"I do, and I think I know who took her," Jess replied. He told Hector the whole story of Buck's obsession with Addie, then reminded him of every detail of Pearl's untimely death, of Jasper's discovery that his brother had murdered his wife, and with each word he felt his panic grow. "I have to find her," he said. "Before . . ."

Finishing that sentence was impossible — and unthinkable.

The district attorney put his hand on Jess's shoulder. "One step at a time, Marshal Porterfield. I'll wire Dr. Boyle at his sister's just to confirm there was no appointment with Miss Wilcox."

Jess felt his fear and rage fill his throat with bile. "How does that do any good? She's been gone three days now — that monster could have . . ."

"We'll find her, Jess."

But by day five, they were no closer than they had been two days earlier. Jess took a room at the hotel — the same room where Addie had stayed. Somehow that helped. At least he was able to get a couple hours sleep. He would try to understand the medical terminology she had been studying, but he would never be as book smart as Addie was. Come to that, he wondered what she had ever seen in him in the first place. She had all the drive and ambition that his father had hoped to find in him, but Jess had looked for the easy way, relying on his charms to carry him through. He didn't deserve a woman like Addie.

"You should go home," Hector told him when the two met for supper later that fifth day.

"I will. I just want to take one more look around the Boyle place. She was there, and I'm reasonably certain that's where she was kidnapped."

"All right. Let's stop by Sheriff Richter's office and ask him to come along. I wouldn't want any of the neighbors to see you snooping around on your own."

But Richter was sleeping off a day and night of drinking when they stopped by. Hector just shook his head and closed the door to the sheriff's office. "If you ever think about maybe running for this job, let me know. Sure as shooting, anybody could do better than that man." He stopped by his office to get his coat and hat. "Let's go."

The Boyle house sat on a residential street that bordered the commercial part of town. Jess didn't bother telling the district attorney that he'd checked the place several times since arriving in town. To his disappointment, nothing had changed, except that the footprints on the porch had been covered or the wind had blown them away. He didn't really expect to find anything this time, but he couldn't keep himself from going back to the only place that might offer a clue to Addie's whereabouts.

Hector walked onto the porch and tried the front door. It was still locked. He checked the windows, which were also locked, and both men could see that the dust cloths over the furniture had not been disturbed.

"Let's check around back," Hector said, leading the way. He had passed by the doors that led to the root cellar and was on his way to check the security of the rear entrance when Jess stopped.

"Something's different," he said. It was a gut feeling more than anything obvious. As

362

many times as he'd walked this way, he'd not had this feeling. He looked around. Hector waited.

"It's the cellar door," Jess said, pointing to where the two oversized wooden doors met. "One side isn't shut all the way."

"Could have been kids fooling around trying to find a way in," Hector said as he knelt and tested the lock. He stood and dusted off his hands. "If somebody's down there, then how did the lock get closed?"

"I don't know, but I aim to find out." Before Hector could stop him, Jess pulled out his six-shooter and fired two shots at the lock. Then he holstered his gun, bent and freed the broken lock, and pulled one side of the double doors open.

Both men waited a beat. Both men stared into the blackness of the cellar.

"Got a match?" Jess asked as he started down the rickety wooden steps. In the dim light, he had spotted the stub of a candle. Hector passed him a match. He lit the candle and moved slowly around the cramped space.

"Did you find anything?" Hector called.

"Yeah. A bedroll, some empty cans, and whiskey bottles."

"But any sign of Miss Wilcox?"

"Not yet," Jess muttered. "Come on,

Addie," he said softly, speaking to himself. "I know if you were here, you were smart enough to let us know."

Something caught the light and his attention. He bent down for a closer look and found himself looking right at a pair of eyeglasses — Addie's glasses.

"She was here," he whispered, and then he repeated the words, shouting them to the district attorney. "She was here, Collins."

Addie kept count of the passing of time as best she could and fought to stay conscious whenever Buck was around. He had struck her twice, slapping her so hard across the face that she tasted blood. There seemed to be no reason for his sudden bouts of rage. He would drink and mutter to himself, all the while watching her as she huddled in the protection of the sacks filled with potatoes and onions. He always untied her whenever he returned from wherever he went. Sometimes he tossed her a can of beans and then giggled when she pointed out that she had no way of opening them.

"You get hungry enough, and you'll figure it out," he told her as he opened a fresh bottle of whiskey and took a long swig.

Later he would toss her his empty can of

beans, and she would scrape out the remains with her fingers. But hunger wasn't the worst of her problems. She'd had little to drink, making do with sucking the liquid from onions when Buck slept. She was getting weaker by the day. Three days in, she was alone in the cellar, tied and gagged, when she heard footsteps outside the door. She fought to make a noise — any noise — but it was impossible. Even her attempts to cry out were nothing more than whimpers muffled by the gag. Eventually, the footsteps went away.

When the person came back — the next day and the next — Addie began to plan how she might sweet-talk Buck into not tying her up when he left. And then the worst possible thing happened. Buck came back late one night and announced, "We're leaving. Now." He tossed her the shoes he had taken from her that first night. "Hurry up."

That was one of the times he slapped her. The hit came so suddenly and with such force that her glasses went flying. She scrambled to retrieve them, but before she could, Buck had hold of her arm and was dragging her up the four steps that led outside. She gulped in the fresh air, and at the same time, realized it was night. Glancing around, she saw no lights in the surrounding houses, heard no activity, and knew that her chances of raising a ruckus that would lead to her rescue would be a dangerous choice for anyone brave enough to come to her aid. Better to go along quietly, and see if she could figure out a way to escape. They were outside now, and that gave her more of an advantage.

"Get in," Buck ordered as he pushed her toward a wagon.

"Where are we going?"

"Well, now first off, we're gonna go over to Haversville to a justice of the peace there and get hitched proper and all. After that, we're heading back to the ranch that's half mine and taking what's ours. Git in."

She crawled aboard, aware that the inactivity, along with the lack of food and water, had left her barely able to move. Buck gave her a shove, and she fell forward. Buck was over her instantly, tying her to the back of the wagon seat. When he was satisfied that she was secure, he made half a dozen trips down to the cellar and back, hauling sacks of potatoes and onions and tossing them on top of her, until only her face was free.

Somewhere nearby, a horse whinnied. She turned to the sound. Buck pulled out his gun. "You make one sound, and that man is dead," he warned. "Your choice, girlie."

She closed her eyes and he chortled. "Good choice. Wouldn't want an innocent man's death on your conscience now, would you?"

He swung the cellar doors closed and climbed into the driver's seat, snapped the reins, and they were off. Addie was so exhausted she hadn't the strength to be frightened. Somehow, she had to find a way to escape — to get away from Buck.

To get back to Jess. If she could get out of this mess, forget waiting so she could have the wedding of her dreams. She was going to marry Jess Porterfield immediately. Amanda would not be happy, but this was Addie's life — and Jess's.

Jess didn't know what to do. Now that he was sure that Addie had been kidnapped — that she had been within a few feet of where he had walked those few days in Tucson — he felt helpless. But every time he looked at Addie's glasses, he was determined to find her and bring her home.

For the rest of that day, he and Collins continued to search for clues, to talk to anyone who may have had dealings with the kidnapper. Hector insisted they refer only to "the kidnapper" until a true identity had been made. Jess had no doubts the kidnapper was Buck, and because of that, he tried to think like Buck, as distasteful as that was for him.

Buck had lost everything. He was desperate, and judging by the number of empty bottles in that cellar, he was drowning that fear and desperation in liquor. Jess knew Buck well enough to know that he was a mean drunk. He shuddered when he imagined Buck striking Addie. The truth was that every time Jess thought about Buck, he wanted only to make him suffer the way he'd made Pearl suffer — and now, Addie.

Where would Buck take her?

Everyone Jess spoke to had no information that would help. He was on his way to meet Hector for breakfast, hoping the attorney had more success, when he ran into the blacksmith. He suddenly recalled selling a horse and wagon to a man matching Buck's description two days earlier.

"Said something about going home to collect on a debt," the blacksmith added.

"He's heading for the Tipton Ranch," Jess told Hector.

Hector had been in the middle of eating his breakfast, but he pulled the napkin from his shirtfront and laid a few coins on the table.

"No, you stay here," Jess said. "This is

something I need to handle on my own."

Hector hesitated, then nodded. "She's a fighter, Jess. She'll come out of this."

Jess nodded. "Thanks for your help."

Ten minutes later, Jess had paid his hotel bill — and Addie's — and headed out for the long ride back to Whitman Falls. It occurred to him that a man on horseback could make better time than someone driving a nag and pulling a wagon. He considered the various routes Buck might take. He'd want to stay away from the possibility of encountering others if he could, and with that in mind, he veered off the beaten trail and traveled cross country, weaving his way back and forth, always looking for some sign of a lone wagon or the smoke from a campfire.

For hours he rode one trail after another, circling the vast land looking for a wagon with no luck. As dawn broke he was close enough to his family's ranch to stop and let them know what had happened. If Buck was desperate enough to take Addie captive, no telling what else he might do. He would ask Chet Hunter to ride over to the fort and alert Colonel Ashwood.

His family was at breakfast when he arrived. Upon hearing the news, Maria gripped her husband's hand. Amanda burst into tears. Trey announced he was ready to join a search party and would get the other cowboys to come along as well. Jess's mother got up from her chair and held out her arms to Jess. The gesture was all he needed to realize how much anger and fear and helplessness he'd been struggling to control.

"If I hadn't been such a fool and left her last year, we'd be married by now, and this never would have happened."

"You can't know that, Son, and besides, holding onto regrets won't bring Addie back to us. Now sit down and eat something. You need your strength."

Juanita had already filled a plate for him and placed it at the head of the table. "Your ma's right," she said as she poured him a cup of coffee. *"Siéntense"* — she pointed to a seat at the table — "eat, and tell us everything you know."

It all helped — the food, recalling the details of the hunt for Addie, and most of all, being surrounded by family. How could he ever have been so stupid to think that he could find happiness without them? Addie had known. She'd tried to tell him, but he'd been too full of himself to listen.

"I got to go tell her folks what we know," he said, pushing the empty plate away and taking a last swallow of coffee. "And I should warn Jasper Tipton."

The women of the house surrounded him as they walked him to his horse. Trey begged to come with him, and it was Chet who suggested Trey could help by taking the news to the fort. "Maria and I can go break the news to Addie's family," Chet told Jess. "You head on over to the Tipton ranch. Everything seems to point to the idea that Buck might be headed for a showdown with his brother."

It was a good plan, and Jess was grateful for the help. He shook Chet's hand, then kissed his mother and sisters and mounted up, taking off cross-country for the Tipton place.

Jasper listened to Jess's report with glassy eyes that seemed to be focused on something else. "Do you hear me, Jasper? Buck's got Addie and —"

"He won't hurt her. He loves her."

"He hurt Pearl," Jess reminded him. He felt sorry for the man, but he had no patience or time for Jasper's optimism. "And he was willing to let Addie hang for it."

The mention of his late wife's name triggered something in Jasper. He looked directly at Jess for the first time since he'd arrived. "He murdered my wife in cold blood," he growled, then he shouted for his foreman and gave orders for all hands to be on the lookout for his brother. "He'll have a woman with him. Don't let harm come to her." Then he turned his attention back to Jess. "You got anybody watching the house in town?"

"My deputy's there," Jess replied, but the truth was that he hadn't thought Buck might take Addie to the mansion. Buck must know his brother would not be able to stand being there. The place would be deserted — a perfect hideout right under their noses.

"Lucas Jennings? He's a good man, but not all that bright. I doubt he would notice anything amiss."

"I'm headed back to town now. You'll send word if Buck shows up here?"

"You have no jurisdiction here, Marshal."

"True, but if your brother's got Addie . . ."

Jasper nodded, and then his eyes filled with tears. "If I had realized what he was capable of, I might have saved Pearl."

Jess had always hated both Tiptons, but now he saw something in the way Jasper grieved for his wife and child that made him feel a kinship to the man. He grasped Jasper's shoulder in a gesture of sympathy and was surprised when Jasper took hold of his hand and said, "If Buck's got Addie, then she's in the same danger. I'll be damned if I'll stand by and let my brother destroy another life. Tell me what you need — I can have a posse of my men . . ."

"Just stay here, and send word if Buck shows up. If you can't find me, then get word to somebody — her folks, my deputy . . ."

Jasper pointed to the telegraph in his office. "One of the advantages to being rich," he said. "I'll send wires to you, Colonel Ashwood over at Fort Lowell, and Hector Collins in Tucson."

"Thank you, Jasper. I know this must be hard for you. Buck is your only family and . . ."

"Buck stopped being family when he took my Pearl. I like Addie Wilcox and her folks," Jasper replied. "Right now, I like them a whole lot more than I care for that no-good brother of mine."

As he rode away, Jess realized that two men who had probably once thought they would never have anything in common now shared a bond that would make them allies.

By wriggling her body from side to side, Addie had managed to shift the weight of the potatoes so that they were not crushing her. At least they provided some warmth, and she was even able to doze a little.

When she woke she took stock of her injuries. One eye was swollen nearly shut, and she had a cut on her lip that had scabbed over. Her wrists and ankles bore the burns and bruises of the ropes used to hog-tie her. Her hair had come free of its pins and lay limp and lifeless over her shoulders. Every muscle in her body ached, and she was well aware that she was seriously dehydrated.

Buck continued to mutter to himself as the horse plodded along. The more time that passed, the angrier he sounded, and Addie debated whether staying silent was the best choice. Maybe she should talk to him, try to get him talking to her.

"Are we almost there, Buck?" She tried to keep her tone light and conversational, as if they were simply out for a buggy ride.

"Never you mind," he grumbled.

She waited and then tried a different tactic. "You must be so upset with your brother. I mean, after everything you've done for him. I know I would be — anyone would."

He didn't acknowledge her in any way, but spoke to the horse. "I was the one who handled everything — Joker, Porterfield, even Pearl. They were all problems Jasper couldn't see. They would bring us down."

Joker was a hand who had worked for Jess's family. He had mysteriously disappeared one night and turned up later at a neighboring ranch beaten half to death. Addie had been the one to treat him, but by the time she had been called in, it was too late, and the man had died.

Porterfield? That would be Jess's father. Was Buck actually admitting that he'd had a hand in the rancher's death?

"How could Pearl have been a threat?" she asked.

Buck snorted. "That harlot was after my brother's money. Somebody who looks like her has no other reason for being with somebody like my brother."

"So you . . ."

"I told her I was on to her. Told her she might be fooling Jasper, but to me she was just another dance hall whore." He chuckled. "I poked her good — night after night, I'd go to her room after Jasper was asleep."

"But then she got pregnant."

"That shoulda been the thing that made Jasper come to his senses, but no, she found a way to make him believe the kid was his. She thought she'd beat me then. Got all uppity, she did, and threatened to go to the marshal. Came at me like a mad dog."

"So you hit her?"

"I wanted to break her damn neck, but she tried to run, and she fell and hit her head."

Addie closed her eyes against the image of the fight he was describing. Pearl must have been so very terrified.

He laughed the maniacal laugh Addie had come to fear. "Thanks to you, I had those pills. I knew if I made it look like she killed herself, in time Jasper would come around, and it would be like it used to be. Jasper went all soft once he married Pearl. She was no good for him." He was silent for a while, then spit out a stream of chewing tobacco, wiped his lips with the back of his hand, and turned to face Addie. "Got plans for you too, girlie." He grinned and reached back so he could wrap his hand around her loosened hair. "Big plans," he added, and gave her hair a jerk. "You and me are going to make a hell of a team once we're properly hitched and I've reclaimed what's mine."

Addie gave up trying to keep him talking. Every word out his mouth made her sick with fear. She was beginning to see no way out of her situation. She was beginning to accept that she and Jess would never know the life they had planned. She was beginning to lose hope.

She felt hot tears streak through the dirt that covered her face. She let them come, treasuring them for the balm they were.

Every few hours, Jess made the walk from the jail to the Tipton mansion. Jasper had given him the key, so he didn't just walk the perimeter checking doors and windows. He entered the house, went into every room, and didn't leave until he was satisfied that no one had been there. Each time he visited the place, his heart sank. Maybe Jasper had been wrong. Maybe Buck wasn't coming back to Whitman Falls after all.

And then on the second night after his meeting with Jasper, he was standing outside the jail — wide awake as he tried to figure out where else Buck might go — when he thought he saw a light flicker in an upstairs window. At first he thought his eyes must be playing tricks on him. But there it was again — faint and moving. Now he saw it, and then he didn't. Someone was inside the mansion and moving from room to room.

His heart felt like a lead weight as he made his way to the house. The front door was locked tight, but when he went around to the back, the door was open — not just unlocked, but standing wide open. He stepped inside, his hand sliding slowly toward his holstered gun.

He moved through the kitchen and along one wall to the front hallway. He saw the light coming from upstairs and started toward it. When he reached the landing, he realized it was coming from Pearl's room. The door was partially open. The house was completely silent.

He edged toward the door, pulling out his six-shooter as he did. He nudged the door with the toe of his boot, and it swung all the way open.

Addie was propped up on the bed, her eyes closed, her hands tied to the bedpost above her head. Her face was battered and bruised, and she looked like a rag doll. With no thought for anything except freeing her, Jess holstered his gun and ran to her side. The bedroom door slammed, and he turned to see Buck sitting in a chair, his gun leveled at Addie.

"What have you done to her?" Jess demanded as he untied Addie and gathered her into his arms.

"Nothin'," Buck replied. "We come here, and she passed out. I guess she could be in need of some solid food, maybe some water. I tried to get her to drink my whiskey, but she's above all that. Like most women, she thinks she's too good for me. But she'll change her mind."

"What is it you want, Buck?"

"I want what's mine. I want you to tell my brother to give me my half of the business. I want you to tell that sister of yours to keep planning the wedding — oh yeah, I know all about that. Sorry to tell you there's been a little change in the wedding party. I'll be the groom."

"Over my dead . . ."

Buck leveled the gun straight at Addie. "Don't make me shoot her, Jess."

Addie moaned, and her grip tightened on Jess's arm. Her touch was like a warning. Jess swallowed his rage as he laid Addie back onto the pillows — the same pillows where they had found Pearl.

"I'll send for your brother," he said, "but first we have to get Addie some medical help. Her father . . ."

"No. She'll be fine."

"She's half dead. You say you love her — prove it."

Buck wavered. "She doesn't leave this room, and neither do I," he said.

"Fine. I'll send Doc over while I go to wire Jasper." He edged closer to the door, keeping hidden the side where his gun was strapped to his hip. Trying not to alert Buck, he eased the gun free, but Buck was bigger and faster. He struck Jess with the butt of his weapon, causing Jess to drop his gun. It went skittering across the floor.

"You do that, Jess. You git Doc over here and my brother. We can work this whole thing out as long as everybody does what I say."

"Do it," Addie said, her voice a weak, hoarse whisper. "Go, please."

Once again Addie was telling him to leave her. The last time that had happened, he knew she had believed he would refuse. He hadn't, and it had been the biggest mistake of his life. He wasn't about to make that mistake again.

"Don't make me kill her, Jess," Buck repeated. "I'll snap her pretty little neck the same way I would have with my brother's whore, only this time it will be your fault for driving me to it."

"Just tell me one thing, Buck, since I know you plan to kill me before this is all over — did you and your brother kill my father?"

Buck grabbed Jess's shirtfront and pulled him close. "Not my brother. Why does everybody think he's the smart one? I did it all. If it hadn't been for me, we wouldn't have half the land we have now. It was me who drove the Buchanans and Kellers back east. It was me who took care of that yellow-livered rat, Joker, and yes, Jess Porterfield, it was me who made your precious daddy understand that he was nothing compared to my brother and me."

Every muscle in Jess's body tensed as he ignored the spittle Buck's words had left on his face. *I'll kill this man if it's the last thing I do,* his mind screamed. But then he looked past Buck to where Addie was watching him from the bed.

Don't, she mouthed, her whole body straining against her bonds to reach him — to stop him.

Jess forced himself to relax, then pulled free of Buck's hold. He backed out of the room, keeping his sights on Addie, moving toward the stairs. As he expected, Buck followed him to be sure he left.

They reached the top of the grand staircase, the one that was plainly visible from the street whenever the doors to the house were open. He saw his chance when Buck seemed inclined to follow him all the way downstairs. He charged at Buck. They wrestled for control of the gun, coming closer and closer to the stairway.

As Buck found his balance, he grasped Jess by the throat and raised the barrel of the gun. Jess hooked his foot between Buck's legs and jerked, startling Buck and sending the larger man toppling head over heels to the foyer below them. The gun went off, and Jess heard Addie scream. Below him he saw Buck writhing in pain from the fall and self-inflicted gunshot.

Breathing hard, Jess ran down the stairs and kicked the gun away. He pulled handcuffs from his back pocket and clamped them onto the injured man. Once he was sure Buck wasn't going anywhere, and that the blood from the gunshot was coming from his thigh, Jess ran back to the bedroom, freed Addie from the ropes, and held her close.

"It's over," he whispered.

"I thought the shot . . . I thought . . ." She was incoherent with terror.

At the same time he heard footsteps and voices. Someone banged on the front door. "Go," Addie urged.

Jess ran down the stairs, stepped over Buck's moaning body, and unlocked the front door. Lucas, Eliza McNew, and Addie's parents pushed their way inside.

"Papa," Addie called. She had made her way to the hallway outside Pearl's bedroom. She took one more step and then slumped to the floor.

It was a foot race between Jess and Doc to be the first to reach her. Jess won, scooping her up in his arms and carrying her back to the bed.

"I'll take it from here, son," Doc said. "Alice," he called, "we're going to need some water and my medical bag." When Jess seemed inclined to hover, Doc looked at him. "I believe you have an arrest to make, Marshal Porterfield."

"Luc can . . ."

Doc placed a comforting hand on Jess's shoulder. "She'll be fine, Jess. Go do your duty. Lock the prisoner up, and then come back."

Jess nodded, but as he started for the door, the blast of a shotgun reverberated throughout the house. Jess ran to the bannister in time to see Addie's mother drop the pitcher of water she was carrying. Lucas stood protectively in front of Eliza, and Jasper Tipton was standing over his brother — a shotgun in his hands.

After a moment, he dropped the gun next to Buck's lifeless body, turned, and walked out the door. By the time Jess reached the porch, Jasper Tipton had crossed the street and was entering the jail.

"Luc, help Doc deal with this," Jess said, turning back to indicate the bloody mess at the foot of the stairs. When he entered the jail, Jasper was seated on the cot in one of the two cells, his hands dangling between his knees, his head bent. As Jess approached the broken man, he realized that the spots of water on the floor were tears — Jasper Tipton was weeping.

The healing power of water and rest never ceased to amaze Addie. With each passing hour, she felt her strength returning — and along with it, her curiosity. What had happened? Where was Buck?

Her mother kept saying, "In all the excitement, you fainted. It's all over now, and you needn't worry. What you need is to rest, not be asking questions. That Tipton boy cannot ever hurt you again."

"And Jess?"

"He's been here, honey. Wouldn't hardly leave your side. He had to take a prisoner over to Tucson."

"Buck?"

Her mother ignored her question. She fluffed the pillows. Addie was back in her own room. She thought of Pearl's ornate bedroom, the place where Buck had taken her once they left the cellar in Tucson. That room had been filled with Pearl — her clothes, her crystal bottles filled with colognes, a silver-framed photograph of Jasper, and the silk-covered pillows piled on the bed.

"Buck was the one who murdered Pearl," she said.

"We know that, honey. It's all over now. Get some rest. I'm going to make you some soup for your supper. Amanda Porterfield is in town. Would you be up to a visit?"

"Oh, yes, please have her come by." Amanda would give her the details of everything that had happened — details others seemed determined to protect her from knowing.

And as Addie had hoped, when Amanda arrived, she relayed the sordid details of how Jess had apparently tripped Buck and made him fall down the stairs, and of how Jasper had simply walked through the open front door, shot his brother, and then marched himself off to jail. "What I really want to know is who is that?" Amanda was sitting on the side of Addie's bed and pointing to a man standing just outside the bank.

The man was tall and slim with broad shoulders. He was dressed all in black — trousers, boots, hat, even his shirt and the gun belt that sat low on his narrow hips. He was leaning against a post, one ankle crossed over the other, and his arms were folded across his chest.

"I have no idea." Addie thought of the day Miss Lillian had interrupted them at the jail — something about a stranger in town who looked to her like a man on a wanted poster. "Have you seen Jess?"

Amanda did not take her eyes off the stranger. "Jess? He took Jasper to Tucson. He said he'd be back by sundown. He looks dangerous, don't you think?"

"Jess?"

"Not Jess — him." She pointed toward the man on the street. "Lucas Jennings told Eliza that there had been word of a gunslinger headed this way. Do you think that might be him?"

Addie laughed, and it felt so good. She realized it had been over a week since she'd felt like laughing at anything. "Oh, Amanda, what if he is?"

"Well, he might not be. I mean, maybe he's just new in town and sort of sizing things up, trying to decide if this might be a good place to settle or not." She primped her hair and pinched her cheeks to bring out the color.

"Amanda Porterfield, tell me you aren't thinking about approaching a total stranger — a total *male* stranger."

"Maybe he'd like to meet some people.

Maybe he'd like to come to your wedding."

Addie understood that it would be useless to try to deter Amanda from the fantasy she was building. She was also well aware that her friend was trying very hard to talk about anything but the last horrible weeks. "And if he agreed, who would he dance with?"

"Me, of course." She knelt on the floor next to the window and rested her chin on her hands, her elbows on the sill. "Oh, Addie, do you know how few eligible men there are in this town? And by eligible, I mean men I would look at twice."

"Seems to me when Chet Hunter came to the ranch, you had similar notions."

"I did, but Chet never saw anybody but Maria. I mean it was as if those two had been struck by lightning or something. The connection was so intense." She turned her attention away from the window and grinned. "Of course, you would know all about that. After all, you and Jess have been fireworks and dynamite from the time you were both ten." She plopped herself back onto the side of the bed. "Now then, getting back to your wedding . . ."

For the remainder of the afternoon Amanda filled Addie's mind with visions of how beautiful her wedding was going to be. Apparently, she had gone above and beyond planning the event itself, down to choosing the perfect gown — or rather, gowns. "Millie Jennings is whipping up a few ideas," she said, as if making one dress, much less several, were that simple. "Whatever doesn't suit, Eliza says she can sell in the store."

"Oh, Amanda, there's no need to go to so much trouble. After all, this is Jess and me. Something simple will be fine."

"Nonsense. The one time in your life that you get to be the belle of the ball, you ought to look like the belle of the ball and . . ." She peered out the window again. "He's going into the mercantile," she whispered. She kissed Addie's temple and fled. "I'll be back tomorrow," she called. "Bye, Miz Wilcox." And she was gone.

Addie watched as her friend hurried across the street and then deliberately slowed her step before opening the door to the mercantile and disappearing in side. She smiled and shook her head. Then she frowned. What if the man *was* a gunslinger? An outlaw? She shuddered as she recalled how Buck had mistreated her — how little he cared if she suffered or not. The last thing she wanted was to see Amanda get caught up in a situation that she couldn't handle.

Addie decided she would speak to Jess

about the man. Jess could find out more about him — and warn his sister to keep her distance. Of course, telling Amanda to do anything that went against what she wanted was a surefire way to have her do exactly as she pleased. Addie sighed and turned her attention away from the window . . . and gasped with surprise.

Jess was standing in the doorway watching her. The way he looked at her made her heart beat faster. It was as if he was touching her everywhere with his eyes, assuring himself that she was there — that she was his.

After turning Jasper over to the sheriff and district attorney in Tucson, Jess had wasted no time getting back to Whitman Falls. He had taken every cross-country shortcut he could and stopped only twice to give his horse water. Ever since Addie had disappeared, he had wanted only one thing — to be with her every minute of every day. Of course, he understood that couldn't be, but he intended to make sure he knew where she was and who she was with when he couldn't be around.

When he reached town, he slid from the saddle, leaving the horse standing outside the Wilcox house. "She awake?" he asked

Doc as he entered the office.

"Last I checked. Your sister was here for a good long visit. Seemed to cheer Addie up some. I heard her laughing."

Jess walked through the kitchen, nodded to Addie's mom, and then took the steps two at a time. When he reached the door to Addie's room, she was gazing out the window. She was waif thin, like some of the street children he'd seen in Kansas City. When he'd last seen her, she'd been sleeping and so pale. Now she was wide awake, sitting up in bed, her color heightened by the light of a setting sun.

And when she turned and saw him, she brought that sun with her. She smiled.

"You're back," she said, and the way she said it made it sound like she'd been waiting all day just for this moment.

"Can't seem to get rid of me, can you?" He set his hat on the dresser and went to her.

She patted the bed and scooted to one side to give him room.

"I'm covered in grit," he warned.

"I don't care," she replied, and held her arms open to him.

Holding Addie and being held in return was like coming home, and he understood that this was what he'd been searching for his whole life — a place to belong and someone he belonged with through the good and the bad.

"We're going to have a good life, Addie. I promise you that."

"Our life will be what comes," she said, always one to look at the practical side of any discussion. "But we'll make it through whatever that is, just like we made it through this."

They held each other for a long moment, and then Jess chuckled. "I'm not so sure I'm going to make it through this wedding Amanda has planned. Last I heard, she wants a carriage draped in flowers to bring us to and from the chapel."

"Amanda's plans for the wedding may be the least of your worries when it comes to your sister."

Jess sat up. "What do you mean?"

"Your sister has noticed a tall, good-looking stranger in town. She thinks he looks dangerous, and apparently to her way of thinking that's an attractive feature."

Jess knew exactly who Addie was talking about. The stranger had ridden into town a couple of days earlier. Miss Lillian had some concerns about the man when he came to her saloon, ordered a rye and soda, and sat down to play cards with some of the regulars. When Gus Abersole had accused the man of cheating and started to pull a gun on him, the stranger had outdrawn him, thrown the money he'd won back on the table, and left.

"Fastest man with a gun Miss Lillian ever saw, from what she said," he told Addie.

"He shot Gus?" Addie's eyes had gone wide with shock.

"No. Just outdrew him. Rumor has it he's on the run. I told Luc to keep an eye on him, but so far he's caused no trouble."

"And Amanda?"

Jess sighed. "I'll talk to Ma about that — or better yet, Juanita. Sometimes I think Amanda is more afraid of our housekeeper than she ever was of our parents. At least she's at the ranch and not staying here in town."

"Well, now, that could be a problem," Addie admitted. "You see, I thought it might be easier for her to stay here until the wedding — save all that running back and forth."

Jess frowned.

"Don't worry," Addie urged. "I'll keep her so busy with plans for the service and the party to follow, she won't have time to even think about that cowboy. And hopefully, he'll be moving on soon anyway."

"That won't be a problem. I'll see to it that he moves on," Jess assured her. He kissed her — then kissed her again. If he lived to be a hundred, he was pretty sure he would never get over the thrill he felt every time he kissed Addie Wilcox.

FOURTEEN

"Adeline, you have a visitor." Her father stood in the doorway of her bedroom the following day. He had a mischievous twinkle in his eye. He stepped aside to allow a small, gray-haired man to enter the room.

"Miss Wilcox, I am Dr. Howard Boyle of Tucson. I understand you came to call on me while I was out of town."

"I'm afraid I was hoodwinked, Dr. Boyle. I must apologize for . . ."

Boyle waved away her apology. "It seems to me, young lady, that it is I who have been remiss. You have become something of a luminary in our community. There are many who have sung your praises to me. This business of reforms for more sanitary and humane conditions in the jail is quite the talk of the town."

Addie blushed. Her father beamed with pride. "Dr. Boyle has a proposition to offer you," he prompted.

"Yes, well, it is my understanding that you have been unable to secure a formal medical education in spite of your proven skills and knowledge."

"Yes, sir."

"My own medical degree was achieved in Chicago, where several years ago my dear friend Mary Thompson — a woman much like you — grew tired of the discrimination against women in the medical field and opened the Women's Hospital Medical College. With your permission, I should like to contact her and encourage her to accept you as a student in her college."

It was a dream come true — and it could not have come at a worse time.

"I . . ." She looked at her father's proud smile. He wanted this for her. It was as much his dream as it was hers. "I am to be married and . . ." Her father's smile turned to a frown.

"Surely Jess would understand that this is an opportunity not to be missed, Adeline."

She thought of how little she — or her father — had understood Jess's dream of new opportunities beyond the ranch and Whitman Falls. "That is not the point."

Dr. Boyle was looking distinctly uncomfortable. "Perhaps I should wait downstairs," he said, and turned to leave.

"No, please," Addie pleaded. "I want you to know what an honor this is for me. That you would intervene on my behalf is overwhelming. Please understand that I need some time to consider your kind offer — and discuss it with my intended."

Dr. Boyle smiled. "You may take as long as you like, my dear. I can see that you have been through a traumatic time. Your friends in Tucson will be glad to know that you have recovered so quickly, and so well. When you have made your decision, you know where to reach me. Until then . . ." He offered her a handshake, and she accepted.

"Thank you, Dr. Boyle — for everything," she said.

"A remarkable young woman," Addie heard him murmur as her father escorted him back downstairs.

Her mind was racing. It was as if she and Jess had come full circle. Once he had asked her to leave everything she cared about and everyone she loved to follow him. Now was it her turn to ask the same of him? And what if he refused, as she was almost certain he would — almost certain he should.

After all, Jess had redeemed himself in the eyes of the people of Whitman Falls. He had proven himself up to the job of lawman. People had come to trust him and rely on him. In his role as tax collector, he had worked out payment plans with those in arrears, allowing them to keep their property — and their dignity. A couple of times he had taken some youngsters bent on mischief in hand and gotten them back on the right path, to their parents' delight. His relationship with his sister Maria and her husband Chet had taken on the trappings of friendship, as well as family, and his devotion to his mother was a thing to behold.

No, Jess was no longer looking to leave Whitman Falls. This was his home, and he had made his place in it. And the truth of the matter was that Addie could practice medicine — as her father had — without benefit of a degree. No one who'd seen her work would question her skills. Already, folks simply assumed that there would always be a "Doc Wilcox" in Whitman Falls.

But an actual degree . . .

She imagined the parchment paper framed and hung on the wall in her father's office. She closed her eyes and could see herself attending classes with other women, working out experiments in a real laboratory, spending hours in the library poring over texts and articles and manuals that were not part of her father's collection. She envisioned herself making rounds with practicing physicians in a Chicago hospital, where patients would be housed in wards or even in private rooms — not in some dark and dust-covered cabin.

The question was, of course, whether or not she could make Jess imagine what she did.

Jess waited a day to cross paths with the stranger. It wasn't especially difficult to find the man. Whitman Falls was a small town, and pretty much anything that went on there, somebody was watching. So Jess followed the trail from Eliza's mercantile, over to the bank, and on to the barbershop, where he found the man enjoying one of Stan Barker's shaves.

"Marshal," Stan murmured when Jess entered the shop.

"Stan," Jess replied, but kept his eyes on the stranger, who had immediately focused on him. He approached the man and offered a handshake. "I'm Marshal Jess Porterfield."

"Is this about that business at the saloon?" It did not escape Jess's attention that the man had ignored his outstretched hand and failed to provide his name.

"Maybe. What do you say you and me have a talk about that once you and Stan finish up here?"

"No time like the present." He reached up and took the hot towel Stan was preparing to wrap around his face and wiped his hands on it. He got to his feet, and Jess realized the man was an inch taller than he was, his legs long and lanky. He also noticed the glint of the gun he wore, the handle a pearly black that caught the light. He flipped a coin to Stan. "I'll stop by later to finish up, if that suits."

"Yes, sir," Stan said. "I'll be right here."

He plucked his hat from a nail by the door and held the door open for Jess. "Lead the way, Marshal."

"I didn't get your name," Jess said as they crossed the street on their way to his office.

"Could be because I didn't give it."

"We're a right friendly town — people like to know who they're dealing with."

"Fair enough. Name's Grover."

"First or last?"

"Seth Grover."

Jess had heard that name. He combed through his memory, picturing wanted posters that had crossed his desk in the months since he'd taken the marshal's job.

They had reached his office, and Jess indicated the lone chair other than his. "Have a seat." He walked to the back entrance and shut the door. The cells were empty. They were alone.

"I hear you're pretty quick on the draw," Jess said as he took his place behind the desk.

Grover shrugged. "Good thing nobody got hurt."

"But if Gus had managed to . . ."

"The man was drunk and spoiling for a fight. He was a sore loser who shouldn't have been playing cards in the first place, not in his condition. If anything, it was his so-called friends who were taking advantage of him."

"So you did your good deed and pulled your gun on them."

"Nobody got hurt, and I left the money on the table." He studied Jess from under the brim of his black Stetson for a long moment. "What's this really about, Marshal?"

Jess was about to say, "It's about my sister," but then he realized just how ridiculous that was. This man didn't even know Amanda. He took a different tack. "Seth Grover — where do I know that name from?"

Again, the almost imperceptible shrug.

"Are you running from something, Grover?"

"Never met a man who wasn't," he replied.

Jess decided he'd had enough. He pushed back his chair and placed his hands on the desk, leaning closer to make his point. "Well, I suggest you keep on running then. We got no place in this town for trouble, and you, sir, have got trouble written all over you."

The man grinned but did not stand up. "What if I were to tell you I've got no reason to be leaving your little town?"

"Look, mister, I've got no time for riddles and games. Now, I'm asking you nice to keep moving on."

"And what if I told you I plan on staying?"

"Then we'd have ourselves a problem," Jess replied, although for the life of him he couldn't think how he might force the man to leave town. "Gus Abersole was mighty upset. He could file charges," Jess bluffed.

To his surprise, the man laughed — a short bark of a sound that held no mirth. "Look, Marshal Porterfield, I'll make you a deal. As soon as I've completed my business here, I'll ride on. Until then, unless you trump up some charge against me, you've got no call to insist on my leaving. The truth is that I need a place where I can stay put for a while. This little town is just about perfect."

"Stay put or hide out?"

"A little of both, I guess. I can't say why, but I'm asking you to trust me."

Jess laughed. "You expect me to believe . . ." Suddenly, he knew why the name was familiar. A wanted poster that showed a man named Sam Grover, a notice Miss Lillian had shown him. The man — more of a kid really — was suspected to be part of a gang of bank robbers and horse thieves.

The stranger must have seen the light dawn. "Sam's my younger brother," he said. "I'd like to find him before he gets himself killed, and I figure maybe the best way to do that is to pretend to have gone down the same trail he took. You've got a kid brother, don't you, Marshal?"

Jess stared at the stranger. He didn't like the fact that the man seemed to know about Trey. "My family is none of your business."

"That wasn't a threat. Just thought you might have a better understanding of where I'm coming from. Sammy is my only brother."

"You're going to bring this town trouble, aren't you?"

"Not if I can help it. Word has it that Sam was last seen around these parts. I believe he's gone into hiding, and the gang he's with is behind the string of stage holdups Wells Fargo has had over the last few months. Sooner or later, they're bound to move on to banks, and the one here in Whitman Falls is ripe for taking."

"And then?"

"If I can find Sammy and join his gang, chances are I can give you fair warning of when the gang plans to pull the job. That way you can arrest him and the others without anybody getting hurt in the bargain." He actually winked at Jess. "Could be quite a feather in your cap. Word around town is you might decide to run for district sheriff."

It also could be the most exciting part of his job as marshal. Now that the Tipton brothers were no longer going to be a problem, Jess realized he was facing months — even years — of breaking up fights at the saloon, collecting taxes, and locking up the local drunks.

"I'll give you some time on one condition," Jess said.

"Name it."

"Stay away from my sister."

This time Grover's laugh was genuine. "Marshal, I don't even know your sister, so we have a deal."

The two men shook hands. Jess could hardly wait to tell Addie the news.

Tired of being cooped up in her room, Addie made her way downstairs and out to the porch. She was stiff and sore, but all of that was temporary. By the time her wedding day came, she intended to be fully capable of walking down the aisle without a limp and dancing the night away with Jess. The image made her smile, and she kicked the porch swing into motion and waited for Jess to come by for his evening visit. But her smile wavered as she realized she was going to have to tell him about Dr. Boyle's offer.

She had tried to consider the matter from every possible angle. They could marry and make the move to Chicago. Her studies at the medical college would take at least a year, maybe more. But then they could return to Arizona. But what would Jess do in the meantime? She couldn't imagine that there was a lot of work for cowboys or town marshals in a city like Chicago.

There was another option — one she did not want to consider. They could postpone the wedding until she had completed her degree. But they had already wasted so much time, and that business with Buck had taught her a valuable lesson about the fragility of life.

"Very well," she murmured to herself. "The fact is that you want to spend the rest of your life with Jess — that is indisputable. But can you make Jess happy, if you are pining for something he can't give you?"

"Addie!"

She looked up and saw Jess running toward her, a huge grin on his face. "Addie, wait 'til I tell you!"

She hurried forward to receive his hug, and he swung her 'round and 'round until they were both laughing and breathless. "What?" she asked as they collapsed onto the swing.

She could barely take in what he was telling her — something about the stranger and his outlaw brother who was likely to rob the bank and how the stranger wanted Jess to help prevent it so the brother didn't get himself killed.

"And he promised to stay away from Amanda," he said, as if that ridiculous detail had sealed the bargain. "The thing is, we can't tell anybody about this, or the whole scheme goes haywire." He hugged her. "Oh, Addie, this is going to be the making of me — of us. If I can bring down a known gang of outlaws, think what that might mean for our future."

"I don't understand." But she did understand the excitement she saw in Jess's eyes. It was exactly the same look he'd had that night he had begged her to run away with him to the city. He wanted this, probably as much as she wanted that medical degree. "It sounds dangerous," she added.

Jess blinked and sat back a little so he could see her more clearly in the fading light. "Well, yeah, I guess you could say that. But I thought you were all right with the idea of me maybe one day running for district sheriff, even if that meant us moving to Tucson."

It was true. They had discussed the possibility. But all of that had been in the future. The opportunity for her to get her degree was imminent — and apparently, so was this business with the stranger.

"Say something, Addie."

She swallowed and grasped his hands in hers, just as her father stepped onto the porch.

"Did you tell Jess the good news?" Her father could hardly contain his pride, and Addie realized again how important this degree was to him.

"What news?" Jess asked, glancing from Addie to her father and back again.

"Your bride-to-be has the unique opportunity to become the first female doctor in the territory," her father said.

Jess looked at Addie. "I thought you already were."

"Oh, did I forget to say, she would be the first with a medical degree — a real degree from a medical college?" With each word out of her father's mouth, Addie felt the tension between Jess and her tighten.

"Addie?" Jess distanced himself a few inches from her.

She could feel him pulling away, feel the slackening of his grip on her hands.

"Papa, Jess and I need to talk," she said quietly, never taking her eyes off Jess or allowing him to fully break contact.

Her father cleared his throat. "I'll be inside," he said as he stepped back in the house and closed the door.

"What's going on, Addie?" His voice was shaking.

"I had a visitor earlier today — Dr. Boyle from Tucson."

"Go on."

As succinctly as possible, she relayed the details of the visit. She tried to keep her voice from displaying the excitement she had felt at his offer — the excitement that had now turned to fear for what it might mean for her future with Jess. Once she finished, Jess was very quiet for several minutes. She waited.

"You want this, don't you?"

"It's something I've often dreamed of achieving," she admitted.

"Like when I wanted to take off for the city?"

"Something like that. I certainly have a better understanding of what you must have gone through then, and I'm sorry that . . ."

"This is different," he interrupted, brushing aside her apology. "This is a big opportunity for you."

"It's a piece of paper, Jess."

"One that represents something special — like a wedding license or a birth certificate."

"I won't do anything you are against," she said firmly, realizing she meant it. "What we have together must always come first."

"Doc wants this for you."

"Yes, but —"

"You'd be a real doctor, Addie. Isn't that what you've always wanted?"

She didn't like the way this was going. Shouldn't she be the one arguing for her future? "I thought it was, but then there was that whole business with Buck, and what if things hadn't turned out the way they did? What if I had . . . ?" She choked on the thought, but finished the question anyway. "What if I had died, or you had been killed? What if . . . ?"

Jess pulled her back into his embrace as he settled them both more firmly in the swing. "We're here, Addie, safe and sound, the both of us."

"I want you to be happy," she whispered. "That's truly what I've always wanted. Even when it seemed you might be happier without me, I still wanted that for you. And now you have this chance to really prove yourself as a lawman and —"

"Shush. There are two things I know for sure. One, we are not postponing the wedding, and two, we're not going to decide how to work out the rest of this tonight."

"But . . ."

Jess released a sigh of pure exasperation. "Woman, there seems to be only one way I know to shut you up." He kissed her, and suddenly nothing seemed more important than being in this moment, in this man's arms.

The truth was that Jess wanted this degree for Addie almost as much as she and her father wanted it. If she could have an actual degree hanging in the office at the little house he'd bought, that would be like icing on a cake.

But her getting that piece of paper — that was the problem. Jess didn't want to wait a day longer to marry Addie. He could go to Chicago with her, but how would they pay the bills? And his wanting to stay in town and be part of this business with Seth Grover was more than him being selfish. It was also about making sure nobody got hurt, keeping his friends and neighbors safe. It was doing his job.

There had to be another way.

He needed more information, so when he saw Doc Wilcox heading out on a call, he followed him. Just outside of town, he pulled alongside the buggy. "Mornin' Doc."

"Mornin'." Doc kept his eyes on the trail ahead.

"I'm not wanting to keep Addie from getting her paper."

"That's good. Problem is, she told her mother and me last night there's no way she's postponing the wedding, so where does that leave you two?"

"I guess that has us getting hitched and figuring things out from there."

"This offer from Chicago won't be there forever."

"I understand," Jess said, "but I've been thinking. Addie's had a lot of experience working alongside you. She's delivered a baby and tended to the dying and all that. And she's always got her nose stuck in some book."

Doc squinted up at him. "What's your point?"

"I was just wondering if maybe the folks in Chicago knew all that, they might make some allowances."

He could see Doc chewing on the idea. "She'd likely still have to go up there."

"But maybe not for the whole time. What if Dr. Boyle could maybe test her and let his friend know she could handle the job? That pharmacist she's been working with on the jail reforms and Judge Ellis might write letters on her behalf. Maybe . . ."

He stopped talking as Doc pulled the buggy to a halt. "And if none of that works?" he asked.

"Then I guess you're going to need a new town marshal because me and Addie would leave for Chicago right after the wedding."

"You'd do that for her, even though you would probably not be able to find work that came close to what you've been doing here?"

"I love your daughter, sir. There were two times when I almost lost whatever chance I had to spend my life with her. I don't intend

411

to test those waters a third time."

Doc grinned. "Let me do some checking around and see what we can make happen, son. In the meantime, let's keep this between you and me for now — no reason to raise false hope."

It was the second time in twenty-four hours that another man had asked Jess to keep a secret. The truth was, it felt good, like other men saw him as somebody to be trusted. "If it's all the same to you, sir — since Addie is going to be my wife and all — I'd like to take care of this myself."

"You'll talk to Dr. Boyle and the others?"

Jess could see that Doc had his doubts.

"Yes, sir. I'll keep you informed," he promised, and turned his horse toward the road to Tucson.

FIFTEEN

Their wedding day dawned cold and blustery, but Addie refused to take that as a bad sign. "It's like our relationship," she said when Amanda bemoaned the weather. "Stormy, unsettled, but in the end, everybody knows the sun will come out."

The ceremony was to take place in the chapel down the street, with a reception to follow at the Wilcox house. At Addie's insistence, it was to be a small gathering — close friends and family. "I won't have people riding for hours just to see Jess and me finally get hitched," she had told her mother.

"But your father's patients — your patients . . ."

"They will feel obligated to come and think they need to bring a gift as well. These are people who are struggling, Ma. I will not add to that burden. Jess and I will visit everyone in spring, once we're settled in a place of our own."

The truth was that she worried about exactly where she and Jess might live. There was a small rundown house just outside of town that could be perfect, but somebody had been working on painting and fixing it up for weeks now, so Addie was pretty sure it was no longer available. Jess refused to talk about where they might live, teasing her that he thought they could always bunk in his room at the jail. He also had said nothing about a wedding trip. Of course, Addie was well aware that money was tight, but maybe a night at the hotel in Tucson might not be completely unrealistic.

"Your problem is that you want to manage everything," Amanda said as she helped Addie dress for the ceremony.

"You're one to talk," Addie replied.

Amanda put the finishing touches on Addie's hair. "Okay, look at yourself, Addie Wilcox soon-to-be Porterfield."

Addie put on her glasses and turned to the mirror — and gasped. She looked so . . . pretty. Her hair was done up in a series of intertwined braids twisted to form a bun at the nape of her neck. The veil to her wedding dress was the one her mother had worn, and its lace edging framed her face. The high neckline of her dress and the straight satin skirt made her look tall and regal.

"Oh, Amanda, thank you," she whispered.

"I have to admit, when that brother of mine sees you coming down the aisle, he is going to either faint dead away, or come running to scoop you up and carry you the rest of the way to the altar."

Jess did neither. Instead he stood perfectly still and watched her coming toward him. His eyes locked in on hers, and when her father placed her hands in Jess's, the two held on tight and grinned like kids at their first party.

We are going to be so happy, Jess Porterfield, Addie thought and knew Jess had the same idea when he nodded and turned with her to face the priest.

As Jess's mother and Addie's father draped their children with their lazo, Addie closed her eyes. Her dreams were coming true, every last one. She felt as if she were floating through time as she and Jess repeated their vows, and he placed a thin silver wedding band on her finger. And all too soon it seemed the priest offered his blessing and pronounced them man and wife.

To Addie's delight and surprise, those attending the ceremony broke into applause and shouts of good wishes, as they walked back up the aisle and out into what had become a cold February day with a clear blue sky and no wind. They rode in a carriage the short distance from the church to the Wilcox home.

"Hello, Mrs. Porterfield," Jess said with a shy smile.

"Hello, husband," Addie replied, and then the two shared a kiss that left them both wanting more just as Trey stopped the carriage in front of the house.

In minutes, they were surrounded by friends and family, and were holding hands as they accepted the congratulations and good wishes of each guest. Amanda brought them each a plate piled high with food. "You have to cut the cake," she said, as if the food were necessary to fortify them for that gargantuan task.

"We have to get out of here," Jess muttered.

Addie laughed. "We can't just leave, Jess. We're the guests of honor."

"I know, but have you looked in a mirror today? You are so beautiful, Addie. All I want is to be alone with you." He smiled and shook hands with the next guest in line.

Addie thought of the beautiful lace nightgown that Eliza McNew had given her as a wedding present. "Or shall I say wedding-night present?" The shopkeeper had giggled, and Addie had blushed. The gown was made of thin cotton that revealed far too much, even if it did cover her from her chin to her toes.

"You're blushing, Mrs. Porterfield," Jess whispered.

"It's warm in here. All these people."

"My point exactly. Let's leave."

"We have to cut the cake."

Jess took hold of her hand and pulled her across the room to where the cake rested on a glass pedestal plate. As he threaded his way through the guests, he made apologies, but did not stop to visit. Once they were positioned next to the cake, he put his fingers between his lips and released a piercing whistle.

"Friends," he shouted when the room went silent and every eye was on him. "Mrs. Porterfield and I would love to spend the evening with you."

Hoots of disbelief interrupted his speech, until Jess grinned and held up his hands. "However," he continued, "I have a very special wedding gift for my bride, and it's a little too large to fit in this room. So, let's all have cake, and then we'll be heading out — alone."

More hoots and hollers as everyone gathered close, and Addie cut the first piece of cake and fed it to Jess. His mouth was ringed in frosting. "Want some?" he asked, as he caught a bit that had fallen onto his shirt.

"Yep," she replied and stood on tiptoe to kiss him — frosting and all.

"Good cake, Nita," Jess announced before taking Addie's hand again and leading her to the front door. "Thanks everybody," he called. He gave his mother and Addie's mother a kiss, shook hands with Doc, and then scooped Addie up in his arms and left the house.

"Put me down, Jess," Addie demanded, as he strode across Main Street and on past the mercantile and the barbershop and the bank, then turned down a narrow street.

"Not until I get you home, Wife."

Addie stopped fighting him and turned to see where they were going, and when she saw that the only place they could be headed was the little rundown house someone had been fixing up, she gasped. "Oh, Jess, really?"

"Welcome home, Addie," he said softly as he pushed open the front door, carried her through the open doorway — the threshold freshly painted in turquoise to ward off evil spirits — and set her down.

"Do you like it?" he asked, suddenly seeming to doubt himself.

"I love it," she assured him. "Think about it, Jess. Think about all the memories we're going to make here. It's perfect. Thank you."

Addie walked slowly from room to room, taking in every detail, but when she came to the room Jess told her would be her office, she was puzzled. An empty picture frame hung above the rolltop desk.

"It's for your medical degree," Jess said, coming alongside her and placing his arms around her shoulders, as he rested his chin on the top of her head. "The one you'll bring home with you from the trip we're going to take to Chicago."

"Oh, Jess, it isn't that easy. I have to take classes and pass examinations and — well, it will take months. Maybe after we've been married awhile," she assured him, "but right now, all I want is to be here with you in this wonderful home you've made for us."

Jess turned her so they were facing each other. "Well now, you see, that could be a problem because I went over to Tucson last week and had a talk with Dr. Boyle. Then he wired his friend at that medical school in Chicago and, well, things are pretty much all set."

Addie bristled. This was just like Jess to

take over and not consult her. "All set for what?"

He reached in his pocket and held up two tickets. "We leave tomorrow for Chicago. Next week Dr. Boyle's friend is going to meet with you, test you and, assuming she's satisfied you already know what she teaches women in that school of hers, present you with your medical degree." He picked up two envelopes that Addie hadn't even noticed lying on the desk. "It will probably help that we've got these letters of recommendation from the good doctor and Judge Ellis. The way I see it, we'll be back home here in about ten days — maybe two weeks, if we decide to stay awhile and see the sights — and you will be officially Dr. Adeline Wilcox Porterfield."

For once in her life, Addie was speechless. She opened and closed her mouth, but no words came out. She looked from the tickets he held to the letters of recommendation to the empty picture frame. And then, with tears of joy running down her cheeks, she wrapped her arms around her husband — this incredible man who made all things seem possible — and kissed him.

When he broke the kiss, he was grinning. "Does that mean I did right?"

"Yes — but don't let it go to your head,"

Addie instructed. Then she looked around as if lost and said, "I'm not sure I got a proper look at the bedroom."

Jess grinned. "Right this way, ma'am."

ACKNOWLEDGMENTS

I can take little credit for the richness of the setting in this series, for I have a secret weapon in the person of Melody Groves. She knows the country and its history, and enriches the story with her suggestions for details that bring it all to life. *Thank you,* Melody.

My editor, Mary Altman, has an incredible eye for detail as well — details about character and plot that make the story stronger.

And my friend and mentor and agent, Natasha Kern, puts up with my insecurities and rants and, time and again, gets me back on a safe track.

ABOUT THE AUTHOR

Award-winning author **Anna Schmidt** resides in Wisconsin. She delights in creating stories where her characters must wrestle with the challenges of their times. Critics have consistently praised Schmidt for her ability to seamlessly integrate actual events with her fictional characters to produce strong tales of hope and love in the face of seemingly insurmountable obstacles. Visit her at www.booksbyanna.com.